"Kissing you was unprofessional of me."

The flat way Cal said it made her eyes suddenly sting. Then he added in his soft drawl, "It happened because I'm attracted to you, and when I had you in my arms I forgot the rules."

The admission stunned her, but Beth could not, would not allow herself to think of the meaning of those words. Instead, she took a step back. "About this case," she said. "I'm not going to fool anybody into thinking we're married. So I'm not going to help you catch the killer."

"You can help me, Beth. And you will. But only if you let yourself feel comfortable with me. Please give it a try. I won't hurt you."

Oh, but you will, she thought. Her pulse was hammering in her throat. Partly from fear, partly from needs that were impossible to deny. She was sure he didn't understand how vulnerable she was to him. She raised her face to tell him, but the words remained locked in her throat as she saw his eyes, dark and intense.

"Give us a chance," he whispered.

The simplicity and the honesty in his voice reached straight to her heart, and against her better judgment she went into his arms....

Dear Harlequin Intrigue Reader,

We have another great selection of exciting Harlequin Intrigue titles for you this month, kicking off with the second book in Rebecca York's 43 LIGHT STREET trilogy MINE TO KEEP. *Never Alone* is a very special story about the power of love and the lengths to which a man and woman will go to find each other—no matter the obstacles.

One down—three to go! Our MONTANA CONFIDENTIAL series continues with *Special Assignment: Baby* by Debra Webb. A covert operation and a cuddly baby are just a day's work for this sexy cowboy agent. And Caroline Burnes scorches the sheets in *Midnight Burning*, a story about one man's curse and his quest for redemption.

Finally, come play HIDE AND SEEK with Susan Kearney as she launches her new three-book miniseries with *The Hidden Years*.

So pick up all four for a dynamic reading experience.

Sincerely,

Denise O'Sullivan
Associate Senior Editor
Harlequin Intrigue

P.S. Next month Harlequin Intrigue proudly welcomes back Anne Stuart and Gayle Wilson in *Night and Day*, an extraordinary 2-in-1 keeper!

NEVER ALONE

REBECCA YORK

RUTH GLICK WRITING AS REBECCA YORK

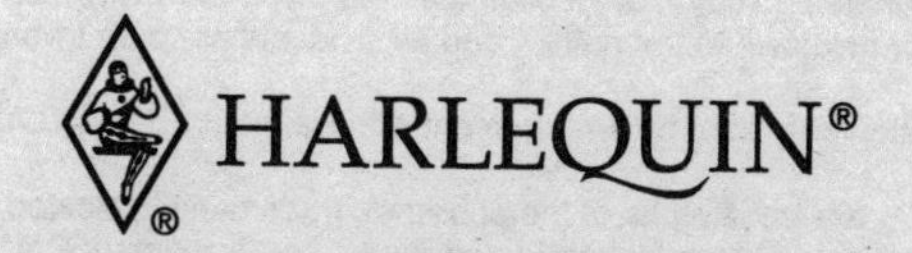

TORONTO • NEW YORK • LONDON
AMSTERDAM • PARIS • SYDNEY • HAMBURG
STOCKHOLM • ATHENS • TOKYO • MILAN • MADRID
PRAGUE • WARSAW • BUDAPEST • AUCKLAND

ISBN 0-373-22633-0

NEVER ALONE

This edition published by arrangement with Harlequin Books S.A.

Visit us at www.eHarlequin.com

Printed in U.S.A.

ABOUT THE AUTHOR

Award-winning, bestselling novelist Ruth Glick, who writes as Rebecca York, is the author of close to eighty books, including her popular 43 LIGHT STREET series for Harlequin Intrigue. Ruth says she has the best job in the world. Not only does she get paid for telling stories, she's also the author of twelve cookbooks. Ruth and her husband, Norman, travel frequently, researching locales for her novels and searching out new dishes for her cookbooks.

Books by Rebecca York

HARLEQUIN INTRIGUE

143—LIFE LINE*
155—SHATTERED VOWS*
167—WHISPERS IN THE NIGHT*
179—ONLY SKIN DEEP*
188—BAYOU MOON
193—TRIAL BY FIRE*
213—HOPSCOTCH*
233—CRADLE AND ALL*
253—WHAT CHILD IS THIS?*
273—MIDNIGHT KISS*
289—TANGLED VOWS*
298—TALONS OF THE FALCON†
301—FLIGHT OF THE RAVEN†
305—IN SEARCH OF THE DOVE†
318—TILL DEATH US DO PART*
338—PRINCE OF TIME*
407—FOR YOUR EYES ONLY*
437—FATHER AND CHILD*
473—NOWHERE MAN*
500—SHATTERED LULLABY*
525—AFTER DARK
"Counterfeit Wife"*
534—MIDNIGHT CALLER*
558—NEVER TOO LATE*
582—AMANDA'S CHILD*
606—BAYOU BLOOD BROTHERS
"Tyler"
625—THE MAN FROM TEXAS**
633—NEVER ALONE**

*43 Light Street
†The Peregrine Connection
**43 Light Street/Mine To Keep

Brazilian Green Beans

Here's the green bean recipe Beth makes for Cal. It's from my new cookbook, *Fabulous Lo-Carb Cuisine.*

Makes 6 cups

6 cups snapped fresh green beans
1/2 cup mayonnaise
2 tsp Dijon-style mustard
1 tsp cider vinegar
1/2 sweet red pepper, diced
2 tbsp chopped chives or green onion tops
1/4 tsp salt, or to taste
Dash white pepper

1. In a small pot, cook green beans to desired degree of doneness, 10 to 20 minutes. Cool under cold running water in a colander.
2. Meanwhile, in a large bowl, stir together mayonnaise, mustard, vinegar, red pepper, onion, salt and white pepper. Stir to mix well.
3. Stir in green beans. Serve at once, or cover and refrigerate overnight (the beans will keep in the refrigerator for 2 or 3 days).
4. Stir before serving. Garnish with additional chopped red pepper and chives, if desired.

CAST OF CHARACTERS

Beth Wagner—She wanted to be left alone; then she found herself smack in the middle of a police investigation.

Cal Rollins—He wanted Beth as he'd wanted no other woman—but could he trust her?

Hallie Bradshaw—Was she dead or alive?

Len Patterson—He forced Cal into a role he didn't want to play.

Tim Fillmore—Did he know more than he was letting on?

Hannah Dawson—Would she ever lead a normal life again?

Lucas Somerville—He was sticking close to Hannah.

Sam Lassiter—He needed Cal's help.

Howard Mason—Why was he hanging around Beth's place?

Wayne Jenkins—Was he guilty or innocent?

Damion Hardon—He'd turned his whole life around.

Deep Throat—What secrets did he have to tell?

Alex Shane—He had a job to do, if his boss would let him do it.

Jamie Naylor—He was out to avenge his brother's death.

Dear Reader,

If there ever was a man who needed the love of a good woman, it was Cal Rollins. But Cal's mother abandoned him when he was just a baby, and his father raised him to think that falling in love was the prelude to pain.

So Cal has kept his relationships superficial, which wasn't all that difficult to do—until he met Beth Wagner. The moment he laid eyes on Beth, he wanted her. Yet there had never been a woman Cal would be less likely to trust.

Cal's push-pull relationship with Beth is only one of the problems he faces in *Never Alone*. He's a police detective trying to track down a serial killer. He needs Beth to give him access to the next potential victims—and perhaps the murderer. So now he's working closely with a woman he wants, a woman he can't quite trust, a woman with extraordinary abilities he doesn't understand. And to make things worse, he finds he's putting her in grave danger.

It's a situation from which Cal desperately needs to escape. And the escape hatch he picks could spell his doom.

I'd tell you more, but I don't want to give away the strange twists and turns of this plot.

So I'll just say that Cal's very survival depends on Beth and the link she forges with him—against his will.

All my best,

Ruth

Ruth Glick, writing as Rebecca York

P.S. Don't forget to pick up the conclusion of the MINE TO KEEP trilogy in December!

Chapter One

The jolt of pain took Beth Wagner by surprise.

One moment she was working at her loom on a half-completed wall hanging. In the next her hand jerked off the shuttle as if she'd been zapped by a bolt of electric current.

Her vision went blurry, then snapped back to the subtle blend of dyed yarns she was using to weave a scene of marsh grass against a background of sea and sky. Disoriented, she struggled to catch her breath as she stared at the soothing combination of greens, blues and browns that had absorbed all her attention until a few moments ago.

From the rug in the corner, her dog, Granger, pushed himself up and trotted toward her, laying his massive head in her lap.

"Good boy," she murmured, absently stroking one of his soft ears. He was a large mutt. The result of an unfortunate liaison between a rottweiler and a German shepherd, the combination giving him a menacing look, if you discounted the warm brown eyes. He was great for chasing away anyone who wandered up her road uninvited.

He raised his head, looking at her as if inquiring whether she was all right and if she intended to go back to work.

"I'm fine," she told him.

He stared at her for a moment longer, then settled comfortably at her feet where she sat at the big loom, the one that she'd bought eight years ago when her commissions started becoming more serious. This wall hanging, for the Columbia Bank lobby, was going to earn her fifteen thousand dollars, enough to do much-needed repairs on the barn.

When her parents had run the Howard County, Maryland, farm, it had mostly been planted in corn and alfalfa—with a side business in pick-your-own fruits and vegetables for the ex-urbanites moving to the new town of Columbia. Dad had bought a few farm animals, including sheep, to amuse the children who came with their parents. As a teenager, Beth had gotten interested in using the wool for weaving.

Now here she was with fifty head of prime wool producers, a big ugly dog and a growing reputation as a master craftsman who dyed her own yarns for the wall hangings she'd sold to wealthy clients as far away as France and Japan.

Beth sat with the work resting beneath her unmoving hands and her breath shallow in her chest, praying that the pain wouldn't come again. Sometimes it was like that. A jolt out of the blue, then nothing more. As the seconds ticked by, she began to relax, began to let her mind drift.

Sensing the tension ease, Granger licked his large tongue across a brown paw, then closed his eyes.

Beth's own eyes closed for a moment as she stroked the animal's head. Here on the farm, away from people, she had the peace she needed. The long lane, the beds of wildflowers she'd planted near the house, the sheep quietly nibbling across the green fields, her intimidating dog. Each in its own way formed a barrier between herself and the rest of the world.

She had a sudden image of herself ten years ago. Rising from her seat in the back of a yellow school bus as it stopped at the end of the lane. Most of the kids had simply ignored her, except Hallie, who'd given her a smile as she passed.

Hallie Bradshaw. Her friend. At least they had been friends when they were little, their moms taking them to each other's houses for visits.

Beth blinked, wondering why she was thinking about Hallie now. Maybe it was that letter she'd gotten about the Glenelg High School tenth reunion. It had been a form letter, asking if she wanted to be on the planning committee.

Probably it had gone out to everyone, because she'd be the last person they'd ask. Not the girl who'd sat by herself at a table in the cafeteria and scurried to the safety of her house as soon as she got off the bus.

The pain of those old days stabbed at her. She'd never fit in. Never enjoyed any kind of easy give-and-take with her classmates. She'd been too uptight, too on guard.

She sighed, then went back to the weaving, the rhythm of the shuttle moving back and forth and her foot rising and falling on the treadles soothing her as they always did.

She had just started working with a strand of cerulean blue when the pain jolted through her once more, this time accompanied by the sound of a woman's scream and a voice pleading, *''No, please. Don't hurt me. Please.''*

The words reverberated in her head, bouncing painfully off the inside of her skull, bruising her brain. Through the agony, she struggled to make her mind work. Had she really heard that cry for help? Or was this like the other times—an echo of reality in her mind?

Her eyes shot from the brightly lit workroom to the yard where floodlights blazed, holding the night at bay. Beyond them was the darkness of the fields. Someone was out there in the dark. Someone in trouble.

Someone.

A face formed in her thoughts. A young woman her age. A woman with straight black hair and dark eyes, her features twisted by fear. A trickle of blood was running from her scalp.

It was Hallie, she realized with a sudden stab of understanding. Her friend Hallie was out there. In the dark. That's why she'd been thinking about her moments before. She'd known.

She was on her feet, flying down the hall, the dog at her heels, barking furiously when she opened the locked cabinet where Dad's guns were still kept. Out here in the country, you needed protection, he had taught her. And he had made sure she knew how to use the weapons, taking her out in the woods where she could shoot at tin cans and bottles.

"Help me!" she heard Hallie cry, her friend's voice rising in terror. Then, "God, no!"

Granger growled as Beth opened the door, shadowing her as she stepped into the yard.

Outside it was absolutely still, the spring air cool and damp.

She crouched beside the dog. "Granger, can you find her, boy? Can you find Hallie?"

He looked puzzled, his gaze swinging from her to the blackness beyond the spotlights, but he didn't move from her side.

Beth flicked her own eyes from the dog to the darkness and back again. Granger was an excellent watchdog, but he hadn't heard anything. He hadn't smelled anything. Which meant Hallie couldn't be close to the house.

Beth thought about calling her friend's name. But what if someone else was there? Someone who would come after *her*. Someone whose presence she'd felt here before.

She knew then that it would be foolish to try to handle this on her own. She had to call the police.

HOWARD COUNTY police detective Cal Rollins stood silently in the front hall of the west Columbia town house rented by Hallie Bradshaw, his dark, assessing gaze taking in the obvious details of violence—the overturned lamp, the trail of blood across the trendy Berber carpet. Then he asked himself the first question he always asked at a crime scene—who had been in this room and why?

Karen Philips, certainly. She was the one who had called the police. At eight o'clock the night before, she'd been scheduled to meet Bradshaw and some of their other friends at McKinley's, a restaurant in downtown Ellicott City, where the two-hundred-year-old stone buildings had been converted into a quaint shopping area. When Hallie hadn't shown up, Philips had phoned her. Then when Bradshaw still hadn't surfaced in the morning, she'd been worried enough to stop by—and the evidence of a struggle in the living room had sent her dashing to the phone.

Cal had caught the investigation.

He stood where he was for several moments, observing, making mental pictures, running scenarios through his mind in the soft North Carolina drawl that he hadn't lost since coming to Maryland ten years ago.

Had someone been waiting inside for the woman, or had the perp followed her in? And who was he—an acquaintance or a stranger?

Pulling out his Polaroid, Cal snapped some pictures that would recall the scene to him later. At the same time, he started making a mental inventory of the support staff he was going to need: an official photographer and some crime scene techs, a computer expert to check Bradshaw's hard drive.

After calling for the techs, he started searching the woman's personal stuff. He found a phone book, which he bagged and tagged as evidence, then thumbed through her bills and mail. Next he started on the bedroom drawers and closet. She had a half-empty box of condoms in her nightstand and some pretty hot-looking erotic novels, but no kinky sexual paraphernalia, unless it was hidden in a heating duct or somewhere else her mother wasn't likely to stumble over it.

When he came out of the bedroom, a technician was sweeping lint from the rug into a small plastic bag. "I'd appreciate an analysis of that blood as soon as possible,'' he said.

''You got it.''

If luck were running his way, Bradshaw's address book would have the name of her doctor, and her medical records would give him her blood type.

He had a lot of work ahead of him, Cal thought as he stepped into the sunshine and closed the door, eyeing the knot of rubberneckers gathered on the other side of the court.

He'd already had a long talk with Karen Philips, who'd had nothing but good things to say about Bradshaw. She was a loyal friend. A hardworking mortgage analyst who liked to relax with some of her co-workers at the end of the day. She'd been married for a brief time after college but had no children. Now she was single again and wasn't dating anyone special. She and the ex-husband had parted amiably. The guy lived in California, and probably hadn't flown in to town to manhandle his former wife. As far as Karen knew, she had no enemies, nobody who wanted to do her harm.

But it was an almost sure bet that someone had invaded her town house last night, maybe stabbed or shot her, then spirited her away. Unless she'd staged her own disappearance. That was always a possibility if she was up to her ears in debt or if she had some other dark secret she was hiding from her friends.

Stepping off the curb, Cal strode purposefully toward the group of rubberneckers, hoping one of them had something useful to tell him—either about Bradshaw's background or about last night.

He spent another two hours doing interviews. Either the neighbors hadn't spotted anything out of the ordinary last night, or nobody was talking. And none of them knew Hallie Bradshaw well enough to rate her dates.

By the end of the morning, he was feeling frustrated. Maybe the crime scene report would lead to something, he thought as he pulled into the parking lot behind the Warfield Building, Howard County Police headquarters.

As he started for the back door, the conversation of two uniformed officers—a man and a woman—drifted toward him. One of them was complaining loudly about a call he'd answered the evening before.

"You think my shoes look bad this morning, you ought to have seen them last night after I spent an hour mucking around a sheep farm out by the fairgrounds. There was this weird broad out there. She must be kind of cracked." He stopped and tapped his head. "Called 911 to report a friend was in trouble. She kept saying her name over and over, Hallie Bradshaw. Kept telling me she'd heard Bradshaw calling for help."

Cal felt a zing along his nerve endings. Whirling, he approached the officer with the complaint. Miles Brodie, his name was. Cal had worked with him before and found him to be a pretty straight shooter.

"How's it going?"

"Fine, except for my ruined shoes."

"Did I hear you mention the name Hallie Bradshaw?" Cal asked.

Brodie looked up. "Yeah. That mean something to you?"

"She was reported missing this morning, and there were signs of a struggle at her town house."

Brodie whistled through his teeth. "Wonder what that sheep-farm lady knows about it. She was pretty insistent that I check her property last night. Wouldn't let me leave until I'd tramped around a couple of disgusting fields."

"Give me her name and address. I'd like to ask her some questions."

Brodie dug his notebook out of his pocket and flipped through the pages.

"Beth Wagner," he said. "Thirty-two fifty Old Bridge Road. In Friendship."

Cal copied down the address. "So this old bat who had

you shifting through the sheep droppings—is she gonna shoot me for trespassing?''

Brodie laughed. ''Well, she did have a gun. And a big dog that looks like he could rip out your throat if she gave him the word. Got your Mace?''

''Yeah.''

''But she's not an old bat. She's young. In her late twenties, I'd say. Good-looking. Long blond hair. Blue eyes. Nice little figure.'' He started to gesture with his hands, then stopped abruptly and glanced at the female officer still standing in front of him as he realized he'd gone one beat too far in the description.

''Thanks,'' Cal drawled.

''No problem.''

Reversing his direction, Cal headed back toward his car wondering how the lady in Friendship was going to react to the news about Hallie Bradshaw. Of course, he wasn't going to spill the beans right away. Instead, he'd act as if he was just following up on Brodie's investigation. Then he'd spring the bad news and watch Wagner's reaction.

IT WAS A BEAUTIFUL spring day, the sun shining on beds of daffodils and tulips adorning the front yards of the old farmhouses along Route 144. Cal saw the flowers as a blur of color, his mind on the nutcase he was going to interview. Really, he wished Brodie hadn't made the observation about the woman's mental condition, since he preferred to form his own impression.

Musing on mental instability led his thoughts to his friend Hannah Dawson, the former Baltimore police detective who'd quit the force after watching a teenager bleed out on the street. For a couple of months there, he'd been worried as hell about her, afraid she was taking a plunge off the deep end. Then she'd joined the Light Street Detective Agency and gotten hooked up with a client named Luke Pritchard, whose real name was Lucas Somerville.

Now he answered to either Luke or Lucas. Cal had mistrusted Lucas when he'd first met him.

In fact, the guy had gotten her into a heap of trouble investigating a drug deal gone bad. And now they were both lying low for a couple of reasons. Luke thought Hannah wasn't safe until whoever was out to revenge the death of that dead teen was apprehended. And there was another loose end—from Luke's own past. The crime boss trying to kill him had disappeared, which meant that Luke himself was still a target.

As soon as they were in the clear, they were getting married. A pretty radical step, as far as Cal was concerned. Sure, Luke had been good for Hannah. But in Cal's experience, relationships didn't last. And tying the knot was the ultimate risk—a risk he had vowed never to take. Heck, his parents had only been hitched long enough to keep him from being labeled a bastard. It was Dad who had raised him, Dad who'd earned his respect and his loyalty. Which was why he was working in Howard County instead of the city—because he'd moved out here to be closer to the old man when his health had started failing. Now Dad was dead, and Cal had inherited a house that was twice as big as anything he needed.

His thoughts were focused so far inward that he realized with a start that he must have overshot the turnoff to Old Bridge Road.

Up ahead was a new development of tract mansions—obscenely big houses on three-acre lots, eating up prime farmland, if he was any judge. He pulled into one of the driveways, made a U-turn, then backtracked to the crossing, focusing his mind on how to play the interview with Beth Wagner for maximum effect. Sometimes the initial approach to a witness made the difference between getting the information you needed and coming up with squat.

Maybe he'd go with the disarming country charm and

exaggerate his North Carolina accent to put the crazy lady at ease.

Once on Old Bridge, he started checking numbers on the mailboxes, his gaze taking in the still-unspoiled land, wondering how long it would be before the acreage was gobbled up by some developer.

Thirty-two fifty was at the end of a long lane that wound upward through a stand of hardwood trees, then rolling fields. He couldn't even see the house from the road. Apparently it was in as isolated a spot as you could find in the county these days. In fact, if you were up to something illegal, this would be a great place to locate your business.

He saw the sheep in the corner of one field, puffy beige shapes accented with black at the face and legs, and imagined Brodie scattering them as he floundered through the field at night looking for Hallie Bradshaw.

Did Wagner tend the flock herself or did she have help?

As he rounded a turn in the road, a red painted barn came into view. Then a two-story farmhouse with a wide front porch. The property looked pretty well kept up, which meant that Wagner was either doing exceptionally well with her sheep or she had another source of income.

Before he could exit his car, the dog Brodie had warned him about leaped off the porch, barking at the top of its lungs and snapping its jaw as it lunged for the car.

Cal was glad there was a metal door and a shatterproof window between himself and the incredibly ugly brute. No way was he planning to get out of the car without a suit of armor—or an order from the woman to call off her beast.

He thought about honking the horn, but he figured Wagner could hear the barking about as well as he could. So he sat there waiting.

It didn't take long for the woman to appear. Momentarily startled, he stared at her, thinking that Brodie hadn't nearly done her justice in his brief description.

She was wearing jeans and sandals under a long, soft

shirt with stripes of peach, mint, aqua and other pastel colors that blended in a shifting cloud of color as she moved.

Her wavy blond hair was long and loose, reaching halfway down her back. Rapunzel, he thought, the hair and her delicate features making him think of the old fairy tale. A captive in her tower.

Only now she was out there walking around, and he was the captive—in his own vehicle, he reminded himself sharply.

He rolled down his window enough to be heard, but not so far that the dog's snapping teeth could connect with any part of his anatomy.

"Cal Rollins, Howard County Police," he said, holding up his badge.

She studied the shield, then turned to the animal.

"Granger, it's all right. The man is all right. He's a friend."

Her voice tightened on the last word. Interesting. Was she still smarting from her encounter with Brodie? Or did she have something to hide?

He watched the graceful way she moved, watched the way the dog instantly responded to her words, as if he could understand what she was saying. Still, she reached down and snapped a leash onto the dog's collar, keeping him at her side.

Cal squared his shoulders and stepped out of the car.

"Let him smell your hand," she said, making it more of an order than a suggestion.

Remembering that Brodie hadn't sported any bloody stumps, Cal bent at the waist and extended his arm. The dog gave him a good sniff, keeping his eyes on him.

"Good boy. What's his name?"

"Granger."

"Hello, Granger. I'm Cal Rollins," he said, progressing from allowing himself to be sniffed by the large black nose to squatting beside the dog and petting the massive head.

He liked dogs, liked making friends with this one. But he also had an ulterior motive. Keeping himself busy with the animal gave him the perfect opportunity to delay announcing his purpose, to let her wonder why he was following up Brodie's late-night visit.

From the corner of his eye he watched Ms. Wagner shift from one sandal-clad foot to the other, brush back a lock of that spun-gold hair as she waited for him to speak.

After several moments, she asked, "Is this about Hallie?"

"Yes," he answered, giving nothing more away as he stood up again and regarded her with a neutral stare.

She looked nervous. Achingly vulnerable. And sexy in a fresh, innocent way that set off a little buzz inside his skull. He caught himself starting to shake his head to clear his thoughts, then squeezed his hand into a fist at his side instead, surprised and annoyed by his reaction to her. *Keep your mind on business, Rollins,* he silently warned himself.

She made a barely audible sound in her throat then asked, "Would you like to come inside?"

"Yes."

They started toward the house. Apparently the dog wasn't accustomed to the leash, because he dashed across her path, heading toward the porch.

The mesh cord hit her across the legs, and with a startled exclamation, she lurched forward, automatically letting go of the strap as she fought to keep her balance.

Cal moved swiftly, reaching for her as she tumbled toward the hard concrete of the front walk. She landed heavily against his body, her hands coming up to grasp his shoulders as she drew in a strangled breath.

"Easy. You're all right," he murmured, unconsciously drawing out the words as he supported her in his grasp. He was thinking that he would just make sure she was steady on her feet and then let her go, but his hands stayed where they were. His senses were already cataloging a dozen impressions as he held her, and his arms failed to turn her loose. He felt her fragile, fine-boned body, inhaled her scent—like a field of fresh flowers after a spring rain, responded to the way her breasts pressed against his chest and her hands cupped over his shoulders as she clung to him for support.

It was the most natural thing in the world to keep hanging on to her, holding her upright as she swayed slightly in his embrace.

His eyes closed, and for several heartbeats his befuddled brain forgot the reason he had taken her into his arms in the first place. All he knew was that he was holding a very desirable woman—a woman who had given herself into his care, given him her total trust. At least for these few moments in time.

Perhaps she was just as addle-brained as he, because she stayed where she was, her head drifting to his shoulder.

It felt right—as right as stroking his fingers over her sun-drenched hair, running his hand up and down her delicate back, then lowering to the curve of her hip.

He made a low sound in his throat. His own private rule number one was "Never lose yourself in a woman's arms." Total surrender was too dangerous, so there was always some part of himself he held back. Now he felt adrift in a dream—a daydream full of warm sunshine and an even warmer woman. Turning his head, he buried his nose in her hair and breathed in the floral fragrance.

The sound of a loud bark brought him back to reality. He didn't know he had closed his eyes until they blinked open—at the same moment the pliant woman in his embrace drew back and stared up at him, a questioning look in her blue eyes.

He felt as if he were drowning in the deep pools of those eyes, eyes that asked questions he couldn't answer.

When he didn't speak, she stepped quickly away from him, her hand smoothing down the side of her jeans.

How long had he been holding her? Five seconds? Ten? An eternity?

Her voice sounded thick as she said, ''Thank you for catching me.''

He cleared his own throat and spoke with some difficulty. ''Are you all right?''

She nodded, looking as if she wasn't quite sure it was the truth. Then she turned on her heel and started for the house.

He stood there on her front walk, still feeling the impact of her body pressed to his, while he silently cursed his unprofessional behavior. He was supposed to be interviewing the woman on a missing person's case, not making love to her.

The dog stayed on the porch. That was good. At least he and Wagner weren't going to do an impromptu tango with the leash again.

Lips pressed against his teeth, Cal followed her up the three steps to the porch, across the beige painted boards and into a front hall that seemed dark after the bright sunshine outside.

Keeping his eyes pinned to her flowing blond hair, he followed her into a sitting room filled with old-fashioned furniture—stuff that might have come from a fancy antique shop, although he suspected that it had probably been in this house for a long time.

The faded upholstery was enlivened with colorful pillows that looked as though they'd been created by the same artist who had executed the modern tapestries that adorned the walls.

For a moment she stood with her back to him. Under other circumstances, he might have put that down to being nervous about talking to the police. This afternoon he knew it had as much to do with his catching her in his arms and failing to turn her loose.

He'd blown the interview before it had even started. Now the best he could do was damage control. Resisting the impulse to swipe his fingers through his dark hair, he pulled out his notebook. ''You called 911 last night,'' he said. ''And an officer came out.''

She turned around. ''Yes.''

''I haven't listened to the tape. What was the reason for the message, exactly?''

''If you haven't listened to the tape, why are you here?''

Score one for her. ''A routine investigation,'' he snapped.

At least he had the satisfaction of seeing her look uncomfortable, evasive. ''I thought I heard my friend Hallie Bradshaw calling for help. I thought she might be somewhere around my farm. But when the officer checked—Officer Brodie—he didn't find anyone here.''

''You were in the house alone last night?''

''Yes.''

''You run this farm by yourself?''

''I lease out some of the fields for corn and other crops. The same man takes care of the sheep.''

''His name?''

''Tim Fillmore. He lives a couple of miles from here. He wasn't at the farm last night, if that's what you're interested in.''

''I'm interested in what you know about Ms. Bradshaw.''

Wagner made a fluttering motion with her hand. ''We were friends when we were little. She went to school with me—elementary school, middle school, high school. I haven't kept in touch with her recently.''

''But last night, specifically…'' He let the question trail off.

''Last night I thought I heard her calling for help.''

He kept his voice businesslike. ''Last night she was supposed to meet friends for dinner at a local restaurant. When she didn't show up, one of them—Karen Philips—called her house several times, then checked at her town house this morning.''

He saw the tension gathering in her features and her

body as though she'd been dreading this moment since he'd shown her his badge.

"Ms. Philips found signs of a struggle. A lamp was overturned."

"And blood," she added, her voice barely above a whisper.

As she spoke, his gaze took in every detail of her face, her body language. Her skin had turned pale, almost translucent, and she looked as if she was going to snap in two.

"You were there? You saw the blood?"

"No."

"I didn't mention that detail. How do you know it, then?"

She gave him a helpless look, touched her hand to her temple as if she had suddenly acquired a headache. "I saw it. In my mind."

He felt his throat clench as comprehension dawned. Then anger washed over him as he realized he'd been reeled in like a trout who had gone for a bright lure. "Are you trying to tell me you're plugged into the psychic hot line? You expect me to fall for that?"

Brodie was right. He was face-to-face with a certifiable nutcase.

Chapter Two

Beth struggled to keep the pain and frustration from her features as she stared at the man facing her. No, not just a man. A Howard County Police detective, she reminded herself with a stab of chagrin. He'd lured her into a trap with his easy manner and his soft country voice—then had snapped the metal teeth around her neck.

Was it possible that a few minutes ago he'd held her in his arms, and she'd felt both his strength and his gentleness? Or had she made that up? That and a whole lot more.

He'd cradled her against his tall, supple body, stroked his hand down her back, caressing her hair, and she'd felt an unaccustomed connection to him, an awareness building between them. He'd made a low, urgent sound in his throat, and she'd forgotten why he had come out to the farm, forgotten the reason why he'd put his arms around her.

Her response hadn't been appropriate, she knew. And when she'd pulled away from him, she'd been embarrassed and unsure of herself.

His dark eyes had still been warm when they'd looked at her. But slowly that warmth had evaporated so that only a tough, probing expression remained.

Now she knew for certain there hadn't been anything of substance building between the two of them. It had all come from her too-vivid imagination.

Or maybe it was worse than that. Maybe he *had* felt something and now he was cursing himself for letting down his guard with a woman he couldn't trust.

Too bad she wasn't a real psychic. Then she'd know for sure what he was thinking. Unfortunately, whatever power she had wasn't something she could turn on and off when she wanted to. Images, sounds, impressions came to her when she was least expecting them. They were always dark. Usually painful, and she had no more control over the process than she had over the rain or the wind.

As he waited for her to answer the question he'd asked half a minute ago, the arms that had held her close became unnaturally rigid at his sides. Like his chiseled jaw. Like the skin stretched over his cheekbones.

Her tongue felt thick in her mouth as she faced him, but she managed to say, "No, I don't expect you to believe it. Not when you're looking at me like I just grew a pair of Martian antennae."

"You'll pardon me, but I don't believe in anything I can't verify through normal means."

"Okay."

He folded his arms across his chest. His eyes had gone as hard and shiny as obsidian. "What do you mean, okay?"

"I mean I accept your rules. You're not going to believe I heard anything out of the ordinary. I can't prove that I did. So Hallie must have been out here last night, and I heard her calling for help. If you want, you can search my property to find out whether or not she was here."

"I think Brodie did an adequate job of that."

"He was here in the dark. It's light now."

"Let's not get off the subject of your, uh, special abilities. What did you hear exactly?"

She hated the way he used the word *special* as if it was a curse. Actually he was right. The abilities were a curse, but she wasn't going to explain all that now. Instead, she simply murmured, "I heard her say, 'No, please. Don't hurt me. Please.'"

"That's all?"

She closed her eyes, wishing she could make him vanish in a puff of smoke, or turn him into a frog and watch him hop away. But none of that was going to happen, so she forced herself to confront his disapproval. "A little later she said, 'help me' again." She gulped. "Then, 'God, no.'"

"You heard those words. That's all there was to the experience?"

She shook her head, wondering how much detail she had to go into for this man who so obviously believed she was somehow making up a story. "At first I heard a woman calling for help and didn't know who she was. Then I saw her face in my mind, saw she was terrified, saw blood dripping down from her hair. I knew it was Hallie."

He made a snorting sound. "Did you happen to see if anyone was with her?"

"No."

His features twisted into an expression she didn't much like.

"How do you explain my knowing about the blood?" she asked quickly.

"Easy. You went to her town house. You saw what happened."

She carefully considered the implications of his words. "So now you're trying to insinuate I was involved? If I were, why would I have called the police?"

He stared at her impassively. "Can anyone verify that you were home last night?"

"Granger and I were here alone—until Officer Brodie showed up."

"Right, I'll interview your dog. No doubt you can translate his barks for me," he said sarcastically, then asked,

"So how often does this happen? How long have you been having these, uh, mystical experiences?"

The phrasing and his tone of voice told her that he still didn't believe her but was playing along because he still wanted information. Balling her hands into fists, she rested them against her hips. "You think they're something I enjoy?"

"Do you?"

"No! That's why I live out here in the middle of nowhere. That's why I stay away from people. I don't want it to happen. It's never anything good. It makes my head hurt. Sometimes it scares me. So I try to shut it out. But sometimes I can't! Despite everything, it gets through to me." The last part came out as if she was a character in a television show and someone had just turned up the volume. Deliberately she took a steadying breath, then inquired evenly, "Do you have any more questions?"

"Did you tell Officer Brodie that you thought you'd picked up vibrations from Ms. Bradshaw?"

"No."

"Why not?"

She looked down at the worn Oriental carpet, twisted her hands together in front of her. "I felt embarrassed about saying anything."

"You didn't think it was relevant, after he didn't find anyone out in the sheep pasture? You were worried about your friend, but you kept your mouth shut because you were *embarrassed?*"

When he put it that way, she didn't like the sound of her own motivation. But she still tried to explain. "He already thought I was hysterical. I didn't want him driving me to a mental hospital."

"But you told *me* how you tuned in to some kind of extrasensory distress call from Ms. Bradshaw."

"It was either that or have you think I went after Hallie with a hatchet last night." She swallowed. "You're the one who told me she's missing and that someone had been in her town house."

"That's not precisely what I said."

"Right, you're trying to see if you can trip me up. Punch holes in my story about hearing voices in my head—or my claim that I was home alone all night last night."

He gave her a small shrug.

"Do you have any more penetrating questions?" she asked.

"Not at the moment, but I'd like you to stay available."

She nodded tightly.

Turning, he stalked out of the parlor. Beth remained rooted to the spot, listening to the sound of the door opening and closing, then a car engine starting.

With a deliberate shake of her shoulders, she tried to release the viselike tension gripping her body. Moving toward the door, she stepped out onto the porch, watching the trail of dust that his car had left down the long driveway. Granger thumped his tail, then stood. Absently, she stroked his big head. When she turned back toward the house, he followed her down the hall to the room where she kept her loom. Picking up the shuttle, she went back to the wall hanging again. But after a few minutes she realized that she wasn't concentrating on the work and she was going to make a mistake.

Sighing, she pushed her chair back, an image of Cal Rollins filling her mind. His features had been tight and strained when he left. In her mind, she managed to wipe that expression off his face and replace it with the one she'd seen in the yard after he'd held her in his arms. The warmth in those dark, deep-set eyes. The relaxed line of his jaw—a masculine jaw that carried the shadow of a dark beard this early in the afternoon.

Unable to stop herself, she imagined rubbing her fingers over that rough surface, or touching his dark, short-cropped hair.

Would her touch bring back the slight smile at the corners of his lips? His lips were too thin to be called sensual, yet she couldn't help ascribing them that quality.

When she realized that her body was starting to feel heavy and hot, she clamped her lower lip between her teeth. Why was she thinking about him that way? Why was she allowing herself to respond to him?

She didn't want to. She wished she'd never met him. But the meeting had happened, and she *had* felt something when he'd held her in his arms. It wasn't merely sexual. It was something strong and deep arching between them. It had drawn her closer to him, even as it had frightened her. Not just the physical sensation of her breasts brushing his chest or his knee pressing against her thigh. Those details had been memorable enough.

No, it was something below the surface, something far more powerful then mere physical sensation—a yearning she couldn't remember experiencing before. It had made her weak and needy and vulnerable—emotions she wanted to avoid. Especially with a man like Cal Rollins—a man who thought she was either crazy or, worse, a criminal.

A DULL ACHE POUNDED in Cal's temples as he drove away from the farm. It had been a long time since he'd made such a mess of a simple interview. He'd touched Beth Wagner in ways that were totally inappropriate, felt emotions he shouldn't be feeling, then he'd overcompensated by turning the interview into the Spanish Inquisition. God, when had he ever been this off balance with a suspect? Never. And now he was going to have to hustle to regain the ground he'd lost.

Not only was he going to have to dig into Hallie Bradshaw's life, he was going to have to do a thorough background investigation on Beth Wagner, psychic.

He'd made it pretty clear to her he didn't believe in that kind of garbage. But that left him with a basic problem. If she hadn't had a flash of inspiration from the cosmic consciousness, where had she picked up her information about Bradshaw?

He was going to investigate her, all right, because she was a suspect. Not simply for his own satisfaction.

He'd start with civil records—utilities, DMV, a credit check. She looked totally innocent, sweet, vulnerable, like a sixties flower child transported from San Francisco to Howard County. But for all he knew, she might have been involved in a messy divorce, a custody battle. She might have been arrested for something. And she might have some hidden connection to Bradshaw that he'd be interested to know about. He'd find out where else she'd lived. Where she'd been employed. Whether this farm was her sole source of income. He'd dig up every damn thing he could—until he figured out how she fit into the Hallie Bradshaw case. Not because he had any personal interest in her, he assured himself.

When he realized his hands were fused to the steering wheel, he deliberately loosened his grip, deliberately rolled his tense shoulders against the backrest.

Half an hour later, he was back in the squad room. He made a stop at the coffeepot and poured himself a mug of high test. Then he read the pertinent reports from the uniformed officers—Brodie's from last night and the one from Al Faraday, who had responded to Karen Philips's call. He wanted to talk to both officers, but neither one was in the building.

So he went into fallback position—research. Logically, he should start by digging into Hallie Bradshaw's background. But he had reason enough to start with Beth Wagner, he told himself.

He began with the Department of Motor Vehicles. He found out she was twenty-eight, that she hadn't gotten so much as a parking ticket in her driving career, that her address had been the same since she'd first applied for a license when she was sixteen.

Then he checked for a criminal record. There was none. Next, he put her name into the Web—just for kicks.

What he got made his eyes widen. Apparently she was a weaver with an international reputation whose commissions ranged from the low thousands upward.

After making requests for phone company and credit card records and other similar information, he took a break from Ms. Wagner and started looking for cases that were similar to Hallie Bradshaw's disappearance.

He found one. A woman named Lisa Stapler. She'd disappeared from her apartment in Long Reach and later her body had been discovered in a culvert near Route 175.

She'd been the same age as Hallie—and Beth Wagner.

Going to another database, he found out that all three of them had graduated from Glenelg High School ten years ago.

Interesting, he thought, rocking back in his chair. Maybe that was a coincidence, but one thing he'd learned over the years was that coincidence was rare in a homicide investigation.

He glanced at his watch. He'd been deep into the case and hadn't realized it was seven-thirty, way past his quitting time. Turning off the computer, he stood and stretched, aware that the guys on the evening shift were watching him. He knew they didn't like finding him still at work when they came in. Probably they thought the new guy in the squad room was trying to prove something by working overtime, trying to show them how things were done in the city.

With a shrug, he headed for the parking lot and climbed into his unmarked car. After a short hesitation, he drove down the hill into the historic district, figuring he might as well eat at McKinley's and get a look at the crowd that hung out there.

THE RESTAURANT-BAR was crowded and noisy. From a table in the corner, over passable chicken fajitas, he watched young men and women eye each other, laugh, make contact and pair up.

Some of the women looked in his direction, but he made it clear by his body language that he wasn't interested. He'd played the game at places like this. But tonight the scene depressed him. Everybody seemed bound and determined to make sure everybody else knew they were having a good time. But there was an undercurrent to the festivities that conveyed a sense of loneliness. Or perhaps it was simply his own detachment from the scene that gave him that impression.

It hadn't been that way with Beth Wagner this afternoon. No, when he'd held her in his arms, his pulse had started pounding and awareness had zinged along his nerve endings.

In his mind he saw her again, saw her incredibly long blond hair, then pictured his fingers combing through that spun gold. His imagination drifted from her hair to the multicolored shirt that had given only tantalizing glimpses of her breasts. But he knew their shape. He'd felt them against his chest when he'd caught her in his arms.

With a low sound, he pulled his mind away from that dangerous direction, reminding himself sternly that she was a suspect. But if she was skating on the wrong side of the law, why would she have made that call to 911 and saddled herself with a story that was impossible to verify?

He had no answers to his own questions. So he deliberately yanked his mind away as he watched the men and women mingle.

Men and women, he thought as a sudden idea struck him.

He'd checked for cases similar to Bradshaw's in which women had disappeared or been murdered. He hadn't checked out the guys.

It was a strange angle to be playing. Usually serial murderers went after one sex or the other. But his hunches were often right. Maybe he should buy a crystal ball and join a carnival, he thought with a snort as he signaled for the check.

BETH STOOD in the kitchen with her arms wrapped around her shoulders. She should be fixing some dinner, but all she could do was stare out the window into the darkness beyond the floodlights.

Long ago, she'd discovered that holding back the night was more important than curbing her electric bill. She'd learned to fear the dark, because it was at night that the bad stuff dug its claws into her mind.

The first time...

No, she wouldn't think about the first time.

But she couldn't stop the memory from leaping into her head.

She'd been twelve and miserable with a bad case of flu, propped up in bed against a mound of pillows, trying to sleep when she could hardly breathe.

Then the headache had struck, a sharp pain inside her skull like a dagger piercing her brain.

The pain brought a scream to her lips. Then Mom was dashing into the room, coming down beside her on the bed, her face white with alarm.

"What, honey? What is it?"

She tried to speak, but she couldn't get the words out because images had superimposed themselves on the pain, a truck hurtling along a country road, taking a curve too quickly, careening into an oncoming pickup.

Dad's pickup!

As she saw the scene in her mind, her father's truck plowed off the road, bumped through a cornfield and bounced into a low metal fence.

"Daddy! No. Daddy!" she screamed again, then began to sob hysterically as she saw his body jerk forward before the seat belt pulled him back.

She sat there shivering and crying, her mother trying to comfort her, trying to tell her she must have had a bad dream, that Daddy was at his monthly card game with his friends.

"He didn't get there. He's hurt. We have to go help him," she sobbed out.

"You're too sick to go out. Maybe I'd better call Dr. Hamilton," her mother answered, probably thinking the fit of hysterics had been brought on by a high fever.

"No. It's Daddy. I *saw* his truck crash. In that field off Underwood Road."

Her mother hadn't understood—not then. She'd given Beth aspirin, put a cool cloth on her forehead and tried to soothe her fears.

She'd almost convinced Beth that she'd imagined the whole thing—until a policeman had come to their door to tell them that Bill Wagner was in Howard County Hospital with a broken shoulder.

That had been the first day of the rest of her life. Until then she'd been a pretty normal kid. After that...well, her parents had treated her differently. It was subtle, but in a way, it seemed as if they were afraid of her, in awe of her, so that there was no way to turn to them for help.

Instead, she'd fought the scared, helpless feeling on her own, even as she started withdrawing from people.

On that long-ago night she'd seen her father injured. There had been plenty of other terrifying images since then. Mostly the experience came to her in visual terms.

With Hallie, it had been different, and she'd thought at first that she might actually be hearing something outside the house and close by. Even when she'd known in her heart that she was fooling herself, she'd kept pretending it was real, because that was better than the alternative.

Beth Wagner, harbinger of disaster.

That was what she was. Because the sights, and now the sounds, that came to her with a knife-sharp pain in her head were never anything she wanted to know.

That was bad enough, but along with the unwanted knowledge came the torment of being different from everyone else. She'd seen the way that cop, Brodie, had looked at her. He'd thought she was a nutcase, just from the way she was acting, and that had cut her to the core. But that was nothing compared to what had happened with Cal Rollins. He'd put his arms around her, and needs she seldom acknowledged had surged through her like a riptide carrying away everything in its wake. She'd *wanted* him to see her as normal. She'd *wanted* him to think she was like everyone else.

She'd *wanted…*

She wasn't willing to put a name to the rest of it. And what did it matter, anyway? In the end, she'd understood that she had to confess her sins and understood that he wouldn't grant her absolution. So she'd told him what she knew and how she knew it and watched the expression on his face harden into something that shredded the tender core of her being.

THE STATE PARK was a good place to bury a body, Damien thought as he opened the trunk of his car and removed the bundle wrapped in plastic garbage bags.

''You dig deep, then scatter the leaves and debris back over the ground, and nobody will ever find the grave,'' he said, speaking aloud. He did that a lot: talked to himself. But there was nothing wrong with it. He liked his own company best, after all. So why not voice his thoughts when he wanted to?

The cops hadn't found the other four graves up here. They wouldn't find Hallie Bradshaw. He was sure of that. Sure all his plans would work out just the way he wanted.

Lisa Stapler was different, though. Special. He'd *wanted* them to find that body. Wanted to humiliate her, even in death. The way she'd humiliated him all those years ago.

So he'd used her as his calling card. His announcement that something important was going on. But he'd just given them a hint, a teaser, when he'd left her where he knew the body would be discovered.

But up here was private. Safe. Anonymous.

He had tramped this ground before, so the three-quarters full moon was enough to light his way as he marched through a stand of trees, then into a meadow where he knew the soil was easy to work.

He was smart and careful. He'd bought the textbooks from the criminal investigation courses at the University of Maryland. He knew how to make sure that the police wouldn't find any trace evidence they could use at Bradshaw's house. Just the way they hadn't found anything at the other crime scenes.

"And the neighbors?" he asked himself aloud, continuing the dialogue with his own favorite conversationalist. "Don't worry about the neighbors. They didn't see anyone besides a carpet cleaner go into her house. And they didn't notice there was a woman wrapped in the Oriental rug the carpet cleaner carried out."

Bradshaw and the other women hadn't been all that much of a challenge. The men had been more difficult to control. They were bigger, heavier. But his hours in the gym had paid off and he had been able to handle them, too.

Hallie had been alive after he'd hit her over the head and spirited her away from the town house.

That was part of his plan. He'd taken her to the locked basement room in his Mom's old house—where the two of them had looked at the Glenelg High School yearbook together. Looked at all the pictures of her in the Spanish Club, the Booster Club, the cheerleader squad and the homecoming queen's court. They'd gone over all her stupid achievements—each one a nail in her coffin lid. There were no pictures of him, except in the pages where there were head shots of all the seniors.

Like all the rest of his victims, she hadn't even remembered him. That was how important he had been to her.

"But you knew me pretty well by the time I finished

with you. Didn't you?'' he asked as he set her plastic-wrapped body on the ground and began to dig.

While he worked, his mind was busy making plans to punish the next hotshot member of her graduating class.

AFTER LEAVING the restaurant, Cal headed home—to the computer system that duplicated many of the features he had at the office.

Dad had inherited the redbrick rambler off Frederick Road six years earlier from his older sister, Martha. Cal had seen her only sporadically over the years, because she'd lived in Maryland and they'd lived outside Greensboro, North Carolina. But she'd urged him to consider the University of Maryland for college. And he'd liked living in the state. Then Dad had retired from a job in the Greensboro finance department and had wanted to make a change, so he'd followed his son north.

After college, Cal had applied to the Baltimore Police Department because that was where the action was. He'd gotten accepted to the same police academy class as Hannah Dawson. They'd both been good patrol officers. Young recruits on the fast track, with undercover assignments and other special gigs that had led to quick promotions to the detective squad.

It was a system that chewed up and spit out promising talent. Hannah had burned out after the shooting of that kid, Sean Naylor. Cal had opted to move to Howard County where there was less crime and less pressure—and where he could help take care of his dad, after he'd been diagnosed with congestive heart failure. Two months after he'd moved to the county, his father died. And now here he was, in an unfamiliar environment, wondering if it was where he really belonged.

He'd left a pressure-cooker job for one that should give him some breathing space. But he was still pushing himself—partly because the habit of working overtime helped fill up the long evening hours.

So as soon as he got home, he changed into comfortable clothes—jeans and a T-shirt—then he warmed up a mug of coffee from the pot that was still sitting on the kitchen counter from the morning and took it into the spare bedroom that he'd set up as an office.

Pulling up his chair in front of the computer, he booted the machine. Before the Windows program took over the display, he could see the shadow of his features reflected on the monitor like a ghost.

He rubbed his hand over his face, wondering why he'd chosen that particular metaphor. There were no ghosts. No spirits called up by little old lady psychics at seances who imparted information from the afterlife. Spirits didn't solve crimes. Psychics didn't solve crimes. Stuff like that was a total bunch of crap invented by Hollywood to fill movie theaters.

Crimes were solved through hard work, persistence and logical deduction.

When the machine had finished booting, he went back to the database he'd been studying earlier, looking for murder victims over the past two years who were twenty-eight and twenty-nine years of age. By midnight he'd found eight unsolved cases.

THE NEXT MORNING in the squad room, Cal kept looking for patterns that would link the victims. Following his earlier theory, he went to the Glenelg High School Web site, to the alumni roster compiled by some gung-ho former student with a lot of time on his hands.

In an hour and a half he'd found three men and one other woman besides Stapler. Five stone-cold disappearances—all the victims presumed murdered—and a probable sixth if you assumed Hallie Bradshaw was dead, which he did. All the previous crimes were still unsolved.

Rocking back in his chair, he stared at the computer screen. It sounded like a plot for a teen horror movie. Only, the victims had long graduated from school. Six homicides all involving classmates of Beth Wagner.

Cal reported his findings to his boss, Lieutenant Patterson. Three hours after that, Patterson called him into his office, closed the door and laid out the most dang-fool undercover assignment Cal had ever heard of.

Chapter Three

A good cop did his job, Cal thought as he turned onto Underwood Road. A good cop didn't question the decisions of the boss. So Cal had held his objections to Patterson's nut-brain scheme to a couple of mild observations.

But violent crime was up in Howard County, and the lieu was anxious to be the one to free the logjam of unsolved cases. He was also anxious to take credit for arresting a serial killer operating in Howard County and surrounding jurisdictions.

Because, thanks to Cal's research, that was what the situation now looked like. He'd made connections between cases that nobody else had seen, connections that pointed to a serial killer knocking off members of the Glenelg High School tenth-reunion class.

Which was why Cal was presently on his way out to Beth Wagner's sheep farm.

As he drove, he was thinking he should have called her first. But he'd been pretty sure that if he presented Patterson's plan over the phone, she'd simply say no.

So he'd come out here in person to convince her to do something that she wasn't going to like. Actually, something *he* wasn't going to like, if the truth be told. But he supposed he was willing to give it a shot.

He slowed when he drew close to her turnoff and saw a dark blue car parked near her rural mailbox. There was a guy inside the vehicle. Was he just checking a map or was he specifically interested in Beth's property?

The man pulled away as Cal approached, but not before he copied down the license number on his notepad. He'd run the plate later and find out who he was.

As Cal drove up the long lane, he saw a man in one of the fields. Probably the farmer Wagner had mentioned.

Quickly he corrected himself. *Don't refer to her as Wagner. From now on when you think about her, she's Beth. And you'd better get used to it.*

Looking to the right, he saw the guy in the field staring at him. He slowed down, and made a point of returning the interest. After thirty seconds of uneasy eye contact, the man turned back to whatever he was doing with the sheep.

Pulling up near the house, Cal cut the engine. This time there was no barking from the big ugly dog named Granger. Instead, the animal came up to the unmarked car, wagging his tail. Well, at least somebody was glad to see him, Cal thought as he exited the vehicle and squatted to stroke the animal.

"Good boy," he drawled. "So you remember me. That's good."

He and the mutt moved toward the porch, and Cal rapped on the front door. There was no answer.

"Beth?" he called, trying out the name.

She still didn't answer, but he could hear music drifting toward him from somewhere at the back of the house. Something classical that sounded vaguely familiar, although his musical education was too sketchy to serve up the name of the piece or its composer.

He tried the door, found it unlocked, and thought that folks out here in the country were too trusting. It could be the damn serial killer with his hand on the doorknob.

His chest tightened at the thought.

"Beth?"

He and the dog passed the old-fashioned parlor where he'd interrogated her a few days ago.

He followed the music, stopping at a room at the end of the hall that was bare of furniture except for a huge loom in the corner and a desk chair. Beth was sitting in the chair, totally absorbed in weaving. He stopped where he was, arrested by the sight of her—the long blond hair flowing down her back and the graceful way she moved as she worked. He didn't know anything about weaving, but she made it look like an exotic dance as her hands did something with the threads and her foot moved the pedals near the floor.

He cleared his throat and went back into formal mode, just for the moment. "Ms. Wagner."

She jumped, then spun around in her seat, her eyes wide. When she saw who it was, she gave him a pained look. "What are you trying to do—scare the living daylights out of me?"

"I knocked. I called out. Nobody answered."

Her reproving gaze shot to the dog. "Granger, you're supposed to tell me when someone comes up the driveway."

The animal lowered his head slightly, looking for all the world like a little boy who had been caught lighting matches behind the barn. "I guess he likes me," Cal murmured.

She gave a noncommittal shrug, then asked, "Do you have some information on Hallie?"

He watched the way she clenched her jaw as she waited for bad news.

"Not specifically on your friend."

"Then why are you here?"

"To ask for your help in the investigation."

She raised her chin. "You think my special talents are a bunch of baloney. Why would you want my help?"

"It wasn't that kind of help we're after."

"Then what?"

He dragged in a breath and let it out. Here it was, the

moment when he had to make Patterson's crazy plan look like something reasonable.

BETH WATCHED HIM shift his weight from one foot to the other. He wanted something from her, and he was uncomfortable about it. Good.

Well, maybe good. Because the look in his eyes suggested that he knew she wasn't going to like what he had to say, either.

She struggled to keep her own expression neutral, struggled not to let him discover that her throat was suddenly dry and aching.

Since he'd come here three days ago, she'd lain in bed making up fantasies about this man, sure that she was never going to see him again. Here he was, back in her house looking and sounding just as appealing as he'd been before his dark eyes had turned hard and the soft southern drawl had turned scornful.

She'd blocked out those parts in her fantasies. Now the remembered look of contempt hurt just as much as when he'd turned that laser gaze on her.

"Can we go in the other room and sit down?" he asked.

She nodded, glad he was giving both of them a little more time before he asked anything of her. When he turned, she filled her lungs with oxygen, held it for a moment, then followed him down the hall. Granger trailed behind her.

As she stepped through the door to the parlor, Cal was looking around the room as if he were just seeing it for the first time.

Keeping her eyes averted, she perched on the sofa; he settled his large frame into her father's easy chair.

Granger hesitated as if his loyalties were torn. Traitorous dog, she thought. When she gave him a stern look, he trotted toward her and settled at her feet. Reaching to pet his head, she hoped the slight tremor of her fingers didn't show.

Cal took a notebook out of his pocket, flipped it open and stared down at a page of black script. "After I interviewed you, I started looking for similar cases. In the middle of the search, I got a hunch and started making some interesting connections."

She continued to stroke her dog's head, refraining from asking him if the hunch had been some sort of psychic intuition.

"I discovered that five other members of your high-school class have disappeared. Three men and two women. They all vanished for no apparent reason. I mean, they weren't suicidal or in any kind of financial trouble. They weren't embroiled in any domestic disputes. They're all presumed murdered."

"No!" came her automatic response.

"Lisa Stapler was the first. She's the only body we've found. The other class members are Will Huttonson, Donna Misk, Andy Preston, Jim Vogel."

She felt a wave of cold sweep over her. "No," she said again. She knew all those names. Will had been a star running back on the Glenelg winning football team. Lisa had been a cheerleader. All of the others were prominent class members that anyone from the same year would recognize.

"That's too many to be a coincidence," Cal said.

When she nodded tightly, he went on.

"The conclusion is obvious. Somebody has a grudge against the members of the class. Most likely a former student."

That wasn't a conclusion she wanted to draw, so she simply sat there staring at him.

"We have to catch the guy before he does it again. I've also learned from my supervisor that the class is gearing up for a tenth reunion. That there's a planning meeting of class members coming up. We want to see who comes to that meeting and why—get a handle on the class members.

But we can't just pretend that someone who didn't even go to the school is suddenly a member of the class."

"And?"

"We figure the best way is to have a spouse of a class member join her at that meeting. Get on the committee."

"What does all this have to do with me?"

"My supervisor suggested that you're our most logical candidate."

"What?" She heard her voice go high and thin. "I'm supposed to be married?"

His gaze was steady as it remained focused on her, but she saw his fingers had tightened around the notebook.

"The last time you came here, you were acting like I was the one who had abducted Hallie," she managed to say. "Now you're asking for my help?"

"I didn't say you'd abducted her."

"You were thinking it."

He gave a small shrug. "I have to think of every eventuality. I stopped considering you as a suspect when I figured out that we're after a serial killer."

"Thanks for the vote of confidence—I think."

He ignored her sarcastic interjection and continued. "What we've got here is a killer operating within a confined population."

"Then why don't you just interview everybody in the class?"

"Right, we can narrow it down to over four hundred individuals. Besides, it might not be someone in the class. It could be a former cafeteria worker who'd developed a grudge against the class members. It could be a former teacher. A maintenance worker. Someone who lives near the school."

"So why do you want to infiltrate the reunion committee?"

"Because that's our best shot. The killer might be arrogant enough to come to the meeting. Or he might be lurking around outside, taking down names. Or someone who comes to the meeting may already be targeted for stalking.''

She shuddered.

The detective plowed ahead. ''If he's there, we want to know. But that doesn't mean we're not going to work on the other angles.''

Folding her arms across her middle, Beth answered, ''I can't help you.''

''There's been a pattern established. There will be other murders. You want them on your conscience?''

She considered that, then answered in a small voice, ''No.''

''Then don't turn me down before you hear what I've got to say. We'd have to do a lot of research to find someone as suitable as you to help us. You haven't had much contact with your former classmates, yet you live right here in the county.''

''That's right. I haven't had much contact with them because they barely knew I was alive in high school. So why should I suddenly decide to join the reunion committee?'' she asked, being as blunt as she could.

''Your new husband's a salesman type. He wants access to your former classmates as potential customers.''

She thought about the implications. ''So I've married some slime who wants to use me to get to my old schoolmates?''

''I wouldn't put it in exactly those terms. Particularly since I'm the slime,'' he drawled.

She couldn't stop her jaw from dropping open. When she recovered enough to speak, she gasped out, ''You and me… *We* would pretend to be married?''

He had the grace to look uncomfortable, but the determination hadn't left his face.

She sat there, letting the idea sink in. On the face of it, the plan sounded harebrained. Unworkable. Dangerous. Yet below the surface was a tantalizing pull that she couldn't deny. She'd be doing something valuable—saving people's lives—and at the same time, she'd be getting closer to this man who had stirred something within her, something that she hadn't come close to feeling before.

"You're a Howard County police detective," she said. "How are *you* perfect for the job? Won't people know you?"

He started giving her arguments he must have memorized on the way over. "I've only been in the county for a few months, so I've had only limited contact with the public. I didn't grow up in the area. Nobody's likely to know me. When I was with the Baltimore P.D. I did a lot of undercover work and found out I have a fair amount of acting ability. We'd keep my first name, to avoid confusion, and I'd take a similar last name. Like maybe I'd be Cal Roberts."

She licked her suddenly dry lips. "If I agree, then what?"

"I move into your spare room. We tell anyone who asks that we're married."

She knit her hands together in her lap, thinking about him sleeping right across the hall from her. Deliberately she forced her mind to another problem. "There's something else that I'd better remind you of. I told you the last time you were here that I tend to stay away from people because…sometimes I pick up, uh, vibrations."

He kept his expression neutral.

She gave him points for not sneering. But then, he'd come to ask for her help, so he was probably on his best behavior.

"What happens if we're at this committee meeting and, uh, I have one of my spells?"

"We'll tell them you have a headache, and I'll take you home."

There was one more question she didn't want to ask. But she forced the words past her dry lips. "And what happens afterward? I mean after this whole charade when we're not married anymore?"

"Marriages go bad all the time. Some of them are pretty short," he said with a bitter note in his voice.

"Are you speaking from personal experience?"

"I'm not married. Never have been. I was thinking about my parents."

She studied the closed expression on his face and saw old anger and pain. She thought again that she should tell him his proposal was the most ridiculous idea she had ever heard. Instead she asked, "Are you expecting me to give you an answer immediately?"

"The sooner the better so we can figure out how to catch the guy who killed your friend Hallie."

"You're sure she's dead?"

"Ninety-nine percent."

She thought about that for a moment, then moistened her dry lips. She'd never been impulsive, never been quick to make decisions, but she heard herself saying, "All right."

"All right, what?"

"I'm willing to let you pose as my husband."

She watched him heave a massive sigh. Of relief, she hoped.

"Thank you."

She cleared her throat. "When do we start?"

"I'm going back to the office to clear some things off my desk and turn over my investigations to a couple of the other detectives. Then I'll go home and pack some of my stuff." He stopped, looked thoughtful. "And I want to check with a P.I. in Baltimore on another matter. So I should be back around six. Is that a problem?"

Her chest was suddenly so tight that she could barely speak. Cal Rollins was coming to live with her. The idea had been seductive. Now cold reality was setting in. Images flashed in her mind. The two of them eating dinner together… Cal in the bathroom in the morning…*her* in the bathroom…the two of them circling each other in this house. It was real. It was going to happen. And now as the images swirled in her mind, she understood that agreeing had been an act of insanity.

She should take it back. Tell him to find someone else. Instead she said, "Six is fine. I'll fix you dinner."

He reached into his pocket and pulled out a business card. "If you need to get in touch with me before I get back, here's my number."

His fingers brushed hers, and she felt a little frisson of sensation pass from her hand to his.

Her eyes shot to his face. Had he felt it too, or was she the only one overreacting with a show of nerves?

His expression was carefully neutral, and she didn't know whether to be relieved or disappointed.

BY THREE, Cal had taken care of the paperwork on his desk. Then he headed into Baltimore to see Sam Lassiter, another friend from the force who was now working at the Light Street Detective Agency with Hannah.

When he'd been on the job, Sam had been known for his by-the-book approach to law enforcement. But he'd turned in his badge two years ago after his wife and three-year-old daughter had been killed in an automobile accident. When they'd died, he'd gone off on a six-month bender—until Hannah had helped pull him out of his funk. Now he was on the wagon and working as a P.I. in the same office.

The lean, dark-haired detective looked up expectantly as Cal came through the office door.

"What brings you down to Charm City from the pristine open spaces of Howard County?" he asked.

"Pristine. I wish. Anything you've got down here in the city, we've got in Columbia and Ellicott City." He dropped into a chair opposite Sam's desk. "You heard anything on that drug dealer...what's his name—Dallas Sedgwick—who was after Lucas Somerville?"

"Unfortunately, there hasn't been any word on Sedgwick,'' Sam told him. ''Which isn't exactly good news for Lucas—or Hannah.''

Cal made a sound of agreement as he took in his friend's appearance. It looked as if Sam was doing okay.

''But I do have an interesting development in the Sean Naylor case.''

''Oh, yeah?''

''You remember Sean's father was pretty torn up about his son's death. And after Ron Wexler was shot in his garage, the senior Naylor was mouthing off about how he was going to get the rest of the cops responsible for his son's death. I was thinking that maybe it was the father who shot Ron Wexler and went after Hannah. Now I'm not so sure.''

''What changed your mind?''

''Well, it turns out he had an ironclad alibi for the morning of the Wexler shooting.''

''Such as?''

''He's got a mistress that his wife doesn't know about, which is why he couldn't give us an alibi for the morning Ron was shot. But when I tailed him, discovered his extracurricular activities and threatened to inform the missus, he came clean with me. When Wexler was killed, Naylor's wife was in Atlantic City with her girlfriends and he was at his honey's house. One of her neighbors confirms that his car was in front of her place all night.''

''He could have slipped out the back, gone to Wexler's and come back in time to be seen leaving through the front door.''

''Not unless he took a cab to the murder scene.'' Sam gave a small snort. ''The neighbor remembers the car sitting in the same spot all night 'cause some cats were yowling outside off and on that night.''

''How does he remember cats yowling on some random night?''

Sam laughed. ''Because he was going in for a lower

G.I. exam the next morning, and he was hoping to get some sleep before the procedure."

Cal nodded. "So do you have a line on who did Wexler?"

"I'm working on that." Sam stopped and cleared his throat. "The trouble is, I've been pressing pretty hard. Some of my sources have stopped talking to me."

"You want some help?"

"Are you referring to yourself? I'd appreciate anything you can do, but aren't you busy with your own cases?"

"Actually, I'm about to go on a hush-hush undercover assignment. But they let me off my leash from time to time. So I might be available if you need me. You've got my cell phone number?"

"Yeah. Thanks. I may just give you a ring."

"Don't hesitate. I like Hannah. I'll be happy when she doesn't have to watch her back every minute. She and Lucas, too."

"Yeah."

They talked for a few more minutes. Then Cal glanced at his watch, realizing he was dragging his heels. He should already be on his way to Beth's house, but he'd come down here instead because deep in his gut the idea of moving in with Beth Wagner was playing hell with his insides. First, there was the crystal-ball stuff that he didn't want to think about too hard. Then there was his inconvenient physical attraction to her, which was going to make the assignment hard—pun intended.

With a sigh, he heaved himself out of the chair.

"You look like you're going to a funeral," Sam commented. "Want to tell me about it?"

"Some other time. I'm already late," Cal answered, turning and heading for the door.

ELLICOTT CITY WOMAN VANISHES.

Damien read the account in the *Baltimore Sun* of Hallie Bradshaw's disappearance. There wasn't much information. The police had no leads. There wouldn't *be* any leads, or anything that was going to pan out.

He carefully cut out the article and used two-sided tape to fix it in the scrapbook he was keeping of his triumphs.

Then he turned to the page with the notice that had been sent out by the reunion planning committee.

"Who's going to show up at that meeting?" he asked, starting one of his dialogues.

He grinned as he thought about appearing at the meeting.

"I could go and sit around with those morons who are so proud of their high-school days. They're probably telling each other what great stuff they've done since then. But none of them can compare to me. I'm not the jerk they used to pick on. Now I'm Damien, the devil's spawn. Just like in that movie. I've gotten rid of my name, and I've gotten rid of some of them!"

He laughed aloud at that.

It was so tempting to let them see how he'd changed, what he'd done. But he knew it was a lot smarter not to walk into that meeting. A lot smarter to stay in the shadows, take notes and maybe give the committee a surprise or two.

He put down the scrapbook and picked up the copy of the yearbook that he'd showed to Hallie and the others.

Slowly he flipped through the pages, looking at the candid shots, the group pictures from the various clubs, the sports teams, the cheerleader squad. What crap! It had all been so important to those jerks. Well, if they hadn't already found out, they'd learn pretty soon how valid it was.

A warm little thought floated to the surface of his mind. He could plant a bomb at the reunion committee location. That would get rid of a whole bunch of them at once. It would be satisfying. But would it be as satisfying as picking them off one at a time?

He'd have to weigh the pros and cons.

He flipped to the section at the back with the seniors' pictures.

He'd already drawn a big X through some of them. Lisa Stapler, Will Huttonson, Donna Misk, Andy Preston, Jim Vogel. He hadn't marked out Hallie Bradshaw yet.

But now was a good time for the little ceremony.

Getting a bottle of sparkling white wine from the refrigerator, he popped the cork and carefully poured the bubbling liquid into a long-stemmed flute.

Taking a sip, he savored the taste on his tongue. Then he got out his marking pen and drew an X through Hallie's picture.

Next came another sip of wine as he began looking at the other smiling faces.

''Silvie Weston is a good candidate,'' he mused. ''I'll have to find out what she's doing now—where she lives.''

Then his eyes traveled to Beth Wagner.

''Beth, your blond hair was so beautiful,'' he said as his finger softly touched the shining strands. Then moved lower, caressing her lips and her breasts.

A smile flickered over his face as he thought about what the two of them might do together.

He'd always had a thing for shy, quiet Beth, he thought as he continued to stroke his finger tenderly across her picture while sipping his wine. But he didn't see any reason to go after her. She wasn't like the rest. She hadn't been a big deal at school. She wasn't going to the reunion committee meeting, so there was no reason to kill her.

Chapter Four

Beth was sitting at the kitchen table, snapping green beans for dinner, thinking that she'd at least show Cal that she could cook. She had a roast in the oven, fragrant with herbs and surrounded by potatoes and carrots. Now she was getting to the green vegetable.

The beans went into a large saucepan, the snapped ends into a small bowl. She'd just picked up another one, when a pain shot through her skull.

One minute she was fine, the next she could barely breathe, barely think. Her scalp felt as if it was on fire, as if the roots of her hair were hot wires digging into her flesh.

And then the terrible sensation traveled down her body, to her face, her throat, her breasts.

It wasn't real, her mind screamed.

But it felt real.

On a strangled cry, she jumped away from the table, sending the bowl of bean ends scattering to the floor.

Swaying on her feet, she reached to steady herself against the chair back. There was a roaring noise in her ears, in her mind, and disjointed, out-of-proportion images she didn't want to see. It was as if she was viewing a picture of herself, and a large hand was hovering over the picture. The hand touched her. Stroked her. As she watched in horror, it descended again to contact her flesh.

Only it wasn't just the picture. She could feel it, too. Someone's hands on her body—touching her in places where he shouldn't be touching.

"No!" she cried out, overturning the chair as she tried to escape the room. Then hands grabbed her again and she screamed.

"BETH, WHAT IS IT? What's wrong? Is someone here?"

She couldn't speak. Couldn't do more than clasp her hands over her ears, trying to block out the sound and the pictures and the terrible sensations of unwanted hands probing her.

Rationality had fled her mind. When she felt massive arms around her, holding her, the terror increased and she started to flail, trying with a burst of desperate strength to yank herself away from the enemy. It was *him.* Somehow, he had her. Not just the picture. He was real. In her kitchen. Come to get her.

Terror grabbed her by the throat. Hysterical sobs welled from deep inside her as she tried with all her strength to wrench herself away.

"Beth. Stop it, Beth."

He was speaking to her, his words low and commanding. Aeons later, the familiar voice penetrated the roaring in her ears. Cal. It was Cal who held her.

"Beth. Shh. It's Cal. You're all right. It's Cal," he soothed, the words slurring in that southern cadence she found so sexy.

Her eyes focused on his face hovering above her. They had turned black as onyx as they stared down, full of concern, into hers. She had known him for only a few days, hadn't really trusted him except for a few brief moments. But now she gave herself over to his care, just as she had when Granger had tripped her.

"Are you hurt?" he asked, his tone urgent. As he felt her struggles cease, he loosened his grip so that he no longer held her captive.

"He...touched me. I felt him touch me. It was terrible," she choked out.

"Who?"

"I don't know," she shouted in frustration.

Then, sensing that she was on the verge of hysterics, she dragged in a shuddering breath as she buried her face against his shoulder.

Shifting her weight, he lifted her into his arms, then carried her down the hall to the parlor. Lowering himself to the couch, he held her on his lap, cradling her close as though she was precious to him, while he murmured low, soothing words.

For long moments she could only huddle there, feeling the steady beat of his heart. It was as if he'd wrapped her in a magic cloak where nothing bad could ever reach her. All she wanted to do was stay there, safe and secure, because she knew he would never let anything happen to her.

His hand stroked her hair, and she shifted in his arms, settling herself more closely.

Cal was the one who broke the spell. "Someone was in here?" he asked. "In the house?"

She swallowed and pressed her face into his shirt so she wouldn't have to see the terrible moment when the look in his eyes changed from concern to scorn, the way it had before.

"You're going to act like you did the other day, when you came to ask me about Hallie. Like I'm some sort of madwoman," she whispered.

"Just tell me what happened."

She kept her head bent. "All right. I was in the kitchen snapping beans. I got a headache. The same kind of headache I had the night...the night I knew Hallie was in trouble." She stopped, sucked in a breath and let it out before forcing herself to go on. "Then I felt him." She gulped. "I mean not really. Well, you wouldn't think it was real. It was just in my mind the way it is when images, sounds come to me. This time..."

Her breath hitched. "This time it wasn't someone in trouble. It was different. I saw *him.* He was looking at my picture, focusing his attention on me. He started touching me...touching the picture, I mean. But I could *feel* it." Again it was several seconds before she could go on in a shaky voice. "I felt his hands on my hair. On my face. Other places."

She heard him utter an expletive.

"You don't believe me, do you? You just think I'm crazy, and that something weird happened inside my mind. Maybe you think I wanted someone to touch me." She pushed herself away from him and landed on a sofa cushion, finally lifting her head, her eyes defiantly meeting his.

He ran a hand through his dark hair. "I don't know," he said in a low voice. Then, "What else do you remember? Did you see the guy's face?"

"Just his hand."

"Did you see where he was? Anything you can tell me about his location that will help us find him?"

She tried to give him what he wanted, tried to come up with details. "It was a tight focus. I knew he was looking at my picture. In a book. The book was on a table. I could see a cigarette burn in the wood. Then when he touched me—touched the picture," she clarified, "I didn't see anything else. I just *felt* him." She shuddered, not expecting him to understand how awful it had been to feel those fingers crawling over her flesh like thousands of insect feet.

"So you don't have any clues besides a cigarette burn on the table that could help us figure out who he is?" he asked, and she caught a note of accusation in his voice.

"I can't choose what I see and feel in a vision." Since that first time when she'd seen her father's truck go off the road, she'd never talked about what happened when these strange episodes took her over. Not to anyone. Certainly not to her parents after their reaction to what had happened. There had been no one she'd trusted with her fragile emotions. Now Cal was forcing her to describe the experience. Fumbling for words, she added, ''I'm not like one of those psychics who leads people to kidnapped children or bodies buried in the woods. But that wouldn't make any difference to you. You'd still doubt the story I just told you.''

''Something frightening happened to you. That's obvious.''

''Right. A psychotic break.''

''Stop it!''

She stared at him, seeing the concern and uncertainty warring in his eyes. She wanted to make demands then. At the very least, she wanted to hear him say he believed her. That he didn't think she was wacko. That he didn't think she was so needy that she'd made up the contact. But she was afraid to ask for reassurances, so she simply kept her mouth closed.

When he spoke, it was to ask another question. ''How often do you experience this sort of thing?''

Again, he was posing a question nobody else had ever asked. ''There's no regular schedule. I can go for months, years, without anything strange happening. I've never had anything like this twice in three days. Never before.''

''Do you have any explanation?''

She gave her head a firm shake. ''I've never had any explanation. I just want it to leave me alone!''

''Okay. I can see you're upset. I'll go out and bring in my stuff—if that's okay.''

''It's fine!'' she snapped, then made an attempt to control the tone of her voice as she added, ''I've changed the sheets on the bed in the room on the right at the top of the stairs. You can put your things up there.''

''Thanks.''

Emotions roiled through her as he turned and headed for the door. She was relieved he had the sense to give her some breathing space. At the same time she was thinking that bringing in his clothing made this whole marriage charade seem real.

As soon as he was out of the room, Beth pushed herself off the sofa, then walked rapidly down the hall to the kitchen. Bending, she righted the chair she'd tipped over, carefully setting the legs against the floor. Then she knelt beside the table and started picking up the green-bean stems that had scattered in all directions.

She'd told Cal that her quota of weird experiences had escalated since the night with Hallie. She could have said that they'd escalated since he'd first come out here. But she saw no advantage in tying those facts together for his benefit.

A few minutes later, Cal appeared in the doorway. Ignoring him, she kept working. Silently, he knelt beside her, helping her put the stems back into the bowl.

Neither of them spoke as they finished the task. Then she washed her hands, sat down at the table and began snapping more beans, working with ruthless efficiency.

Cal washed his hands, dried them on the dish towel, then pulled out a chair. "Can I help you do that?"

"You don't have to."

"Show me what to do. I don't want to make extra work for you because I'm here."

"It's not rocket science." She demonstrated how to snap the end off a bean with one hand while she used the opposite thumb to break the bean in half.

He laughed. "It may not be rocket science, but you're going to have to slow down a little so I can see how you're doing all that in one blinding motion."

For a few minutes, they focused on the bean-snapping lesson. She'd never thought of what she did in the kitchen as anything unusual. Not until she watched him fumble to get it right.

His efforts barely augmented the pile of beans going into the pot. But her own efficient motions helped her get back her sense of balance.

"Dinner smells good," he commented.

"It's just a roast," she answered, transferring the beans to a pot of water she'd started boiling on the stove.

"For me, that's a pretty fancy home-cooked meal. Dad never made one. He was more the hamburger-on-the-grill type."

"You lived with your dad?"

"Yeah, he got custody of me when I was nine months old."

"That's unusual, isn't it?"

"Well, my old lady deserted us. It wasn't too hard to convince the courts that she wasn't a fit parent."

"Oh," she answered as she set the pot of beans on a burner.

"You lived here with your parents?" he asked, switching the conversation away from himself.

Granger came into the kitchen, pushed his dish with his nose to tell her he needed water.

"Yes," she answered as she washed out the bowl and filled it again. "They were pretty old when they had me. Dad died before I graduated from high school. Mom passed away five years ago. What about your dad? Is he still living?"

"He died a couple of months ago."

"I'm sorry."

He nodded, his gaze fixed on the dog.

She measured out dog food from the large metal container in the pantry, the one Mom had used to boil home-cured hams.

"Let me give him the food," Cal said.

Understanding why he'd made the request, she handed him the dish, and he set it on the floor. Granger started eagerly chomping, his noisy eating filling the silence.

"Did you have a dog when you were a kid?" she asked.

"There was always a mutt around. None quite as distinctive-looking as Granger."

She nodded, then went back to work. While she drained

the beans, cooled them under cold running water and made the dressing for the bean salad, Cal set the table. As far as she could tell, he was acting as if nothing unusual had happened when he'd come charging into the kitchen. Which was good, she supposed.

When she took the pan out of the oven and set it on the stove, his eyes widened as he stared at the perfectly roasted meat surrounded by crisp, golden potatoes and tender carrots.

"That looks even better than it smelled in the oven."

Trying not to let the praise swell her head, she carved slices of meat and arranged them with the vegetables on a platter. Then she finished the bean salad.

They took chairs at opposite sides of the table. It was strange to glance up from her plate and find this particular man sitting across the table from her. As though they really were married, she couldn't stop herself from thinking.

She was about to sink into a little fantasy about that until she brought herself up short. She'd better not enjoy this too much. He might like her cooking, but the only reason he was here was that he wanted her help catching a serial killer. A killer who had focused his attention on *her* not long ago.

That realization sent a nasty shiver slithering down her spine. Looking up quickly, she saw that Cal was watching her and knew that he'd caught the reaction.

"What's wrong?" he asked.

"Nothing."

"Something," he corrected.

She looked down at her plate, pushing a couple of green beans around with her fork.

"Beth, if we're going to work together, we have to communicate with each other."

She swallowed, then raised her head. "Okay, I was thinking about your assignment. Then I was thinking about what happened just before you got here. I mean, the feeling of being touched." She stopped, closing her fingers around the handle of her fork. "I guess that means the killer was focused on me."

"Not necessarily. It could be somebody else."

"Like who?"

"Like anybody," he answered as if they were having a normal, rational conversation.

"Then why did I feel...like I was being pawed?" She didn't go into any more detail because she didn't want to think about the experience again.

"It could be that you're hypersensitive," he said slowly. "Because of what's happened to your friend."

Again she fought the impulse to ask if his comment meant he believed her. "Maybe," she murmured, silently conceding that he could be right. She'd never been in quite this state, so she had no idea what to expect.

Picking up her knife, she cut off a piece of meat and forked it into her mouth. Cal did the same.

"So, I looked you up on the Web," he said.

Her head jerked up. "You did?"

"Yes. You're a weaver with an international reputation."

She could only nod.

"Your work is beautiful. Where do you get your ideas?"

She was pleased by his interest until she reminded herself that the question was just part of his assignment. "I don't know. They come to me. A lot of times the inspiration is from nature, like the hanging I'm doing now. Other times I'm just playing around with color combinations or shapes."

"You obviously have a talent for it."

The compliment was gratifying. So was his enthusiasm for her dinner. He put away a considerable portion of meat and vegetables before pushing back his chair and sighing. "That was a great meal. I guess there are some advantages to this job."

"I hope so," she murmured, then felt her face heat, wondering if she'd implied too much by the answer.

His voice turned businesslike again. "We need to talk about how we're going to work together," he told her as they cleared the table.

"Do you want to do it over coffee and cookies?"

"I won't turn down that offer."

She made coffee and set the pot on a tray, along with cups, plates and the chocolate chip squares she'd baked that afternoon in honor of the occasion.

After polishing off one of the cookies, he set another on his plate, then cleared his throat.

"For, uh, our marriage act to work, we've got to look like we're comfortable with each other," he said.

"That's a tall order, since I wasn't comfortable with the idea from the beginning."

"I figure if we hang around together for a while, that will help."

"Are you going to sit and watch me weave?"

"I'd like to."

"We'll see." She cleared her throat. "So what am I supposed to tell people about the mysterious stranger in my life?" she asked, unable to actually say the word *husband.* "How did I meet you? Why did I marry you?"

"I came out here because you answered an ad for financial planning. We hit it off and ended up tying the knot."

"What company?"

He pulled a card from his pocket. It was a different card from the one he'd given her on his first visit. This one said Alliance Financial Services.

"What if somebody calls the number?"

"They'll get an answering machine. I'll pick up the messages, make some appointments."

"You're going to go through the whole shtick—doing a financial analysis?"

"I did some undercover work in a financial firm. I can

pull it off if I have to. But my plan is to come across as so super-slick that nobody will hire me."

"That will certainly reflect well on me," she answered dryly.

"It will be a good reason for you to boot me out."

She gave a tight nod. Then, because she couldn't bear to sit there facing him, she stood and turned toward the window. To her surprise, she'd been so absorbed in the conversation that she hadn't noticed the sun setting. It was almost dark outside, and she felt the familiar tug of fear that always grabbed her as the blackness closed in. Automatically, she moved around the room, turning on lamps. Then she walked to the front hall and flipped the switch that activated the floodlights around the house.

OUT IN THE FIELD, a man watched the lights flick on. He knew the range of the illumination, knew where to walk, how close he could come to avoid them. And the dog. Avoiding the dog was another priority.

Beth was a little late tonight. Maybe because of that guy who had come up the driveway and parked in front of her house. The guy who'd carried in a couple of suitcases.

An expletive tumbled from the watcher's lips.

What the hell did it mean? That guy being here? Were he and Beth lovers?

"No!" He'd damn well know if she had a lover. Maybe the man was an out-of-town relative.

The watcher took an involuntary step forward, then checked himself. Beth had no idea he was out here in the evenings. And he wasn't going to have her finding out about his after-hours visits—not because some guy was staying with her.

But that was certainly a complication he didn't like. He'd have to find out who the visitor was and what he was doing there.

Then he'd have to figure out what to do about it. Or

maybe the best course was to speed up the timetable he'd set for himself.

Yeah, that was it. Make things happen faster, he thought, a plan starting to solidify in his mind.

Because Beth was his, and if he couldn't have her, he'd make sure nobody else could, either.

Chapter Five

Cal watched Beth walking around the room turning on lamps as if it were the most natural thing in the world to illuminate the house like the national Christmas tree.

He was even more interested when she hurried down the hall and started flipping more switches. In moments, the area around the house was almost as bright as day.

That certainly wasn't normal behavior. She was afraid of something, and he was going to find out what.

She came back down the hall, stepped into the parlor and saw him looking at her.

"I was just turning on some lights," she explained quickly.

"I can see that. But why so many?"

"I—" She stopped, taking her lower lip between her teeth. "I...like to be able to see the yard. And I like it bright in here."

"Why?" he asked again, letting her know he wasn't going to accept a simplistic answer.

"Some things happened," she said in a small voice.

"What things?" he pressed.

"Well...the sheep." She cleared her throat. "Tim found some of them dead. It looked like they'd gotten into some grass where there was a pesticide spill."

She'd mentioned the guy before. "Tim Fillmore, the farmer who works for you?"

"Yes."

"You use pesticide?"

"No. But, uh, but someone could have dumped it on my property. We moved the sheep to a different field."

"Did you call the police?"

"It didn't seem like a matter for the police."

"Uh-huh," he answered, suggesting mildly that he didn't share her judgment. "Anything else you haven't mentioned?"

"No." The way she looked away was like a sign announcing that she was lying.

He kept his eyes fixed on her. "Come on. What else don't you think is worth telling me?"

"Well, there was a fire."

Automatically, he looked around the room for signs of damage. "Where?"

"Not in the house. In one of the fields down by the road."

"And?"

"A thunderstorm put it out."

"Lucky for you. I suppose you think it was caused by someone tossing a lighted cigarette onto your property?"

"Or a match."

"Which came first, the sheep poisoning or the fire?" he asked, keeping the questions coming in rapid succession.

"The sheep."

"And the time frame?"

She folded her arms across her chest. "Is this an interrogation?"

"Just answer the question."

"A year ago."

"And the fire was?"

"Six months ago."

"So all this happened after you acquired a bunch of new neighbors in that development down the road?"

"Yes."

"You have a run-in with any of them?"

"No."

"And when did you install the outdoor lighting system?" He kept his gaze fixed on her as she crossed to the chair by the fireplace and carefully sat down.

"Eight years ago."

"Because something happened back then?"

"No. I just felt more...secure with lights around the house."

"Why?"

"Stop asking me questions with that edge in your voice, like you did the other day."

"Stop acting like a hostile witness. All I'm trying to do is help you."

"I don't need your help."

He watched her carefully, noted the way her blue eyes flicked away from his gaze, flicked toward the door. Wondering if she was going to try to make a break for it, he stood and moved to the arched doorway so she'd have to dart around him to get out of the room.

As he propped his shoulder against the wall, she sank into her seat looking small and vulnerable and very feminine, and he felt his insides clench. He was going at her like a murder suspect again, when all he was trying to do was help her. Lord, what was it about her that brought out the worst in him?

Softening his voice, he asked, "Why don't you want to take advantage of the fact that you've got an experienced detective willing to help you with something that sounds like an ongoing problem?"

"You don't have to help me with anything."

The way she said it had his aggressive instincts flaring again. "What are you hiding?"

"What do you think—that I've got a drug-distribution operation going on in one of my pastures?"

"Do you?"

"No!"

"Then what? Why are you being evasive?"

She dragged in a shaky breath and let it out slowly. "Because I'm tired of having people think I've got a couple of screws loose. You think so. I don't want to give you any more ammunition."

It was obvious she wanted to drop the discussion, but he couldn't give her the luxury. Not when the two of them had to find a way to deal with each other before that reunion committee meeting.

"Such as what?" he asked.

Her chin jerked up. "Okay, you want to know the answer. I'll give you the damn answer. Sometimes I feel like there's someone out there watching me. I can feel him out there in the dark. Beyond the range of the lights."

"Who?"

"I don't know! The other night I thought—I thought he might have something to do with what happened to Hallie. That's why I had some reason to believe she might really be here."

"You've seen someone out there?"

"No. I—I just felt him...with my sixth sense, or whatever you want to call it."

"Has he given you one of your headaches?"

"No. What I feel isn't that strong."

"Why not? He could be a danger to you."

"I told you. I can't control what comes to me and what doesn't."

He heard the exasperation in her voice.

"Okay," he muttered. Then another thought struck him. "You sense him during the day, too?"

"I get headaches during the day, but the extrasensory experiences are always at night."

"When I came here, you were having one of those episodes."

Her face contorted. "Yes!"

He kept his gaze tightly focused on her, watching for any sign of duplicity. "When I got here, it wasn't at night. That was during the day."

Her face drained of color as she took in his words. "Oh my God," she said in a barely audible voice.

BETH STARED AT HIM in numb shock.

She'd known someone was looking at her picture. Felt the awful touch of fingers against private parts of her body. But she hadn't been thinking about the time. Now he was telling her it had been during the day.

The day!

Cal must have seen the panic on her face, must have seen her lips trembling as she tried to speak. Only a groan came out of her mouth.

He crossed the room and sat down next to her on the sofa. Too stunned to speak, she could only continue to stare at him as he lifted her cold hands and sandwiched them between his warm ones.

"Lord, you're freezing."

The words were like a trigger making her teeth start to chatter. He pulled her closer, his arm going around her shoulder, his fingers stroking up and down her arm. The contact felt good. Reassuring. She closed her eyes, allowing herself to lean into his warmth and strength.

But as his hand stroked her arm, she felt her body suddenly stiffen as she realized she was doing it again—letting him comfort her. And the worst thing in the world she could do was let herself need him or depend on him for anything. He was only here for a little while—and he was only pretending that they had a relationship. As soon as the job was over, he was walking away, and she had to make sure he didn't leave a hole in her life. She'd survived all these years alone on the farm. She could damn well do it now.

Straightening, Beth pushed herself away, stood and smoothed a hand over her hair. "I'm fine."

"Are you sure?"

"Yes. I'm going to work for a few more hours," she said, making her tone brusque. "The television reception's not all that great out here. I don't have cable, but you're welcome to watch, if you want."

"I'm not much for TV. I can amuse myself."

"There's a towel in the bathroom for you. The pink one. And you've already put your stuff in the guest room?"

"Yes. Thanks. I'll try to stay out of your way."

"I appreciate that," she said in a clipped manner, then turned on her heel and exited the room before he saw her hands were still shaking.

Squaring her shoulders, she marched down the hall, then slowed when she heard her traitorous dog hesitate the way he had earlier in the evening. When he finally followed her down the hall, she let out the breath she hadn't realized she was holding.

In her workroom, she sat down at the loom and picked up the shuttle. But it was impossible to focus on the wall hanging when her heart was pounding so hard in her chest that she couldn't catch her breath.

Daylight. It had happened in broad daylight!

Previously the night had shadowed her weird experiences, and the daylight had been safe.

Now everything was suddenly different. Including her need to flee her own parlor—to flee from the man whose presence filled that room. She turned her head, staring toward the front of the house, picturing his dark hair and those dark eyes that saw too much. She'd left him standing in the middle of the room. Was he sitting on the sofa now, or had he gone upstairs?

What did that matter, she asked herself fiercely. What did *he* matter? She turned deliberately back to the loom and sent the shuttle sailing through the threads.

CAL STARED DOWN the hall after the woman who had fled his presence. He'd tried to comfort her, but she hadn't wanted his comfort. Which was good, he told himself. In a remarkably short time, he was getting very wound up with her.

She brought out his protective feelings. And his sexual feelings. The first he could handle, the second was damn inconvenient. It had been easier when he'd been able to simply think of her as a liar or a suspect.

A harsh sound rose in his throat. Now that he was getting to know her better, he was torn by doubts he'd never confronted before.

He'd never believed in phenomena he couldn't measure, couldn't experience for himself. And he'd always thought that anybody who relied on information from a crystal ball reader ought to have his head examined. But if psychics were pure frauds, what had been happening to Beth?

He'd doubted her original story about Bradshaw. But that left him with no explanation for how she'd known about the woman's disappearance or the blood.

Then he'd come here this afternoon and found her in the throes of some kind of attack that he couldn't dismiss. Now he was almost a hundred percent positive that she wasn't faking.

He cursed under his breath.

It was clear that something had happened to her. Something she explained in terms that left him baffled and uneasy.

But he wasn't going to mentally take a flying leap off a cliff because he didn't understand her.

For damn sure he wasn't going that far!

He sighed and pushed himself off the couch. Part of the problem was that he had nothing else to occupy his thoughts. He was used to being busy. But Ken Patterson had taken away his active caseload because Cal couldn't risk being seen going into the Warfield Building when he was supposed to be spending his time peddling financial investments.

He walked into the hall, opened the front door and stepped onto the porch, staring into the brightly lighted yard and the darkness beyond.

In the past, when he'd been on an undercover assignment, it hadn't been that difficult to play the role of a drug buyer or a dealer or the owner of a fencing operation. But the rules had been different. He'd been working to arrest the scum of society. There had been no moral ambiguity about his role.

He hadn't liked this charade from the first. Now he was finding out just how difficult it was going to be playing Beth Wagner's husband.

He wasn't sure how to cope with the shaft of guilt that stabbed through him. Raising his right hand, he pounded his fist against his left palm in frustration. In the middle of the blow, he was struck with a feeling of self-consciousness. Beth had said she'd sensed someone out there, someone watching her.

Watching him, now, too. Because, with the lights turned up, he was about as visible as a character on a movie screen out here.

The thought of being spied on made him edgy. And angry. If some bozo was coming out here harassing Beth, he wanted to know who it was and why.

Could it have something to do with the missing class members? Was the guy who had abducted the others and presumably murdered them going after Beth?

It didn't seem likely. All the victims had been movers and shakers during their high-school years. Football players, cheerleaders, members of the homecoming court. Beth had been nothing like them. According to her own account, she'd been an outsider.

Of course, she could be lying to him. But he didn't think so, not from the look on her face and the emotion in her voice when she'd talked about her high-school days.

So who had come sneaking around here? Was the watcher just a figment of her imagination? Or was she lying to him about that?

He clenched his teeth, then deliberately eased up in the pressure. He hated second-guessing everything she told him, hated making a value judgment about every encounter.

And suddenly he remembered the car he'd seen parked at the end of her lane. He still had the license number in his notebook. But he'd forgotten all about it with everything else going on. Well, he couldn't do anything about that until he got back to his computer.

Resolutely, he climbed down the stairs, then headed toward the large bulky barn. As soon as he stepped around the side of the building, he was shrouded in darkness. Good.

He stood there for several minutes, breathing in the country air, which was perfumed with a generous dollop of sheep manure, he noticed. He stood with his back to the solid bulk of the barn wall, allowing his eyes to become accustomed to the dark, thinking that the three-quarters full moon gave him just enough light to see by. As he stepped away from the building, he remembered Brodie's complaint about his shoes, and gave a low snort. If the shoes got messed up, he could always leave them on the porch and clean them up in the morning. Beth must be used to stuff like that since she lived out here.

BETH'S HANDS WORKED the shuttle, her feet worked the pedal of the big loom, her motions automatic, the familiar rhythm of her work and the low classical music coming from the radio helping to take the edge off her nervous tension.

She had almost managed to forget about her disturbing houseguest, when a stab of pain in her head made her body jerk as though she'd been shot.

"Oh God, no," she moaned the words aloud. It was happening again. And the last time had been only hours ago.

A sob of mingled protest, fear and frustration welled in her throat as she waited helplessly for some unwanted sound, some terrible vision to invade her mind. Or the feel of hands on her body.

At first she felt nothing concrete. Heard nothing, saw nothing. All that came to her was a vague and shadowy impression of darkness. And then a man walking in a darkened field. She could see his legs and his feet, but not his face.

Despair threatened to overwhelm her.

Please, God. Please, not again, she silently begged, pressing her palm to her forehead, willing the image to go away.

Was it the man who had been watching her?

She should try to see his face. Rationally she knew that. Instead, she fought the mental invasion with everything she had.

Her hands trembled, sweat broke out on her forehead and her whole body went rigid.

She had tried in the past to make the terrifying experience stop. Always before, her will had been weaker than the invisible energy waves bombarding her, and the unwanted experience had taken over her mind with a death grip she was helpless to control. But this time her determination was stronger than it had ever been in her life.

Cal had come in once and found her hysterical with fright. The thought uppermost in her mind now was that she couldn't bear his seeing her like that again.

Every muscle in her body clenched as she fought the invasion with more determination than she'd thought she possessed. Slowly, slowly, the picture in her mind grew dimmer, wavered, defused. And for the first time in her life she felt as if she had some control over the forces invading her mind. For long seconds, she sat there, breathing in and out, marveling at her victory.

It had happened again. But this time she'd gotten some control over the experience.

The only residue was a dull ache in her head. Standing

on shaky legs, she steadied herself against the frame of the loom, then walked down the hall to the bathroom.

Opening the medicine cabinet, she found two ibuprofen tablets and downed them with a glass of water.

Had Cal heard her walking down the hall? Would he wonder what she was doing, why she had stopped working? Where was he anyway?

With a grimace, she realized the focus of her thoughts. It didn't matter what Cal was doing or what he thought about her walking around her own house. Firmly she put him out of her mind and hurried back to the workroom.

But instead of picking up the shuttle, she sat there thinking about what had just happened, trying to evaluate the experience.

It wasn't like the last time when she'd felt as if questing fingers were assaulting her body. This time had been different. Not like something was happening. But like something was going to happen.

But what?

She stopped herself with a jolt. Why was she trying to bring it back when she'd just worked so hard to make it go away?

CAL TIPPED his head up, looking at the blaze of stars above him. They were so much brighter than he'd ever seen in Baltimore, or even in Ellicott City where he lived now.

It reminded him of Greensboro, and he suddenly realized how much he missed the open space and the solitude of his boyhood home.

He stood for a moment, listening for any sounds around him. There was nothing to hear but the buzz of insects and the distant bleat of a sheep.

The bleat came again, more plaintive, he thought. Then it was joined by another. And another.

Did sheep get stirred up like that all by themselves, or was something—or someone—spooking them?

Turning in the direction of the sound, he reached for the

small but powerful flashlight he carried on his key chain. Then he thought better of it.

If someone was out there in the pasture with the animals, he didn't want to announce his presence with the light.

Instinctively crouching low, he moved as silently as possible through the darkness, heading for the field with the sheep, their fluffy white shapes coming into view as he drew closer.

Weeds tugged against his pants legs, then grew more sparse as he moved under the branches of a giant tree.

It was darker here, the stars and the moon blocked from view and the ground uneven, and he stumbled over a tree root. Moments after he'd righted himself, his lead foot stepped off into empty air. Then, before he could jerk himself back to safety, he was falling through space, an involuntary cry tearing from his lips.

BETH HAD BEEN WORKING for a few minutes when the pain attacked her again—fast and ruthless, like a knife plunging into the soft tissue of her brain.

It was worse than the attack she'd fought off a few minutes ago, and this time she knew it wasn't a premonition of disaster to come. This time the breath whooshed out of her lungs in a strangled gasp as she felt herself falling, falling through space in a terrifying plunge.

A silent scream clogged her throat. The hand that automatically shot out to keep herself from falling closed around the solid wooden frame of the loom.

The plummeting sensation stopped with a sudden sickening jolt that made her body feel as if it had slammed into a stone wall.

Disoriented, she dragged in a rattling breath, even as Granger stood and moved to her side, pushing his nose against her leg, silently asking her what was wrong.

She couldn't tell him, couldn't speak. Her head was spinning, the pain almost unbearable. But somewhere in her mind she knew that she wasn't the one who had fallen. It was Cal.

Something had happened to Cal. And she wasn't prepared for the surge of panic that swept over her. Wasn't prepared for the way it gripped her by the throat, cut off her breath.

With a strangled sob, she jumped up and ran toward the front door, the dog at her heels. Heedless of her own safety, she dashed into the night.

There was no hesitation. She made straight for the pasture to her right, her feet eating up the yards as she plunged ahead into the smothering darkness.

IT TOOK SEVERAL SECONDS for Cal to realize that his foot had struck something solid, breaking his fall before slipping off again. But his reflexes had been good enough for him to grab for purchase.

In the pitch blackness, he could see nothing. Cautiously, he shifted his body, and winced when he felt a twinge in the leg that had taken the weight of the fall. Flexing it, he decided it wasn't broken, thank the Lord.

For long moments all he could do was hover where he was, fighting to catch his breath, clinging to whatever it was that had broken his plunge into oblivion.

Then, being careful not to loosen his hold, he slid his palm over the solid surface under his hand. Rough fibers tore at his bruised skin, and he winced.

Where in the hell was he? he wondered as he cataloged sensory impressions. It felt as if he was clinging to a tree limb. Well, not a limb exactly, a root maybe.

Careful not to dislodge himself, he shifted so that he could crane his neck upward. Above him he could see a patch of star-studded sky, partially blocked by branches. The view was further blocked on all sides by some sort of circle. From below him, the smell of dampness wafted upward. Reaching out the foot that wasn't throbbing, he touched a wall. A curving wall. When he kicked at it, a small piece of masonry dislodged, falling into the darkness below him and finally splashing into water.

Silently, he considered what he knew. A curved shaft around him, water below him, a tree root sticking into one side of the shaft and continuing through the other. He must have fallen into an old well. Who in the hell was stupid enough to leave a hazard like that around?

Shifting his position again, he manually inspected the tree root. Yeah, that was it. The root must have grown through the side of the well. Lucky for him, because if he hadn't caught himself on it, he'd have plunged a lot farther.

Now the question was, how far was he from the top?

Not far enough to be seriously injured. At least he knew that much.

He looked upward again. The top of the well must be about level with the ground, which was why he hadn't seen it. From this vantage point, it looked as if he was about nine or ten feet into this damn thing. Too far to climb up, unless there were other protrusions he could use.

Running his hands over the wall, he felt nothing useful and cursed. Then he decided there might be a way. What if he wedged his back against one side of the shaft and his feet against the other? Cautiously he shifted his position and found the shaft was narrow enough so that he could brace his back against one side of the tube and his feet against the opposite side.

Slowly, with difficulty, he began to move upward, the rough surface scraping his skin through the fabric of his shirt.

After a few minutes, a section of concrete or whatever it was crumbled under the pressure of his heel, and he slipped back a foot. Without sparing the breath to curse, he hung there panting. Then he started inching upward again, his teeth clenched with effort.

He had managed to move himself about five feet toward

the surface when he heard Beth calling his name, her voice high and strained.

"Cal! Cal! Are you all right? Answer me!" she cried, her voice edging toward the hysterical. Her dog barked in concert with her frantic words.

A surge of emotion flowed through him—part worry, part anger. Whether with himself or with her he wasn't sure.

"Stay back," he ordered, his voice echoing and re-echoing in the hollow space. "I'm in a damn well. Stay back before you fall in, too."

"Oh Lord, are you all right?" she asked again. Then, speaking more sharply to the dog than he'd ever heard her do before, she ordered, "Granger, quiet."

The dog stopped barking at once, and Cal answered her question. "I'm more or less okay. I caught hold of a tree root, so I didn't fall too far. I'm on my way up."

She was close enough so that he heard a breath sigh out of her. Then she was leaning over the rim above him, blocking out most of the light so that all he could see was her darkened shape above him.

"I told you to stay back, dammit."

She remained where she was. "I can't see you."

Perhaps because he was embarrassed about his current indecorous position, he growled, "Why didn't you have the sense to cover this damn thing up? What if one of your sheep fell down here?"

"Cal, it *was* covered. It's supposed to be covered."

"Oh, yeah? Then what the hell am I doing down here?"

"I don't know," she whispered and he could tell from her sudden note of panic that she was telling him the truth. She'd thought this hole in the ground wasn't a hazard, but it had turned into one.

He'd give that careful consideration later. The task for the moment was to get himself out. With a grunt he started moving upward again.

The pressure was killing his back, pulling the muscles, scraping the skin raw, but he kept moving.

He wanted to ask how she'd happened to come running out here looking for him, but there was no question of sparing the breath, not when he was already panting.

Above him, he heard Beth breathing almost as hard as he was himself. He thought about telling her she'd be in the way when he reached the top. But he kept his jaw clenched as he inched his way toward freedom.

The goal was within reach, when a section of the curved surface gave way under his foot, and he felt himself lurching downward again. His fingers clawed at the sides of the well, but there was nothing to stop his fall.

Chapter Six

"Cal! Oh, God, Cal!"

In a frantic lunge, Beth grabbed his arms, her fingers digging through his shirt to his flesh as she yanked him upward. She was almost sobbing, panting hard, but somehow she stopped his downward progress without going headfirst into the well with him. Then she hauled his body over the upper rim.

He was holding tight to her shoulders as they tumbled together in a heap on the ground under the tree, the performance accompanied by the loud barking of her dog. But the sound blurred in his ears, wiped away by more pressing considerations.

He was on top. She was on the bottom, and he knew he should heave himself off her. Still, for long moments all he could do was lie there panting after the hazardous climb up the cylinder and the frantic scramble at the end. When he could find the strength to move, he shifted to the side.

Somewhere in his mind he was thinking that he should loosen his grip on her shoulders. But it had become impossible to break the contact, as though the silken strands of her hair that slid against his fingers were holding him captive.

She breathed his name, and he raised his face to look at her. Her skin was so white in the moonlight, her eyes so intense, her slightly parted lips so inviting.

One of her hands lifted, and he thought she intended to push him away because that was sure as hell what she should do. Instead, the hand flattened against his shirt. He felt the pressure of her fingers, felt her stroking his flesh through the thin layer of fabric.

He wondered if she knew what she was doing, if she knew that the sensation of her fingers touching him like that was setting up a buzz in his mind and in his body.

Again, he ordered himself to pull away. But those fingers on his chest made him powerless to break the contact. Craving more of her, he gathered her close, simply absorbing the feel of her body against his. She felt good. Too damn good. That was his last coherent thought as he slanted his mouth over hers.

She tasted of homemade sweetness and innocence and the richness of the night. One draft of that potent combination was not enough. Not nearly enough. On a surge of need, he increased the pressure of his lips on hers, urging her to open for him.

There was a moment of resistance. Then she gave him what he wanted, so naturally and generously that he felt his heart melt.

When she murmured something incoherent, he deepened the kiss as needs he never knew he possessed welled inside him.

Warmth flowed through his body. Rocking against her, he devoured her mouth, using his tongue, his lips, his teeth in an assault that should have gotten him arrested.

He was aware of so many sensations, all of them swimming in his head. The silky feel of her hair as he plunged his fingers into the golden strands. The insistent pressure of his lips on hers. The sweet taste of her. The feel of her breasts pressed to his chest. His legs, one wedged between hers, one to the side so that his erection was pressed to her thigh. The faint surprised sound that she made as his mouth moved over hers.

"Darlin', you're so beautiful. So sweet," he murmured against her mouth.

She didn't answer him in words, only cleaved to him, her hands restless as they moved over his back and shoulders.

For long moments, nothing existed in the universe besides the two of them giving and taking pleasure in the other. Every reaction, every nuance ricocheted through him, each sensation reinforced the others until his senses were swamped.

Then from somewhere outside the protective bubble that surrounded them, the barking of a dog filtered into his consciousness. A large dog. Very near his ear.

He lifted his head and found himself staring into Granger's liquid eyes.

A startled exclamation tumbled from his lips. Sitting up, he looked around, aware for the first time in minutes that he'd been lying in the middle of a sheep field with a woman he had no business holding in his arms.

"I'm sorry."

The apology sounded lame to his own ears. And the confused, stunned look in her eyes made his chest tighten with unfamiliar pain.

He was feeling just as confused as she looked. Because it was damn difficult to think when his insides were tied in knots. It wasn't simply from lust—although that was a big part of it. But tangled with the lust were feelings he dared not articulate.

Standing, Cal dusted off his pants, thinking that they should go straight into the washing machine when he got back to the house. That is, if she planned to let him back in the house after his demonstration of extreme unprofessional behavior.

"We can't stay out here," he muttered.

"Yes," she answered in a voice so low he could barely hear her.

He started to offer his hand to help her up. Then he

pulled it back, not knowing if she would welcome the contact.

As she got awkwardly to her feet, he turned slightly away, so that he was momentarily startled as she walked past him, heading at a rapid pace for the house, the dog trotting ahead.

He caught up with her, limping because one foot felt as if he'd caught it under a bulldozer.

She didn't look at him, only kept walking, speeding up so that she was practically running as they neared the house.

He might have reached for her shoulder. Instead, he kept his hands to himself—something he should have thought about in the first place.

"You said there was a cover on that well," he said in a voice that came out more sharply than he intended.

"Yes. My dad had it covered a long time ago, after we dug a new one. That tree's grown up since we used it last."

"And the sheep couldn't have pushed the cover off? Or Granger?"

"Of course not. It's concrete."

"Then how did it turn into a death trap?"

"I don't know!"

He wanted to ask more questions, but not out here, not when somebody could be listening.

She charged through the front door, then barreled down the hall to her workroom.

He started to follow, then hesitated, realizing she was right. What they both needed was some time to cool off, literally and figuratively. But that didn't mean they could skip the discussion period.

If the sheep or the dog hadn't moved the cover from the well, then some person had done it. The murderer?

That didn't seem to fit the pattern. But if not the murderer, who, then? Someone else who was out to get her? The same person who had set the fire in her field and poisoned some of her sheep? The guy parked at the end of her driveway?

The thought of someone stalking her sent a shiver through his body. He was suddenly very glad that he was staying here, that he could protect her.

He stayed downstairs for several more minutes, waiting to see if she would reappear. He still wanted to ask her more questions, but he wasn't willing to follow her down the hall, because he didn't blame her for being shy of him now.

Finally, he decided that if she wasn't coming out of hiding anytime soon, he should go ahead and get cleaned up.

Back in the guest room, he opened his suitcase and took out fresh jeans and another T-shirt. As he looked over the other items in the bag, he realized he'd made a strategic mistake. He didn't own pajamas, but somewhere in the back of his closet was a bathrobe he should have brought. Now he was going to have to undress and dress again in the bathroom.

Actually, the bathrobe was pretty ratty, he decided as he carried a change of clothing and his Dopp bag down the hall. Tomorrow he'd buy a new one at the Columbia Mall. Too bad he couldn't deduct it as a business expense.

After using the facilities, he turned on the shower, and pulled off his shirt. The back of it was shredded from the contact with the rough wall of the well. After tossing the shirt in the trash, he stepped under the hot water. The showerhead was leaking slightly, running down the tile wall and making a streak. He'd fix it for her tomorrow, he thought as he washed his hair, then lathered his body.

When he turned so that the water hit his back, he winced, fingering the skin. It must be cut up as badly as the shirt.

To take his mind off the pain, he brought his thoughts back to the well—and the moments before he'd plunged in. He'd heard the sheep bleating, and he'd started off in that direction. Did that mean someone had been out there in the darkness, luring him toward the gaping hole in the ground?

There was no way to answer the question. Not tonight. Not in the dark.

Finished with his shower, he shut off the water, stepped dripping wet onto the bath mat, and was hit by an unexpected draft of air much cooler than the steamy bathroom.

His head swung toward the hall, and he saw the dog standing in the doorway, his dark brown eyes inquiring what Cal was still doing in the house.

Damn, either the lock on the door didn't work properly or the dog had learned how to turn knobs with his teeth.

"Go on," he scolded. "Get out of here and let me close the door."

Granger didn't move. And it was then that he heard footsteps. Lord, Beth had picked this moment to come upstairs. And he was standing here naked as the day he was born.

"Granger, get the hell out of here," he ordered, but the dog still didn't move. The towel rack was on the other side of the room, next to the sink. Making a quick decision, Cal lunged for it, wrapping the towel around his waist a split second before Beth's head appeared at the top of the steps. Her hair was wet and hanging down her back, and she was wearing a woven robe. So she must have had the same idea as he and had gotten cleaned up in the downstairs shower.

Her eyes shot to the bathroom door, to the back end of her dog protruding into the hall, then traveled beyond the dog to focus on Cal as his face heated and he fumbled to secure the towel around his middle.

BETH STOPPED where she was, her feet frozen to the stair treads. She should look somewhere else, she knew. But she was unable to drag her eyes away from the sight facing her. From where she stood on the steps, she was at eye level with the towel that Cal was trying to fasten around his waist. A pink towel.

Totally inappropriate. How could she have given him something so feminine, she thought as she watched his large, masculine hands fumble with the ends of the terry cloth, heard him curse as the covering started to slip.

As he worked at making himself decent, he pulled the fabric tight across his crotch, accentuating the outline of his prominent sex.

Again she ordered herself to look away. Dragging her eyes upward, she was treated to the sight of very masculine and very naked flesh—the flat plane of his belly, then the broad expanse of his chest. It was smooth and hard, except where dark hair spread out in a seductive pattern around his nipples and across his breastbone, then angled downward toward the pink towel. Again she pulled her gaze up, focusing on the brown nipples and the dark hair glistening with water from the shower.

She felt her stomach muscles clench in reaction, felt a wave of heat that was as potent as when they'd been rolling around on the ground beside the well.

He finally secured the covering, looking at her with an expression that was equal parts embarrassment and exasperation.

"I'm sorry," they both said at the same time.

Then, as if that would hide his nakedness, he turned, and she gasped. "Cal, your back."

"What about it?"

"It looks like you've been horsewhipped!"

"Yeah. It feels pretty raw," he allowed in a low voice, as though he was embarrassed to be admitting to pain or weakness.

It flashed through her mind that perhaps his brain was so saturated with testosterone that the cells couldn't function properly.

"You need something on it. I've got some antibiotic ointment."

"Where's the tube?" he said, still with his back to her.

"In the medicine cabinet. But you can't do it yourself. Not on your back," she found herself saying. "You can't reach. I'll have to put the salve on."

She heard him sigh, watched his shoulders heave. "Maybe. But let me get my pants on first."

"Yes. Right." Realizing she hadn't been thinking through the implications of her offer, she practically ran the rest of the way up the steps, scurried down the hall and slid into her room, closing the door behind her and standing in the middle of the braided rug, her breath jagged.

She'd taken a shower downstairs to keep out of his way. But the strategy hadn't exactly worked out the way she'd planned, and now she'd committed herself to taking care of his naked back. Why hadn't she simply kept her mouth shut?

Because the sight of his raw, brutalized flesh had made her insides clench.

Quickly she took off her robe, pulled on underwear, a shirt, jeans.

She wasn't sure how much time had passed, when a knock sounded on the door. With a little exclamation, she whirled around. Her pulse had been pounding so hard in her ears that she hadn't heard Cal's footsteps in the hall. But here he was right outside her door.

"Beth, are you dressed?"

"Yes." Taking a steadying breath, she opened the door. He was wearing only jeans. His chest was bare, as were his feet, like hers.

Unable to meet his eyes, she focused somewhere over his left shoulder, at a crack in the wall across from her room.

"I should have locked the bathroom door," he said. "I keep making unfortunate mistakes."

Like kissing her? Involuntarily she ran a hand through her wet hair, thinking she probably looked as if she'd just emerged from the pond in the west field. "The door doesn't lock. I forgot about that because I'm usually here alone."

"I'll fix it for you tomorrow. And the showerhead."

"You don't have to."

"Since I'm living here, there are things I can take care of for you."

"You don't have to," she said again, aware that she was repeating herself.

She had forgotten why he was standing in her doorway until he held up his hand, and she saw the orange and white tube of ointment. His shirt was in his other hand.

"Maybe I'd better do this myself."

"You'll miss half the raw places."

He stepped into the room and handed her the tube, being careful not to brush his fingers against hers, for all the good that did either one of them. Then he turned his back.

As she stared at the lacerated flesh, she sucked in a little breath.

"That bad?"

"It's worse up close." Quickly she uncapped the tube, spread the ointment on her fingers and lightly touched him, staring at his damaged flesh and thinking that his skin was hot under her touch. Thinking that she had never touched a man this intimately in her life.

She felt his muscles ripple as she worked in the salve as gently as possible, but otherwise he didn't move, even though she knew she must be hurting him.

That made her ashamed at her own reaction, because there was no way she could stop the sensual feelings that traveled from her fingertips to the rest of her body.

"Thank you," he said in a thick voice when she had finished, and at least she had the satisfaction of knowing that he was reacting on the same level as she.

It was several moments before he turned to face her.

When he did, she picked up the tube of ointment from

where she'd set it on the dresser and turned it in her fingers.

"Beth, look at me."

She kept her eyes fixed on the orange letters of the label as she said, "You can put your shirt on now."

He did as she asked, but he didn't move from where he was standing. "We need to talk."

"Now?"

"Yes, now."

"Why?"

"Because we don't know who took the cover off the well. It could have been the killer. Someone was out there. I think he stirred up the sheep to get me curious. Get me walking in the right direction to stumble into the well."

The words sent a shiver traveling over her skin. And the helpless feeling coupled with everything else she couldn't handle made her lash out defensively. "If it's the killer, he's here because of you! Why don't you just go away and leave me alone?"

"If I've brought you trouble, I'm sorry. But it's all the more reason I have to do my job."

"Your job," she repeated.

A look she wanted to read came into his eyes. "It's not just a job. I care about what happens to you."

She couldn't let herself bank on that. And she couldn't believe she was having this conversation with a man who happened to be standing in her bedroom. But as long as he was insisting, she might as well make a complete fool of herself.

"Why should you care?" Before he could answer that question, she piled on another one. "Why did you kiss me?" she asked, amazed that the words had tumbled from her lips as she stood there facing this police detective who had breached her defenses before she had time to realize what was happening.

She saw him swallow. "Kissing you was pretty unprofessional of me."

The flat way he said it made her eyes suddenly sting.

Then he added in his soft southern drawl, "It happened because I'm attracted to you, and when I had you in my arms, I forgot the rules."

Though the admission stunned her, it was difficult to take it at face value. "How can you be attracted to a woman you think is a few bricks short of a load?" she pressed.

She had the satisfaction of seeing conflicting emotions war on his face.

"I don't think you're crazy."

"Everybody else does."

"You're taking this conversation in the wrong direction," he said sharply.

Maybe he was right. It didn't matter what he thought about her. The main point was the murder investigation. She'd let him persuade her to cooperate—a mistake she never should have made.

"About this reunion committee thing," she said. "I'm not going to fool anybody into thinking we're married. So I'm not going to help you catch the killer. The only thing I'm going to do is let him know you're after him."

When she took a step back, he followed her. As his hands went to her shoulders, she stiffened. "You can help me. You will. But only if you can let yourself feel comfortable with me. Please, Beth, give it a try. I won't hurt you."

As if to prove it, his hands dropped away from her body.

"You will hurt me," she whispered, backing toward the closet, knowing that if she didn't keep the barriers in place, he was going to stab a knife into her heart.

Her pulse was hammering in her throat. Partly from fear, partly from needs that were impossible to deny. She was sure he didn't understand how vulnerable she was to him. She raised her face to tell him, but the words remained locked in her throat as she saw his eyes. They were dark and intense, like black fire.

"Give this a chance," he whispered.

When he reached for her, she went still, allowing him to draw her into his arms. Earlier he had kissed her. Now he simply held her, but not so tightly that she couldn't get away if she wanted to. It was a sweet, tender embrace. An embrace that told her he meant her no harm. That was probably what he thought. He just didn't understand the risks. *She* knew them, but she was helpless to keep her head from drifting to his shoulder. Helpless to deny the heady response that surged through her. And helpless to ask for what she wanted. So the two of them simply stood there, quietly, peacefully, deceptively. At least she knew she wasn't being honest. And if she couldn't deal with her own motivation, she certainly couldn't deal with his.

THE NEXT MORNING, after a restless night, Cal tramped across the farm property looking for evidence. He found the field that had burned. And he inspected the well in the light of day. He also went into the barn and found a couple of places where there were chinks in the siding. Places that would be excellent observation spots if someone wanted to watch the house.

Then he drove to the Columbia Mall to get a robe. And after that, he went back to his house and booted up his computer, where he got into the DMV and ran the license plate of the suspicious car he'd seen the day before.

It belonged to a Harold Mason. It took only a little more checking to find out that Mason was a developer with a thirty-lot project not too far from Beth's property.

Interesting. He'd like to have a talk with the guy. Maybe he could do it as Cal Roberts, investments salesman. But he'd have to be careful. Because if he blew his cover, he'd blow the murder investigation.

When he pulled back into the farmyard, a large brown delivery truck was pulled up near the house. The driver and Beth were on the porch, apparently engrossed in conversation. But as soon as they spotted him, the man stepped away and trotted back to his truck.

Once again, Cal felt a surge of emotion he didn't want to name. What was that driver doing talking to Beth? Usually those guys dropped packages on the front porch and hightailed it back to the truck as quickly as possible.

She had disappeared back into her workroom by the time he stepped into the house. He wanted to stride down the hall and ask how well she knew the guy and just what kind of relationship they had.

Then he brought himself up short, realizing that he was thinking like a jealous husband. A controlling, possessive jealous husband.

With a grimace, he forced his steps into a light, even pace as he climbed the stairs to put his packages in his room. But he was too keyed up to stay in there, so he went out into the fields again, not sure if he was looking for clues or walking off nervous energy.

Two hours later when he walked into the kitchen, he and Beth eyed each other uneasily. Pulling open the drawer, he began slapping cutlery on the table.

They were both still wary as they sat down to eat. But as it had the night before, the first taste of her cooking brought a compliment to his lips.

"I love what you've done to these pork chops," he said and saw her flush with pleasure.

"It's one of my mom's old recipes."

"And the sweet potatoes. You put pineapple and walnuts in them?"

"Pecans."

"Yeah, right. Pecans," he said after another appreciative bite.

He relaxed a fraction, thinking the question sounded almost natural as he asked, "I saw the U.P.S. truck a while ago. Do you get many delivery trucks up here?"

"Uh-huh. I order supplies from all over the world."

"So you and that driver are pretty friendly."

She shrugged. "We say hello."

"He's never done anything out of line?"

"Certainly not! What are you implying?"

"You're alone up here. Men who come to the house could...take advantage of you."

"Anyone who tried to take advantage of me would have to deal with Granger."

At the sound of his name, the big dog trotted over.

Beth patted his head, then slipped him a piece of meat.

Cal took a breath and cast around for a change of subject. "Well, I guess if we're going to convince your classmates we're married, I'd better tell you something about my background."

Her grimace made him wish he'd introduced the subject with a little more finesse. "I'm from North Carolina."

"So that's where you get that drawl."

"Do I have a drawl?" he asked innocently.

"You know you do. Where in North Carolina?"

"Greensboro. My dad worked for the city, but we had a place fifteen miles out of town. Not as big as this. We had five acres, part of them wooded."

She nodded.

"You've lived here all your life?" he prompted.

"Yes."

He kept the conversation going, enjoying himself more than he should, then disappearing right after dinner to give her some breathing space.

He followed that pattern the next day, too, doing his job, meeting her for breakfast, lunch and dinner, carefully orchestrating a casual exchange of information, then starting to coach her on what they would do and say at the meeting.

Afterward he always gave her some time alone. Or perhaps it was giving *himself* time to decompress, he silently admitted.

Because despite the easy demeanor and the slow drawl he was able to manufacture, he was more uncomfortable than he had ever been in his life—both physically and mentally. And he didn't know which was worse. Physically, he wanted her with a gut-burning desire that edged into pain.

Mentally, he felt as if the universe was shifting under him and he was hanging on by his fingernails. He'd had his share of women, but there had been a kind of intimacy between him and Beth that he'd never asked for and never expected. He'd seen what happened to his father when he'd let down his guard. And he'd vowed never to open himself up for that kind of grief.

In the past, he'd never had any reason to question his own judgment—or any problem keeping relationships within the bounds he'd set. Then he'd met Beth Wagner—a woman who made him want to throw the rules out the window. Only he couldn't. Because if he did, everything he'd ever thought was true would be false.

TWO AFTERNOONS LATER when Cal spotted Tim Fillmore outside mending a broken fence, he ambled into the fields for a friendly chat.

"How are you doing?" Cal asked.

The man turned, straightened. "Fine."

"You know who I am?"

Tim gave him a measured look. "You're the guy who moved in with Beth," he said, a note of disapproval in his voice.

Cal hesitated, thinking he should have planned what to say. If he said he was married to Beth, this man would know it was a lie in a few weeks. What would embarrass her more? he wondered—his claiming to be her husband now, or something closer to the truth. He settled for, "It's temporary."

"Is that supposed to reassure me or something?"

"You have a personal interest in Beth?"

"I watch out for her—that's all. I've been watching out for her since her father died."

"You watch out for fires? Sheep getting sick from pesticides? Covers disappearing from old wells?"

Fillmore looked uncomfortable. "She told you about that?"

"I had occasion to discover the well on my own."

"She didn't say I had anything to do with it!" the man said with a vehemence that made Cal suspect the questions were making him very uncomfortable.

"I'm not accusing you of anything. I just thought you might be able to give me some information," he said reassuringly.

"Like what?"

"Like who wants Beth off this property."

Fillmore looked down at his right boot and kicked a tuft of grass.

"Beth's land would make a nice little parcel for some developer," Cal prompted.

"She doesn't want to sell."

"She might if somebody made her afraid to stay here."

"Are you thinkin' that might be me?"

"I'm just considering possibilities."

Cal spent a few more minutes questioning the man, pretty sure Fillmore was hiding something but unable to find out what. Maybe if he'd flashed a badge in the farmer's face he would have gotten a little further.

But blowing his cover was out of the question.

Frustrated, he turned and headed back to the house. Toward more frustration. Because it was almost time for dinner—and another session with Beth where he got to pretend that he didn't ache to reach across the table and pull her into his arms.

He tried to marshal his defenses as he approached the front door. But as soon as he stepped into the house, he knew he was in trouble—on an entirely different level. He smelled apple pie. And some spicy meat. Maybe barbecue.

Hell, he was going to gain five pounds before he finished with this assignment. Only a six-mile morning run was keeping his gut from pouching out.

Beth was standing at the sink washing tomatoes. She didn't turn, but he knew from the way her shoulders stiffened that she'd heard him come into the room.

He moved to the drawer in the hutch and took out cutlery.

"I saw you talking to Tim," she said as he set the table.

"Yeah."

"About what?"

"The stuff that's happened around here. The well. The fire. I want to get his reaction."

"He's not responsible for any of that."

"How do you know?"

"He...likes me."

"Oh yeah. You mean as in a man liking a woman, or some other way?"

"First you quiz me about the deliveryman, now Tim."

"I didn't quiz you about the deliveryman! I just asked a couple of questions. Like I'm doing now."

He wanted to cross the room, turn her to face him, show her how strongly he felt about her safety. Instead, he clenched his fingers around the handle of the fork he was holding.

Dinner was as strained as any meal they'd shared. Then after he helped her clean up, he told her he had research to do. The quick stab of disappointment on her face made him duck his head as he left.

But he was too restless, feeling too caged in. He'd never lived with a woman before, never been forced into such intimacy. And he couldn't cope. So he went back to his own house for a few hours, back to his computer where he plugged in Tim Fillmore's name and the names of her other neighbors, just for good measure.

Then he looked up land records, scoping out which developers had bought tracts similar to Beth's in the recent past.

When he came back after midnight, he drove slowly up the lane, probing the silent landscape, wondering if he'd spook some watcher who thought he was safely out of the way.

He could see the light was on in the parlor as he drove into the yard. Granger came to the door when he stepped inside, chuffing softly and giving his hand a lick with his warm tongue.

"Good boy," Cal said, thinking he could go right upstairs. Instead, he was drawn down the hall. Beth was sleeping in the easy chair by the window. Maybe she'd been waiting up for him.

She looked so beautiful with her blond hair falling around her shoulders that he felt his heart squeeze. A heavy book was on her lap, a book on weaving he'd seen her reading. Now it was slipping toward the floor. If it went over her knees, it was going to hit her on the foot, he realized, moving forward quickly and bending to catch it in his hand.

His fingers brushed her knee, and her eyes shot open, focusing on his face.

"The book," he said, hearing the thickness in his voice. He pushed the volume more firmly onto her lap, the touch of his fingers against her leg searing his flesh. Before the fire could consume him, he straightened and took a quick step back.

They stared at each other across four feet of charged space. He couldn't stop himself from picturing what he wanted. In his mind, he saw himself scooping her up in his arms and fusing his mouth to hers. But he knew where that would lead.

As the fantasy took on substance in his mind, her tongue poked from between her teeth, moved across her bottom lip, and he followed the tiny movement with his eyes, even as he pressed his hands against his sides to keep from reaching for her.

There was nobody here besides the two of them. Nobody to prevent him from taking her upstairs to her bedroom and making love to her until the tension building between them was spent.

He stood there for another moment, the blood rushing hotly in his veins. Then he jerked away and left the room before he did something he knew he would regret.

Chapter Seven

The reality was a hundred—a thousand—times worse than the anticipation, Beth thought as Cal pulled up in the parking lot in front of the Fairways Restaurant where the reunion committee was having its first meeting.

Show time.

And she wasn't ready. She'd never be ready to face these people. Not in a thousand lifetimes. Not alone and not with Cal Rollins.

It was not quite six-thirty, and the last vestiges of daylight lingered in the parking lot. Given her choice, she would have elected to arrive under cover of darkness, but that would have brought its own perils, making her and Cal late so that all eyes would be on them when they entered the room.

To her right, a car door slammed, and she jumped. Cal put a hand on her shoulder, and her body stiffened even more.

"Relax," he said in that deep, slow drawl that had become so familiar over the past few days.

Relax?

Impossible. How could she relax when her nerves felt like a bunch of live electrical wires twisting inside her? The reaction came from anticipation of what was just ahead. And sitting next to Cal wasn't helping. Not at all.

She slid him a sidewise glance, thinking that if Tim

Fillmore were her escort, he wouldn't be adding to her case of the jitters. Because she wasn't attracted to Tim, even though she knew he liked her. But the idea of anything physical with him left her cold.

It was just the opposite with Cal. The idea of doing anything physical with him left her hot and edgy.

And she knew he was having the same problems—even if his sense of honor demanded that he do nothing about the feelings neither one of them could repress.

They wanted each other. And if she'd been more willing to reach out and take what she craved, they might have ended up in her bed together. But thinking about the consequences always stopped her, since she knew that any pleasure she gained in the present was only going to lead to pain in the future.

Cal Rollins would walk away from her when this job was over. Because of the man he was. She knew from what he'd told her that his father had done the best he could, raising him without a wife's help. But from some of the comments that slipped out, she could tell he'd absorbed a whole trunkload of negative attitudes about man–woman relationships. If there was one thing she knew about Cal after spending four intense days with him, it was that he was never going to let himself be vulnerable to a woman the way his father had let himself be vulnerable to his mother.

So no matter how well she got to know him, no matter how much he liked her cooking or told her that he was in awe of her weaving talent, there was a line he was never going to cross with her or anyone else. They might be playing husband and wife. But for him it didn't go beyond the superficial level. Which meant that the fantasies she was entertaining about the two of them were going to stay strictly in the fantasy realm. Because she wasn't going to let him leave her with a scar on her heart.

"I can't relax," she whispered now, pressing the back of her skull against the firm support of the headrest. Inside her mind she was silently screaming, *Take me home. Just take me home.*

"You know your lines. Everything's going to be fine."

Impossible. It wasn't going to be fine. She'd known that well enough from the beginning. When she started to nervously twist the strap of her purse through her fingers, Cal reached out and stilled her hand.

The pressure of his flesh on hers made her go very still. Through her lashes she glanced up at him and saw that his emotions were as conflicted as hers. She believed that he cared about her, at least on some level. Yet at the same time, he was a cop with a job to do. And a man who didn't believe in the word *commitment.*

He cleared his throat, and the words that came out of his mouth stunned her.

"Are you, uh, picking up any vibrations?"

He was *asking* for help from a psychic? Lord preserve us.

"I'm trying not to," she answered in a voice that was barely above a whisper. She'd wanted him to believe her story about Hallie. And believe how she'd known he was in the well. But she didn't want to deal with any of that now. Not on top of everything else.

Instead of dropping the subject, he pressed ahead. "I'd like to know if you're feeling anything unusual about this place. I mean do you sense anybody here, like the man who touched you."

"But you don't put much stock in extrasensory abilities."

"I still want your impressions," he said, and she heard the cop speaking.

She dragged in a breath, then let it out slowly as she forced herself to answer his question as honestly as she could. "I feel anxious. I feel on edge. I have a headache, like the kind I get when something's going to happen. But I can attribute all that to a case of nerves."

"Are you sure it's just nerves?" he asked insistently.

"I don't know! Stop pressing me. Don't you have undercover guys here, watching the parking lot? They've got their eyes and ears. They don't need psychic abilities."

"Yeah. We've got a team taking down every license plate."

Before she could ask another question, movement on the other side of the windshield caught her attention, and she seized the opportunity to shift her attention away from him. But the change in focus had just the opposite effect from what she'd intended. As she looked past Cal's shoulder, she saw a group of people she recognized crossing the parking lot. The first one to register was the large bulky form of Billy Nichols, former Glenelg star quarterback. He was still well muscled, still with shoulders as broad as Alaska. With him was Candy Marks, former cheerleader. If anything, she was thinner than she'd been in high school.

Beth had read in the local paper four or five years ago that they'd gotten married. She was surprised that two people with such swelled heads were still together.

Billy glanced in her direction, stopped and squinted, then did a double take as he apparently recognized her. It wasn't as if she was some anonymous nerd who had faded into the background during her high-school years. She'd been known for her odd behavior, like her headaches that struck in the middle of a class, sending her to the nurse's office.

Instinctively, she slid closer to Cal, and he slung his arm around her shoulder as he followed the direction of her gaze.

Then he turned so that his mouth was only inches from her ear. "That Billy Nichols?" he asked, apparently recognizing the former football player from his yearbook picture.

"Yes," she managed to say, her nerves humming, and not just from seeing her former classmate. She and Cal had been careful not to get this close to each other over the past few days, and for several seconds she felt slightly dizzy as she breathed in the scent of his aftershave.

Two newcomers joined the couple looking in their direction. Ted Banner and Libby Humphry. Again, Beth did a quick evaluation. Ted looked kind of stressed out, his face aged more than the ten years that had passed since she'd seen him, and his dark hair thinning. Libby had put on a few pounds. As they all stared in her direction, she wanted to slide down below the level of the window, but Cal didn't allow her to escape.

"Don't let them get to you before the meeting even starts."

"I..."

"You've got your husband in your corner. Your husband who's going to make it very clear to the jerks out there that if anybody gives you a hard time, they'll have to answer to him."

Absorbing the words, she leaned into him.

"Don't you think it would be a good idea for us to show them how your husband feels about you?" he added as he gathered her closer.

There was a stunned moment when she could only stare at him, trying to follow his logic. She saw the intent in his eyes and tried to pull away, but his hand came up to steady her head. When his lips touched down on hers, the world went away.

For days, she'd been trying not to think about how those lips had felt on hers, how his body had felt pressed to hers. Now she was helpless to do anything besides respond to the challenge he'd issued.

Somewhere in her mind she was thinking that nobody was going to be watching this performance with a telephoto lens. As far as she was concerned, all they had to do to convey the impression of a loving relationship was to remain with their lips lightly pressed together. But apparently, Cal didn't think that the light pressure of mouth against mouth was enough.

Beth's brain stopped analyzing the situation when his tongue, wicked as sin, played with the seam of her lips. Helpless to resist, she opened her mouth, granting him the access he requested.

She had lived through what felt like aeons of self-denial since he'd moved into her house. Now the feel of his tongue against her inner lips and the pressure of his hand against the back of her head was intoxicating. She forgot they were in a car in a parking lot, forgot that four of her former classmates were watching them with interest. Forgot why they were here.

Instead, her world was reduced to sensory impressions: the wonderful taste of his mouth, the feel of his hands splayed across her back, the cocoon of his strong arms.

She felt him make a low growl of conquest as he changed the angle of his mouth, plundering her as though he still meant to be kissing her when time stopped.

"Beth," he murmured, his hand stroking through the thick curtain of her hair, then moving lower to skim the sides of her breasts.

When she answered with a small sound of pleasure, his palms slid inward to cup her fullness.

She was helpless to hold back a moan as his fingers found her hardened nipples through the thin fabric of her lacy bra and silk blouse.

At night as she'd lain in her bedroom, vividly aware that he was just across the hall, she had secretly thought about him caressing her like this. Longed for it. And now that he was actually doing it, his touch burned through her. She wanted it to go on forever, wanted more. Wanted things from him that she could hardly articulate.

But just as she was sure she was going to drown in sensations, he broke the contact, leaving her head spinning and her breath coming in small gasps.

His breath was just as labored as he drew back. When her eyes snapped open, she saw his gaze burning down into hers with an intensity that seared her flesh.

"Beth..." Her name sighed out of him. Then he straightened, ran a hand through his hair. "I..." Again, the syllable trailed off.

She saw his face change, saw the moment when he went from lover to Cal Rollins, police detective. "Come on, we'd better go in there," he said.

She wanted to know what had just happened. But she didn't have the guts or the time to ask what the kiss had meant to him. Instead, she gave a tight nod, then looked up to see that their audience had departed while they were too involved to notice. The realization made her flush. Pulling down the visor, she stared at her own face in the mirror. There was nothing she could do about the swollen look of her lips, but she took the time to run a comb through her hair and straighten her blouse.

"We'd better go," he said again.

Knowing there was no way to put off the inevitable, she opened the car door and joined him in the parking lot.

THEY WERE HALFWAY across the parking lot when Cal felt Beth stumble. Automatically, his arm shot out to grab her.

She was leaning on him heavily as she staggered to the side of the building.

"What? What is it?" he asked urgently.

It was several moments before she could talk. "I...felt something. Somebody."

"Here? Watching you?"

"I don't know."

He turned to scan the parking lot, pretending he was watching for new arrivals to the meeting, then moving in close to her. Eyes closed, she leaned into him.

"Are you okay?" he asked, feeling the tension ripple through her body.

"I'll be fine," she said in a voice that sounded far from fine. "Just give me a minute."

Still with his arm around her, he turned his back on the open area and pulled a phone out of his pocket, hiding his action from view with his body. Punching in a number, he waited until one of the men from the plainclothes detail answered the phone, then said without preamble, ''Double-check the immediate vicinity.''

''We have,'' the officer informed him curtly.

''Do it again.''

''You got some reason to get us stirred up?''

Yeah, he thought. The civilian working with me is picking up bad vibes. But he couldn't say that. Because he knew what kind of reaction that would get him. So all he said was, ''I've just got a feeling.''

''Okay. Yeah.''

Lucky that was an acceptable way to put it. When he finished the call, he turned back to Beth. ''We'd better go in.''

She nodded tightly, looking as if she was on the way to her execution. He didn't feel much better as he took her arm and steered her toward the door.

Inside he spoke to the hostess, pretending he needed directions to the meeting room, although he'd checked it out himself a couple of days ago. He cut Beth a quick sideways glance. She was so pale her skin stood out against the darkened interior of the restaurant. And he felt like a slime for dragging her here.

No, not just for that. For the whole thing. He'd told himself that the only way to handle the little husband-and-wife game they were playing out at her house was to keep his paws off her.

So what had he gone and done? He'd come up with an excuse to pull her into his arms and kiss her senseless, telling her he was putting on a show for the members of the reunion committee, when he knew his own selfish needs had been his primary motivation.

He'd always been absolutely sure of what he wanted from the women he dated. Hot sex and the understanding that commitment wasn't part of the package.

Well, he still wanted the hot sex. In fact, he'd never

wanted a woman more in his life. She was tempting him beyond endurance, though this was hardly the place to think about that. He had a job to do, and he was going to do it.

"Get your mind back on business," he muttered, mentally giving himself a kick in the rear.

"What?" Beth asked.

"Nothing. We'd better get in there."

SHE WAS GOING to melt into a puddle on the floor, Beth thought. Or maybe she was going to start screaming. Either way, she would make a spectacle of herself, the way she had so many times in high school. Like the morning when she'd fainted in the middle of an assembly and two football players had picked her up and carried her down the aisle. Later in the day one of her favorite teachers, Mr. Lipman, her social studies teacher, had had a heart attack.

Cal kept his arm tightly around her as they crossed the restaurant, and she wanted to lean on him.

Then a long-forgotten mechanism kicked in. Somehow she was able to summon the invincible aura she'd wrapped around herself like armor when her classmates had been making her feel lower than a worm's belly.

Her head rose, her shoulders straightened, and she took several breaths of the stale, refrigerated air. Cal noticed the change in her immediately. Turning his head, he murmured, "That's my girl."

His girl. She felt the warmth of those words spreading through her, even though she was sure he had only meant them as a figure of speech. Or had he let his real feelings slip out?

Before she could work her way through the implications, they reached the door of the Dorsey Room where the meeting was being held.

Beth took in the scene in one quick sweep. Small tables had been pushed together to make one long conference-type table. Around the room were about twenty people, some sitting in captain's chairs, some loading plates from a snack buffet and some standing in small knots talking. Included in the latter group were the people she'd seen in the parking lot.

She had the feeling they'd rushed inside to tell everyone she was going to be walking through the door with a hunky-looking guy, because as she and Cal entered the room, all eyes turned toward them.

For a moment her facial muscles felt frozen. Then she forced a smile that she knew didn't meet her eyes. "Hi, everyone. I'd like you to meet my husband, Cal Roberts. Cal, these are some of the people I've been telling you about."

Her eyes took in varying reactions to the short speech. A few mouths dropped open. Some people looked as if they wished a weirdo like her hadn't intruded on their private party. But the majority of her former classmates at least made an attempt to look as if they welcomed her presence. Maybe time had dulled their memories of her, she thought. Or maybe maturity had made them more tolerant.

Donna Pasternack, who had sent out the letters inviting people to the meeting, crossed the room to greet her. "Beth, it's good to see you after so long."

"Good to see you," Beth answered automatically. In truth, Donna had been one of the girls who'd made her feel least uncomfortable—although that was hardly a ringing endorsement of their former relationship.

In high school, Donna had been a brunette whose parents were pretty strict with her about wearing makeup or dating. Now her hair was blond and her mascara looked as though it had been laid on with a putty knife. Apparently she'd decided to have more fun.

To her vast relief, Beth didn't have to say anything else because Cal took over, reaching out to shake Donna's hand like a long lost friend, explaining in his warm southern drawl that he and Beth had gotten married recently and that he'd considered the reunion committee a perfect way to meet her former classmates.

Within minutes, he'd introduced himself to everybody in the room. And as five more people arrived, Donna told them who he was. It was obvious he knew how to work a crowd, how to get people to like him. The women were practically eating out of his hand, she thought as she watched them flirt with the handsome new husband of their geeky former classmate. But despite the female attention, he was able to quickly make friends with the guys, too.

Even Skip Sorenson. Beth had always considered him a space cadet. A few minutes ago she'd heard him telling Donna that he had his Ph.D. and was doing research at the Johns Hopkins Applied Physics Lab. Well, good for him, she thought before her attention switched back to Cal.

She watched the people's expressions close up a bit when he steered the conversation down a less pleasant avenue. "You hear about that girl, Hallie Bradshaw, disappearing?" he asked when the noise level in the room dropped a little. "Pretty scary."

The rest of the conversations stopped dead. And the sound of Paul Sampson crunching on a taco chip was the only noise in the room.

The guy Cal was talking to, Jim Fitch, filled the sudden quiet. Tall and thin with a shock of thick sandy hair, Jim had been the president of the business club. Now a successful insurance agent in Ellicott City, he appeared to have combed his hair to the side to conceal a rapidly retreating hairline. "Yeah, I read about it in the *Baltimore Sun.*"

Ned Brentley chimed in, "She was supposed to meet me and a group of friends at McKinley's but she never got there."

"You were friends with her?" Cal asked.

"Yeah. She was a fun kid."

Beth wouldn't have called her a kid, though she knew that was simply Ned's way of talking. Back in high school, he hadn't had much respect for women. Apparently that hadn't changed.

As the conversation turned to speculation about Hallie's disappearance, Beth watched Cal observing the members of the group without appearing to be particularly watchful. Again he used a natural opportunity to widen the discussion. "You remember Lisa Stapler?" he inquired.

"The woman whose body was found in a drainage ditch?" Alice Carpenter asked with a little shudder. She'd been the shortest girl in the class, and she hadn't grown any since then.

Cal nodded.

"What does that have to do with Hallie?" Alice demanded.

"I don't know. But I saw both their names in your yearbook when I was looking to see who might be at the meeting tonight. Isn't that a little strange for two women in your class to, uh..." He shrugged casually, but Beth knew he was carefully cataloging everyone's reaction.

You didn't have to be a psychic to feel the buzz of tension in the room, Beth thought.

"Are you trying to make something of that?" Alice demanded, her chilled voice cutting through the previously friendly atmosphere.

"Uh, no," Cal answered, apparently deciding that it was better to back off than keep pressing the issue right now.

People started talking again, most on deliberately cheerful subjects. Before they got too far though, Donna banged a spoon against a glass, getting everybody's attention and saying that they should get the meeting started.

Cal rejoined Beth, taking the chair next to hers as the rest of the group arranged themselves around the table.

When everybody was seated, Donna passed out sheets of paper with her agenda. Cal read his rapidly, then leaned back in his chair, looking totally relaxed and interested in the proceedings.

But he didn't simply let the business of the evening

swirl around him. Once the committee got into full swing, he had several suggestions for locations they might use for the dance and barbecue they were planning.

Beth was relieved that the meeting settled down to an easy give-and-take. When Donna asked her if she was willing to work on the committee sending out promotional materials, she agreed to help, thinking that she could always back out later.

"I want to kick start this reunion celebration," Donna said as the meeting drew to a close. "So I think we should meet again in two weeks to see what progress everybody has made."

There were murmurs of agreement around the room. With the official business concluded, nobody seemed to be in a hurry to leave.

People drifted into little groups to chat or congregated around the snack table. And Beth noted with a mixture of disappointment and relief that nobody made an effort to come up to her.

Pretending she was perfectly content to sit where she was, she watched Cal help himself to a buffalo wing, then turn and smile as Dee Dee Johnson came gliding up to him. Dee Dee was a curvy brunette who had been considered sophisticated back in high school. Ten years had only accentuated her charms. She and Cal were on the other side of the room, but Beth could tell from the other woman's body language that Dee Dee had no compunction about coming on to another woman's husband.

A jolt of primitive emotion shot through Beth, taking her by surprise. When she realized it was jealousy, she sternly reminded herself that she had no right to be possessive of Cal Rollins. He was only here with her on an undercover assignment. Still, when he glanced in her direction and caught her watching him, he looked a bit uncomfortable. Excusing himself, he crossed the room to her and leaned down.

"Maybe it's time to go home, sweetheart," he said, his

voice loud enough to carry around the room, his hand cupping possessively over her shoulder.

Knowing that he was just playing a part, Beth flushed. But she stood obediently and leaned into him as he slung his arm around her waist.

Still strung tight as an electrical wire, Beth looked up to see that Dee Dee had followed Cal across the room. With a knowing little smirk on her face, Dee Dee asked, "So how did you two meet anyway? Was it a case of opposites attract?"

Beth's mouth went dry as cotton. She could no more have answered Dee Dee's question than she could have sprouted wings and flown around the room. But Cal smoothly gave the response that they'd rehearsed—the story about his coming out to the house in answer to her inquiry about a financial evaluation.

"So you trust him with your money as well as, uh, everything else," Dee Dee observed sweetly.

"Yes," Beth managed to say, thinking that the evening had gone pretty well until now.

Prickles of tension gnawed at her, and the headache she'd pushed to the background was suddenly pounding in her temples like a stereo speaker with the bass jacked up too high. With a jolt, she realized she'd been so focused on the byplay with Dee Dee that she'd been ignoring something else.

Something more important. The air in the room was thick with it. Her brain was suddenly thick with it, too.

Cal's face had taken on a look of concern. Then the feel of his arm tightening around her helped collect her scattered thoughts.

"What is it?" he asked.

His voice seemed to come from a great distance, so that it was difficult for her to focus her attention on him.

"Beth!"

She stared at him, her lips moving, trying to form words, trying to warn him.

''Sweetheart, are you having another one of your migraines?''

''Yes,'' she whispered.

Dee Dee made a little clicking sound with her tongue. ''In school, she was always having them. She spent more time at the nurse's office than in class.''

Cal ignored her, his fingers digging into Beth's arm. ''Is something going to happen?'' he asked, the urgency in his voice making her focus on him.

She hadn't known for sure it was true until he asked the question. ''Yes.'' She forced the syllable through her dry lips. Then, with a tremendous effort, she added, ''He's coming...''

Cal's features tightened.

''Who?

''I...don't know. I can't see his face,'' she said.

Before she could say anything else, the lights went out. In the next instant, the sound of a scream filled the air.

Chapter Eight

A jolt of panic made Beth go rigid in the blackness. Disoriented, she could only stand there with her heart pounding until she felt Cal's hand tugging at her arm.

"On the floor," he ordered, his voice urgent as he pushed her down and pulled her forward, his hand on the top of her head the way she'd seen officers usher suspects into the back of police cars. But in this case it was to prevent her from banging into the tabletop.

She let him move her forward until she bumped into a curved piece of metal. It must be part of the table leg, she thought inanely as she stroked her fingers over the slick surface, thinking it was too bad she couldn't pull it off and use it as a weapon.

"Stay here. Stay down," he ordered, his mouth close to her ear.

Above them in the darkness she heard people crying out. Two voices cut through the babble.

"What's going on?" That was Donna.

"This isn't funny. Turn on the lights, you jerk." That was Ned.

In addition to the voices, Beth could hear scuffling sounds, more screams. In the dark, it was impossible to figure out what was happening. Fighting a wave of sheer terror, she clung to Cal.

When he started to pull away from her, she grasped frantically at his arm.

"I've got to find out what's going on. You stay here," he repeated, his voice firm.

She didn't want him to leave her in the blackness with chaos swirling all around, but she knew he was right.

He gave her arm a reassuring squeeze, then let go and was swallowed up by the darkness.

Holding back a cry of protest, she eased to her side and pulled up her legs. As she huddled on the floor, she listened to the sounds of panic, trying to picture what was happening.

A heavy body crashed to the floor, landing so close that she felt a sudden breeze fan her skin. A man, she thought, judging from his apparent weight. God, was he dead?

Uncurling her body, she strained to see. "Who is it? Who's that?" she whispered, but nobody answered.

When she stretched out her hand, she felt a hairy arm. Moving closer, she encountered a knit shirt. Jim Fitch had been standing near her and he'd been wearing a knit shirt.

"Jim?" she whispered. When there was no answer, she crept forward several more inches so that she could press her hand to his chest. She was relieved to detect the beating of his heart. It felt shallow but steady.

He'd been hurt, but he was still alive.

She was wondering what to do for him when a crashing noise to her right made her freeze. In the next moment, she realized that a door had burst open, accompanied by several bright lights blasting into the room.

"Howard County Police. Everybody freeze," a voice rang out from behind one of the powerful flashlights.

In the next moment, Cal was back beside her, as though he'd never been away from the group, and she realized that he was probably the one who had called in the police. Now he was fading back into the crowd, pretending he was just one of the panicked people who'd been attacked by Lord knows who.

"Everybody put your hands on top of your head," one of the cops said.

"But we're the victims!" someone shouted.

"Hands on your heads. Until we sort this out, everyone is a suspect."

Beth glanced at Cal, saw him comply and did the same. But as soon as her hands were firmly in place, she raised her voice. "There's a man hurt over here. He needs medical attention."

In the flashlight beams, she could see an officer crossing the floor, kneeling beside Jim. Then he spoke into his radio.

"Over here," someone shouted. "We need help over here, too."

Another officer responded.

"He's hurt bad," Candy wailed in a barely recognizable voice.

"Who?" a chorus of voices shouted.

"Ted."

"No!" Libby shrieked, and the room erupted in pandemonium.

"Quiet!" The command had come from Cal, and the sound of his voice was enough to restore some sort of order. "We'd better do what the cops say," he added.

There were restless stirrings in the room. Then the overhead lights snapped on, and everybody was blinking in the sudden brightness.

Beth poked her head out from under the table. The room around looked like a set from a disaster movie. Or a hostage scene, she amended.

"It's her fault. It's her fault," Dee Dee shouted, pointing toward Beth, focusing all eyes to the spot where she sat on the floor. "She did it. It's just like when we were in school. She'd get one of her headaches, and something bad would happen."

Beth cringed. A denial sprang to her lips, but her mouth was too dry for even one syllable to emerge. Deep down she had known that something like this would happen, had known that nothing had changed in the ten years since she'd last seen these people.

She felt Cal's arm around her, offering his warmth and reassurance. Then his voice was cutting through the silence. "Yeah, my wife has a headache. She gets migraines. But they don't hurt anyone besides her. She's in a lot of pain right now. I'd appreciate it if she could leave the room," he said, addressing the cops.

An officer pivoted toward Cal, and a look passed between them. When the man gave a quick nod, Cal helped Beth to her feet and started moving her toward the door.

"Why does *she* get to leave?" Billy Nichols snarled.

Cal whirled, facing the former football player, who had three inches and fifty pounds on him. "You want to step outside with *me,* and we can figure it out together?"

There was a charged moment during which Nichols glared at him, then he said no in a low voice.

"Anybody else?" Cal asked, pressing the point.

Nobody spoke up.

His hand firmly on Beth's arm, he led her through the crowd and out of the room.

As soon as she stepped into the hall, she felt as though a thousand-pound weight had been lifted from her shoulders.

"Are you all right?" Cal asked.

"More or less."

He paused to speak to a detective who was standing nearby. "Where are you doing the interviews?"

The cop pointed toward a door down the hall.

"I'm taking Beth to one of the other party rooms."

"Sure. But we need to interview her, like everyone else."

"I'll do it and turn in a report," Cal said brusquely.

"That's not procedure."

"The hell with procedure. She needs peace and quiet."

Beth blinked, stunned by the emotion simmering in his voice.

Turning away, he took her arm and steered her toward the end of the hall. The light had a dimmer switch, and Cal lowered the illumination as they stepped inside. Looking around, Beth found the room was about half the size of the one where the meeting had been held. The furnishings were similar, only the tables and chairs were arranged around the room instead of pushed into the center.

Gratefully, she pulled out a chair and dropped like a stone into the seat. Resting her elbows on the table, she lowered her head into her hands. Cal came around in back of her, his fingers grasping her shoulders and massaging her tense muscles. His touch felt good. Wonderful. She closed her eyes as his hands worked their way up her neck, wiping away some of her tension, although it was impossible to banish it completely.

"Better?" he murmured.

"Yes."

His hands stopped moving, but he didn't step away from her.

She heard him clear his throat. "I hated like hell to leave you alone in there. I mean, when the lights went out. But I couldn't just sit there hiding under the table. I had to—"

"Let the police know what was happening," she finished for him. "I understand."

"I hope so."

She raised her head and half turned, "Why did they make everyone put their hands on their heads?"

He came around the table and pulled a chair at right angles to hers. Gently, he laid his hand over hers. "Because there was no way to know what had happened, or if the perpetrator is still in the crowd. For all we know, he could be one of the people who came to the meeting."

She nodded, understanding better. "Do you think it was someone from the group?"

"From meeting them, I wouldn't say so. It's more likely

someone who was outside waiting to pull the plug on the lights and come in there.''

''But how did he get into the room? How did he turn off the lights?''

''There are two entrances. One to the outside.''

Beth hadn't even noticed. ''An outside entrance? Where?''

''Behind the curtains.''

She nodded.

''That's where Howard County's finest came bursting through. And it's where I went out.''

''How could you see where you were going?''

''I was here a couple of days ago. I memorized the layout. And I knew where the guys were stationed in the parking lot.''

''If there are police in the parking lot, why didn't they see him?''

''I don't know,'' he answered, frustration sharpening his voice. ''And as for the lights, I can't give you an answer on that one yet, either.'' He pressed his palm more firmly against the top of her hand. ''I know I've put you smack in the middle of a mess. Not just a mess. I've put you in danger.''

''I knew what I was getting into.''

''No, you didn't. Neither of us knew.''

''I'm doing my civic duty.''

''More than your civic duty.'' He dragged in a breath, then let it out. When he spoke again, he made one of his abrupt changes of subject. ''Just before the lights went out you had one of your headaches.''

She pressed her lips together, thinking that every time she felt as if they'd connected on a personal level, he switched back into police detective mode. ''Is that going into your report?''

''No.''

''Then why are you asking?'' she demanded, struggling to keep her voice steady.

"I'm trying to understand what happened. You sensed something wrong?"

"Yes."

"But not much before the room went black?"

She gave a hollow little laugh. "Maybe I would have. I was pretty focused on Dee Dee. I thought she was giving me a headache. Then I realized it was something else."

"Something? Or someone?"

"Someone."

"Can you be more specific?"

"I wish I could. It was just a vague impression of danger. Of a figure moving through the dark."

He made a frustrated sound. "This talent you've got isn't very dependable."

Her chin jerked up. "Why should it be? I've spent most of my life trying to avoid it."

"Maybe you should stop ducking away from it," he said, and she didn't much like the tone of his voice.

"Are you blaming me for not solving your case for you?"

He scraped back his chair, paced to the end of the room like a tiger confined to a cage, then came back to stand across the table from her. "No."

But she knew that in a way he was. She'd gotten involved with him in the first place because she'd heard Hallie calling for help. Cal hadn't believed her back then. Then he'd changed his mind. At least he'd started asking her questions.

"I'm sorry," she answered in a tight voice. "I have no control over what comes to me."

She heard him sigh. She had reached the point where her self-control was just about shredded. Tonight had been terrible. Then it had gotten worse, and somewhere along the line it felt as if Cal had stopped being on her side.

"Did you have something else in mind for me?" she asked, unable to keep a sarcastic note out of her voice. "Like maybe you could lead me around the parking lot the way they lead dogs who are sniffing for dope. Only I'd be taking a psychic reading on all the cars, seeing if I picked up any evil vibrations.''

''Stop being ridiculous.''

She should keep her mouth shut, she knew. But she couldn't stop herself from hurling another absurd suggestion. ''Then what? Listen in on the interviews through a two-way mirror the way they do in cop shows on TV? And tell you if I think someone's lying.''

He made an exasperated sound. ''Let's go home.''

''If you think I can't do anything else for you here.''

''I don't!''

They started to step into the hall, then Cal blocked her path.

''What?''

''One of your fellow committee members is in the hall. You don't want anyone to find out the police let you go home early.''

''You don't have to do me any favors.''

''I'm getting you out of here. It's the least I can do,'' he said, sounding as if he was trying to make a peace offering.

He waited several more seconds, then ushered her down the hall and out a side door into the parking lot. It had gotten dark while they were in the building, and she stood where she was staring at a couple of police cruisers with their lights blinking. Behind them were vans from all four Baltimore television stations.

''Damn reporters,'' Cal muttered. ''I didn't expect them to get here so fast.''

The media types spotted them and waved their microphones, but they must have been warned to stay back, because nobody crossed in front of the cruiser.

A police officer looked in their direction.

Cal strode toward him. Feeling exposed and vulnerable, Beth hurried to keep up. As she reached Cal's side, she heard him speaking in a low voice. ''What's the status on the two people who were attacked?'' he asked.

''Fitch is in stable condition. The other guy, Ted Banner, didn't make it.''

Beth felt her chest tighten. ''He's dead?''

''Yeah,'' the cop confirmed.

She glanced at Cal. His face was tight. ''Cause of death?'' he asked.

''Apparently a knife wound to the heart.''

Beth couldn't hold back a gasp. She hadn't had a clue about what was going on in the dark. Now she knew somebody had been in the room knifing people. He could have gotten her. Or Cal.

Cal spoke for a few more minutes to the officer, then apparently asked for an escort, because another man from the department shooed the reporters away as they crossed to his car.

As he pulled out of the space, she said, ''I'm sorry I lashed out at you.''

''You're under a lot of pressure. We both are.''

He didn't continue the conversation, and they rode toward the farm in silence. She wanted to ask him questions. Not about the case, but about the two of them. Before they'd gone into the meeting, he'd kissed her. Maybe he had done it for show, but it hadn't felt that way. Then when the lights had gone out, he'd found her as safe a hiding place as possible under the table. And later, when he'd massaged her back and neck, he'd been tender, concerned, until he'd gone back into police detective mode.

She wanted to ask precisely what he felt for her, but she wasn't sure she had the guts to hear the answer. Maybe she'd gotten angry at him back at the restaurant because she'd invested too much emotional energy in their relationship when she knew it didn't have a snowball's chance in hell of going anywhere.

CAL DROVE IN SILENCE, wondering what else he was supposed to say. Women wanted you to say stuff. They wanted everything spelled out. But that was impossible in this case. Or, yeah, he could spell it out and hurt her so badly she'd never trust another guy in her life.

Honey, I'm kind of on edge because we just walked out of a pretty bad situation. A situation I got you into because of my damn undercover assignment. I'm real sorry about that. And real sorry that what I want to do when we get home is to take you straight up to the bedroom and make love to you until neither one of us can stand up.

But I've got a good reason not to take you there. Because I know I'm going to walk away from you in the end and that's gonna break your heart. You're too vulnerable, too innocent, too nice to get messed up with me. So the best thing is not to get started. Only, if that's what I really think, why did I grab you and kiss you in the car?

He shifted uncomfortably in his seat. Then, as they pulled up in front of the house, his phone beeped. Thankful for the distraction, he cut the engine and reached into his pocket.

''Rollins,'' he answered.

''I'm glad I got you,'' the man on the other end of the line said. It was Sam Lassiter, the P.I. he'd talked to last week.

He glanced at Beth. ''Things have been a little hectic.''

''Oh yeah?''

When she got out of the car, giving him some privacy, he mouthed ''Thanks.'' Then said to Lassiter, ''You can see it on the evening news.'' Cal watched Beth go into the house.

''I was hoping you might want to make good on that promise to help me out.''

''With the Hannah problem or the Luke problem?'' he asked as he climbed out of the car and stood with his hips propped against the bumper.

''Both.''

Cal wondered if he'd heard right. ''What do you mean both?''

"You remember Luke was working undercover in Texas with a gang smuggling drugs across the border. And Hannah's on the run from whoever is trying to avenge the death of that kid, Sean Naylor, who got caught in the crossfire at a drug bust. Well, it looks like they're related."

"How exactly?"

"I don't know. I'm hoping to find out tonight. I'm meeting an informant in back of a warehouse on Pulaski Highway. Another P.I. was supposed to go with me, but he's backed out. I'm reckless, but I'm not suicidal, so I'm looking for someone to cover me."

Cal glanced toward the house, seeing the blaze of lights that Beth had already turned on. "When is the meeting?"

"Midnight."

"Well, I'm in kind of a situation here," he said, then quickly filled in his friend on the undercover assignment.

"So you're worried that if you leave Wagner alone tonight, she could be in danger?" Sam clarified.

"Not from the guy who crashed the reunion committee meeting. He's gone to ground somewhere. But there was another incident out here. Somebody took the cover off an old well. I damn near broke my neck when I fell into it."

"Deep Throat told me something that will interest you."

"Deep Throat?"

"That's what the informant called himself."

"Original!"

"He says that people associated with Hannah are being watched."

"Oh yeah?"

"Not just watched. Warned to mind their own business. I came out of the office a couple of days ago and found my tires had been slashed. That could account for your well cover."

It was an angle Cal hadn't considered—that the booby trap had been directed at *him.* "Thanks for the heads up. Let me get back to you about tonight."

He stood there by the car, staring toward the darkened fields, his fists clenching and unclenching. He'd suspected Tim Fillmore might be harassing Hannah. Or an unscrupulous local developer who saw an opportunity to buy up prime land in the path of development. He'd even wondered about the deliveryman, for Lord's sake. But now he worried that he was the one who had brought Beth more trouble than she'd bargained for. And at the same time he also felt a surge of relief. Leaving her was the solution to his problems—and hers. He was putting her in danger, and as soon as he got out of her life, the better for her.

With renewed purpose, he entered the house and walked down the hall to the workroom. She was where he'd expected—at her loom.

Her back was to the door, but he saw her shoulders tense as he approached, in contrast to the reaction of her dog, who started slapping his tail against the floor.

"Can I talk to you?" he asked.

She gave him a small nod but didn't turn.

"That was a friend of mine on the phone, a P.I. named Sam Lassiter, with an emergency situation. He needs me to cover him while he meets with a guy who has important information for him about another friend of ours, Hannah Dawson. A few months ago, somebody tried to kill her. And we're trying to find out who."

Beth turned, her face grave as she digested the information. "Then you have to go help him," she said in a low voice.

"I don't like leaving you tonight."

"I'll be fine. I'm used to being alone."

He swallowed. She was giving him permission to bail out, and despite his earlier sense of relief, he was feeling like an absolute bastard. Why couldn't she get mad at him again? Then he'd be justified in stalking away.

"The, uh, thing about the well," he said in a halting voice. "If you're worried about the cover being off, Sam says the informant told him that both he and I are being watched by somebody from Baltimore. It's related to a drug case Hannah was working. Sam found his tires slashed. The well's probably something of the same nature."

"Why would someone expect you to be walking around my fields?"

"Because that's what a cop does in a new environment. He checks things out." He went on quickly, "So it wasn't somebody out to get *you.* At least not now. The other stuff you told me about was several months ago, right?"

"Yes. Nothing recent." She kept her features even and her voice steady as she said, "You don't need to feel guilty about leaving me."

"I don't."

"Then why are we having this discussion?"

"Okay. I feel like a rat walking out on you after what happened at the meeting. Does that make you happy?"

"No."

"What do you want from me, exactly?"

"There's no point in spelling out what I want," she said, her voice barely above a whisper.

The words and the way she said them made his chest so tight he could barely breathe. He was pretty sure what she wanted. The same thing he did. But he was the one who understood the consequences.

For long moments, he could only stand and stare at her, feeling on the verge of doing something he knew he would regret. But he couldn't act on his own selfish impulses. Not when Sam needed him. He took a breath to steady himself. Finally he managed to say, "I have to call Lassiter back and let him know whether I can help him out."

"Then go do it."

He stayed there for another few seconds, torn in so many directions that he couldn't catch his breath. Then he turned on his heel and fled, because this was a chance to help his friend Hannah. And it was also a chance to escape from a situation that had created more doubts in his mind than he had ever experienced in his life.

Up in his room, he called Lassiter and asked where he should meet him. Then he strapped on his shoulder holster with his Sig .40. Thinking he might need an additional weapon, he got out his Walther PPK .380 and slipped it into an ankle holster.

After he'd made his preparations, he checked to see that the windows and doors were secure.

When he came to the front door, Beth was standing there. "Tell me where you're going to be," she asked.

"A warehouse off Pulaski Highway."

"You have the address?"

He fumbled for the piece of paper he'd shoved into his pocket and handed it over. She picked up a pad from the hall table and transferred the information.

"Thank you," she whispered.

"You won't need it. I'll be fine," he told her, then pushed the door open and trotted back to his car, without asking if she had any premonitions. He didn't want to know.

As he drove, he tried to focus on the upcoming meeting, but the only thoughts that filled his mind were of Beth. He couldn't stop thinking about how he'd almost gotten her killed this evening—and about how much he wanted her. Lord, he'd never gotten his professional life and his personal life so tangled up. And he'd never felt so glad to escape as when he'd walked out the door and left her standing there in the hallway because he couldn't face her tonight—and he couldn't face his own feelings.

He was still tied up in knots when he pulled into the filling station where he was supposed to meet Sam. Looking around, he spotted the dark shape of his SUV parked in the shadows.

Seeing the truck made him take a deep breath. He'd

come to guard his friend's back and he'd damn well better get his mind on business.

After getting out of his car and locking it, he slid into the passenger seat of the P.I.'s truck.

"Thanks for helping me out," Sam said.

"No problem," he answered, willing his full attention to his friend.

"Okay," Sam began. "Let me show you a plan of the exterior of the warehouse where I'm supposed to meet the guy. And show you where you can cover me."

Halfway through the briefing, Cal started focusing more closely on the P.I. rather than on what he was saying. His friend had sounded like his normal self over the phone. He'd sounded fine a few minutes ago. Now he was starting to slur his words. Lord, was he drinking again? Cal wondered, thinking about the problems he'd had after his wife and child had been killed.

When Lassiter grimaced and gritted his teeth, Cal asked, "You got something you want to tell me?"

The detective answered with a vehement curse. "Yeah. I'm thinking the damn tacos I had for dinner were bad." He sighed. "I'll be okay. But maybe you'd better drive."

Cal slipped behind the wheel of the detective's SUV. As he drove down the highway, he glanced several times toward the passenger seat. When they passed under a streetlight, he could see that Lassiter was sweating and his jaw was clenched.

Before they got to the rendezvous point, Cal pulled on to the shoulder. "You're in no shape to deal with someone who may have set this meeting up as an ambush."

Lassiter sighed, then answered. "I was wondering how I'm gonna stay on my feet."

"You're not. I'll take your place."

"I can't ask you to do that."

"You're not asking. I'm volunteering. So tell me everything you know about the meeting."

"Not much." The detective paused, drew in a shallow

breath and let it out before continuing. "Like I said, this morning I heard from a guy who said I could call him Deep Throat. He wants ten thousand dollars in exchange for some information about how the Sean Naylor case is tied to Dallas Sedgwick."

"The drug kingpin who's out to get his missing million dollars from Lucas Somerville?"

"Yeah." Lassiter made an attempt at a laugh. "Of course, there's one good outcome. The Peregrine Connection let Lucas keep Sedgwick's money. The new head of the organization, Addison Jennings, says that after what he went through, he earned it."

"Yeah," Cal agreed, thinking how many ways the poor bastard had almost been killed. He and Hannah both.

Lassiter was speaking again in a halting voice. "Deep Throat said it was dangerous for him to be seen with me. That we'd better get together out here. He told me to come unarmed and he would, too."

"You're taking his word on that?"

"No. But this is important for Hannah, and I figured if I brought you along, you could cover me." The P.I. paused for a moment. "I could tell the guy wants something from me. Not just money. He wants me to do something for him." The detective paused and closed his eyes for a moment. "But now the equation's changed. I'm not going to be much good to you, so maybe we should call this off."

Cal's nerves were humming as he said, "And maybe we won't get another crack at him. Besides, I won't be unarmed. I've got an ankle holster." He gave Lassiter a once-over. "Does this guy know you? I mean, will he think I'm you? Or will he realize there's been a switch?"

"I wish to hell I knew," Lassiter answered.

Cal started the engine again. Two miles up the road, he pulled into the parking lot in back of the warehouse where the meeting was scheduled. The setting immediately gave him a bad feeling.

He didn't like the darkness. Or the quiet. Or the isolation. If any spot smacked of an ambush, this was it.

Lassiter reached into his pocket and pulled out a legal-size envelope. "Here's the money."

Cal started to get out of the truck.

"Your Sig .40," Sam reminded him.

"Yeah. Right. Taking off the holster and gun, he laid them on the dashboard before climbing quietly out of the car. Sam also exited, moving to the right, bending slightly at the waist and folding his arms across his stomach as he made for the side of the building.

Cal took a more direct route to the designated spot, thinking that this would have been an excellent time to consult Beth and ask her if she was picking up any evil vibes. Then he reminded himself that her powers were pretty uncertain—if you could call them powers.

He wondered where Lassiter had gotten his plans of the building as he passed a door that he hadn't seen on the drawing of the exterior layout. Stopping, he looked along the wall, thinking about what other surprises he was going to encounter.

He hadn't taken more than a dozen steps when he came to another detail that wasn't in the plans—a recessed space. A space big enough for a man to hide.

The odds had just tipped precipitously against him. Maybe keeping this appointment wasn't such a bright idea after all.

He had started to back up just as a whiny voice called in the darkness, "Hey, man. Don't leave now."

BETH HAD LONG SINCE given up on sleep. But she was too exhausted to sit at her loom. So she'd gone up to her room, kicked off her shoes and lain down on top of the spread, still wearing her clothing because she wanted to make sure that Cal was all right the minute he walked in the door.

That was why she was waiting up, she told herself.

As she glanced at the clock yet again, she knew she

wasn't being entirely honest. That was part of it. But only part.

Tonight, when he'd stood in the hall looking at her like a man balanced on a razor's edge of tension, she'd known that all she had to do was reach for him and he'd come into her arms.

But she'd been a coward—afraid of the consequences, afraid to ask for what she wanted because she knew he was going to break her heart when he walked away from her.

Now, as she lay in her narrow bed, she was thinking consequences be damned.

She'd fallen in love with the man. She ached to give that love physical expression. And it didn't matter that he was never going to make a commitment to her or any other woman.

Well, it did matter. His leaving would be terrible. But she wasn't going to give up what they might have in the present because she feared the future.

She wanted tonight with him. And every other night while he was living in her house.

Eyes closed, she tried to focus on the relief she'd feel when he walked in the door. But relief was beyond her grasp.

Instead, as the minutes ticked by, a terrible feeling of dread began to gather in her mind, in her body. It swirled around her like invisible fog, choking off her breath even as she struggled to hold on to her sanity.

Then an arrow of pain pierced her skull, and she sat bolt upright in bed—a scream on her lips and a terrible image in her brain.

"No! Oh God, no. Cal, get out of there. Please get out of there."

CAL FROZE IN PLACE. For a moment he felt dizzy, disoriented. And the thought came to him again that retreating would be an excellent idea. But he was too close to getting the information Lassiter needed to quit now.

The light was so dim that the informant's face was hidden. "Tell me again—what's the name you gave me over the phone?" he growled.

"Deep Throat."

So the man accepted him as Lassiter. Good. Cal tried to size him up. All he could see in the darkness was a vague shape—about medium height, medium build.

"You said you have some information for me?" he prompted.

"If you've got some dough for me."

"Are you planning to come and get it?"

"How do I know you ain't going to drill me?"

"I was wondering the same thing," Cal allowed. "Maybe we should agree that we've got some mutual interest here."

"Yeah. Okay."

"Then why don't you start talking. What do you know about this drug kingpin?"

"His name's Sedgwick," the informant said promptly. "I know about him because a friend of mine had a buddy named Chad Crosby who worked for him. Sedgwick killed Crosby. My friend is still working for Sedgwick, but that's not the name he's using now. Sedgwick, I mean. Anyway, my friend is afraid he'll end up like Crosby. So he's feeding me information, see? If you take Sedgwick down, my friend can get his life back."

Cal made an instant evaluation of the story. It sounded plausible, especially if you figured this guy was actually taking about himself, not a friend. "What else do you have for me?" he asked. "What name is Sedgwick using now?"

"I'm not telling you any more until you give me the money."

Cal reached slowly into his pocket, pulled out the envelope and tossed it on the ground five feet from where he stood.

The man quickly scrambled forward and pocketed it, then stepped back. He was dressed in black and wearing a cap pulled low over his eyes. When he was back in his original position, he said, ''Sedgwick is calling himself Sierra. But that's going to change. He's in Baltimore making big plans. He's going to be trouble for you.''

''What do you mean?''

Deep Throat opened his mouth to answer.

Before he could speak, Cal heard a spitting sound, a shot from a gun with a silencer. The man pitched forward, and Cal knew instantly that there was nothing he could do for him.

Ambush! Get the hell out of here, his mind screamed as he reached for the gun at his ankle.

Then pain exploded across the top of his head.

Chapter Nine

Beth leaped out of bed, snatching up the paper she'd set on the nightstand, then ran barefoot to the phone and dialed 911.

When the dispatcher came on the line, she had to take a breath before she could speak. "Cal Rollins has been hurt."

"Can you describe the nature of the injury?"

"It's his head."

"Is he conscious? Can he talk to you?"

"He's not here. He's at a warehouse off Pulaski Highway."

"He called you?"

"No." She stopped, gulped in air, then rushed to explain because that was her only option. "He's working with me on the Hallie Bradshaw case. I—I had a psychic vision of Hallie's abduction. That's how I started working with Cal. Now I know he's in trouble. I know the same way I knew about Hallie."

"I'm not familiar with the Hallie Bradshaw case, ma'am. Are you saying you've had a psychic vision of Detective Rollins in trouble?" the dispatcher asked, his voice skeptical.

"Yes!" she screamed into the phone. "Yes."

"Pulaski Highway is out of our jurisdiction, ma'am. I'll transfer you to the Baltimore County Police."

In the next moment the line went dead.

Great! They'd been cut off.

She slammed down the phone, dialed information.

This time she was smart enough to say she'd gotten a tip from an eyewitness who had called her on his cell phone to say a man in back of 231 Field Road had a serious head injury. Once she'd told the dispatcher what she could, she asked which hospital Cal would most likely be taken to. After finding out it was Mercy General, she slammed down the phone, pulled on her shoes and ran down the stairs.

First she let Granger out. While he was doing his business, she filled his water dish and poured out dry food.

Then she checked an area map to make sure she could find the hospital. Twenty minutes after she'd first leaped out of bed, she was speeding down the farm road.

DAMIEN PUSHED the rewind button on the video recorder and waited impatiently for the machine to do its thing. He'd set the tape to record the broadcasting on Channel 13. And he'd kept it on through the evening news.

"Ted Banner's dead," he said, speaking loudly because he was pleased with himself. "Too bad Jim Fitch is still alive. He should be dead, too."

And so should some of the others, like that loudmouth Ned Brentley.

He smiled as he stared at the screen, watching the cute little girl reporter do her thing. She didn't know what was going on. Nobody did. Nobody knew he'd walked into the restaurant, ordered a drink at the bar, then gone down the hall to the men's room, and slipped into the utility closet next door, where the circuit-breaker box was located. He knew which circuit controlled the room where the meeting was being held because he'd scoped them out earlier in the week. With the night-vision glasses in his carry bag, he'd made it down the darkened hallway and into the room within seconds. He'd seen the turkeys flapping around in there—all in a panic—and it had been tempting to pick a bunch of them off. But he'd been afraid to stay more than a minute.

And he'd been right. The guy who'd come with Beth had made for the door. And brought the police back, apparently.

"But by then I was already out the front door and in the clear," he congratulated himself.

The camera switched to a shot of the restaurant, and in the background he saw Beth Wagner coming out with the man.

"Beth!" As he watched, he slapped his right fist against the palm of his left hand. He could see the guy talking to the policeman on duty, like the two of them were working together, which they probably were because ten to one the guy was a cop.

So Beth was working with the police, he thought as his fist slapped rhythmically against his palm.

Back in school he'd liked her. And he'd never considered including her in his plans for the class members.

Now a surge of raw anger swept through him. Anger that she'd fooled him about being so sweet and nice. Anger that she was working with the cops. He'd get her for that. Damn, he'd get her good.

IT WAS AN HOUR RIDE to the hospital, counting the fifteen minutes when she'd gotten lost and had to stop at an all-night gas station to ask for directions. Finally she was pushing open the door of the emergency room and barreling toward the desk.

"I'm here to see Cal Rollins," she said. "Can you tell me where he is?"

"Are you related to him?" the woman behind the counter asked.

From the corner of her vision she saw several people moving toward her. A woman with rich brown hair and two men, both tall and dark. One had a comforting arm around the woman, the other looked pale and sick.

"Who are you?" the sick-looking guy demanded.

She whirled toward him. "Beth Wagner. Cal and I are working together," she said, trying to keep her voice even.

The woman came forward and took her arm. "Come over here."

"Please, I have to see Cal."

"They're working on him. We're all waiting to find out how he is."

"We? Who are you?"

"I'm Hannah Dawson," she said. "This is Lucas Somerville and Sam Lassiter."

Beth rounded on the one named Lassiter. "This is your fault! You got him to walk into an ambush!"

The man's face contorted with a stomach-wrenching guilt. "Yeah, I did," he muttered. "It should be me lying in there—not him."

She saw anguish suffuse his features and knew he had piled more blame on himself than she ever could. "I'm sorry. I shouldn't have accused you like that."

"No, you have a right to be angry with me. I screwed up. I asked him to come along for backup, then I got food poisoning and I was going to call the meeting off. He wouldn't let me do it. He said he'd go in my place."

"It's not Sam's fault," the woman named Hannah Dawson said softly, drawing Beth toward a corner of the room. "Cal was trying to help me and Luke. They both were. So if you want to get mad at someone, it should be me."

Beth sighed. "I'm sorry. I shouldn't be taking out my frustration on any of you. Please, just tell me if Cal's okay."

"He was shot."

She gasped. She'd known it. Knowing it the way she knew about Hallie. But hearing it from Hannah made it all the more real.

The other woman added quickly, "The bullet went

across the top of his head. Not into his brain. Maybe he was ducking down or something. He was brought in here unconscious. They haven't told us anything else."

"Can you tell me how it happened?" As Beth asked the questions, she squeezed her hands so tightly into fists that her nails dug into her palms.

It was Lassiter who answered. "Cal went to meet my informant. Then somebody else crashed the party. Two guys, from what I could tell. The informant is dead. A bullet went through his back and into his heart. Cal was hit from the front."

"I felt it," Beth gasped.

"You felt what?" the one named Lucas inquired, studying her with unnerving intensity.

She wanted to duck away, to fade into the gray walls. Instead, she raised her face toward him and moistened her dry lips. "I'm...I have..." She flapped her arm. "Okay, I have psychic abilities. That's how Cal and I ended up working together. I saw a friend of mine being abducted. I mean, I wasn't there...but I heard her calling for help. I reported it to the police, and Cal showed up at my house. Then tonight I couldn't sleep. I was waiting for him and I...saw where he was. I felt him getting hit. Then nothing. Blackness. You can either take my word for it or not. I don't care either way," she added defiantly.

"You're here," Lucas said quietly. "And you called 911, didn't you?"

"Yes."

"I guess that's pretty convincing evidence you're telling the truth. Either that or you sent a covert agent to tail him." The last part was said with a look that told her he had already discounted that possibility.

At that moment a door opened and a doctor clad in a green scrub suit came out. He looked around the room, spotted the group and walked toward them.

"Dr. Koenig," Hannah said, her face hopeful. "Do you have some good news for us?"

The doctor's expression remained neutral. "We've cleaned up the wound and we have him stabilized. He's in a room up in ICU, but he's still unconscious."

Beth felt her chest constrict. "What does that mean, exactly? You're saying the bullet didn't go into his head? But he's unconscious. Why?"

"We can't say for sure yet," the doctor answered. "He's had extensive skull X rays and an MRI. There's a flesh wound but no skull fracture. And no internal bleeding. The best I can tell you is that the impact from the bullet bruised his brain tissue."

"But—"

"I'm sorry. I simply can't give you any more information at this time."

"Can he have visitors?" Sam Lassiter asked. "Can we see him?"

"Only immediate family."

Beth took a step forward. "I hope that includes me. I'm his fiancée." As soon as she said it, she realized what she'd done. The others in the group were staring at her, since the words that had popped out of her mouth were definitely at odds with what she'd told them a few minutes ago. But Dr. Koenig hadn't heard her explanation and seemed to take the information in stride.

"I can arrange for you to see him for a few minutes."

"I've heard that people who are unconscious retain their sense of hearing," she answered.

"Yes, that's true. Sometimes. The ICU is on the third floor. You can see him for a few minutes now, if you like. When you get up to the desk outside the unit, tell them who you are and that I sent you."

"I'll come with you," Hannah said, putting an arm around her shoulder. "At least to the waiting room."

Beth glanced at her gratefully. The men appeared on the verge of insisting that they come along, too, but Hannah gave them a long look, and they both closed their mouths.

In her present state Beth wasn't sure if she was capable

of finding ICU, but Hannah got directions and led her to the elevator. As soon as they were alone, she murmured, "I guess you and Cal have gotten close, working together."

"Yes. But what I told the doctor—that was a pretty brazen thing to say. We're not engaged. If you know Cal, you probably realize that he doesn't intend to marry me or anybody else."

Hannah nodded and said, "Things can change. Actually, Lucas and I met under similar circumstances—working on a case. He started off with no intention of getting into a relationship with me, but we're going to be married as soon as the Naylor and Sedgwick cases are cleared up. It's a long story, but I realized that the bottom line is if you love the guy, don't give up on him."

Beth absorbed the words, aware of Hannah's eyes on her. When the door opened, she stepped quickly out of the elevator. But the other woman caught up with her just as quickly.

"You do love him, don't you?"

She felt slightly light-headed as she said, "Yes, for all the good that does me..."

Hannah stopped her with a hand turned palm out. "Don't make negative assumptions. I know him pretty well. I know about his childhood. I can also see you're the right woman to change his mind."

"Why?"

"Because you care for him deeply."

"How do you know?"

"From the anguish etched into your face."

They reached the unit and stopped at the desk.

Beth looked at the nurse. "I'm Beth Wagner. Cal Rollins's fiancée. I was told by Dr. Koenig that I could see him for a few minutes."

The tall black woman led her through a set of double doors into an area with television screens that showed sleeping patients lying in beds.

The rooms were clustered around the central area. Each was brightly lit and had a glass wall and curtains.

Cal was lying in a hospital bed pale and still as death. His head was bandaged, and tubes and monitors were attached to his body. The only sound in the room came from the wheezing of the equipment. Seeing him like that made her heart squeeze so painfully inside her chest that she could barely breathe. Lord, she'd been waiting for him to come home, thinking that she would finally tell him she wanted him in her bed. And now...

"Cal," she whispered, taking in the scene from the doorway. It was like an alien spaceship where they kept human captives alive so they could do terrible experiments on them.

She shook her head and fought to shake the horrible chill that had settled in her bones. This wasn't some alien torture chamber. This was a hospital, and Cal was here because they were trying to help him. Still, she felt as if she was invading forbidden territory as she took several hesitant steps into the room and stopped beside his bed.

"Cal, it's Beth," she whispered, so overwhelmed that it was difficult to speak. "I'm here. I want you to know I'm here."

His hand was resting on top of the light covering. She looked down at it, large and strong, the tendons standing out against his tanned skin. Gently she laid her palm over his knuckles, needing the contact. His skin felt warm, and she thought she saw his lips twitch as she touched him, but she couldn't be sure.

He had touched her with the hand she was pressing now. Caressed her. She willed him to turn his palm upward and link his fingers with hers.

But he didn't move. Beth had the sudden terrible sense that he was far away from his body. Far away from her. Out of reach, even though she could feel the warmth of his flesh.

Her voice rose in alarm as she begged, "Cal, come back.

I'm here waiting for you. So are Hannah and Lucas and Sam. We all need you."

Again there was no change in his expression, nothing. A wildfire of fear blazed through her.

Her fingers clenched his, and she stood beside the bed in a kind of daze, not realizing how tightly she was clutching his flesh, not realizing she was digging her fingernails into him until the nurse touched her shoulder.

"Miss Wagner. Miss Wagner, you can't be doing that."

The woman's voice brought her back to reality. Blinking, she looked around the unnatural environment.

"You can come back later," the nurse said kindly but firmly.

Beth allowed herself to be led out of the room. Then she was in the waiting area, and Hannah was beside her.

"How is he?"

"He's not there," she whispered.

Hannah's face registered panic. "What do you mean, not there? Didn't they bring him here?"

"They brought him to one of the rooms back there. His physical body. But his mind..." She trailed off, trying to think how to convey what she meant. "He's not..." She couldn't finish, couldn't say it again.

"I've spoken to Lucas. He's arranged for you to spend the night here, if you want."

"Here?"

"There's a VIP suite upstairs. He's gotten all of us rooms."

Beth was dumbfounded. "Us? But he doesn't even know me."

"He knows you care about Cal."

"I'll pay for the room."

"Nonsense. Cal probably told you that Lucas has money to burn. Not just the million dollars he acquired. He's sold his father's ranch."

"Oh." She didn't know anything about the ranch, or

Lucas Somerville, for that matter. But she could see that these people cared deeply about Cal.

So she let Hannah take her up to the fifth floor, where she found a comfortable sitting area and a bedroom that looked as if it had materialized from an upscale hotel chain—except that it had two hospital beds.

The surroundings were of little interest to her. But she knew she had to rest. So she slipped off her shoes and slacks and crawled under the covers of the nearest bed.

In the morning she'd have to get Tim to let Granger out and feed him. But Tim wouldn't mind doing it, since he'd be working the farm anyway. She'd call him early. That would be no problem because she was too worried to sleep.

That was her assumption. But almost as soon as her head hit the pillow, she found it was too much effort to keep her eyes open. Once they were closed, she felt sleep pulling at her with a kind of supernatural force.

A spurt of fear shot through her. Some part of her knew she had to resist, had to keep herself awake, because sleep meant danger. She didn't know why. She only sensed that it was true.

Heart pounding, she lay there, knowing that if she succumbed, something terrible was going to happen. The feeling was like all the other premonitions she'd had in the dark hours of the night, and she fought for control with all her will.

Then she felt a tiny sliver of doubt come creeping into her consciousness.

You want to help Cal, a small voice urged. *You want him back.*

How will sleeping help him?

I don't know. But it will.

Still, she was afraid to give in, remembering the long history of terrible extrasensory experiences that had seized control of her. Her father's car accident. Hallie. The time she'd known that her old dog, Sampson, had been hit by a car and that she'd find his lifeless body on Underwood

Road. The time she'd known that kids from her school were going to take a curve on Route 108 too fast and crash into a tree.

None of those psychic visions had ever brought her anything but pain—and guilt, because deep down she'd always felt as if she should have done something.

But this time was different. In some strange way, she sensed that maybe there *was* something she could do. Still, fear made her fight. She managed to roll to her side and pull up her knees, her sense of self-preservation struggling against the voice in her head until finally the voice was the stronger of the two.

Within minutes, sleep claimed her.

For a short time she was blessedly inert. And then with a jolt she woke up in a place of nightmares, and she knew that she had made a terrible mistake.

She was in a dark shadowy woods. A woods that had never been part of the familiar Maryland countryside she had known all her life.

This was a horror-movie landscape thick with vegetation and the smell of decay. Around her, towering trees blocked out the sun. At ground level, dense underbrush pressed in against her. Vines hung from the branches and slapped against her face as she tried to make her way through the thick greenery, her feet slipping in slimy mud.

Some part of her consciousness knew she was dreaming. But that didn't make the terror—or the danger—less. In the darkness she could hear deep, menacing animal noises. Shrieks, growls. And then the sound of something coming toward her, moving on padded feet through the darkness.

In her mind, she saw a large jungle cat, its claws sharp, its teeth poised to tear at her throat. She screamed, cowering back against the broad trunk of a tree.

Then from an immense distance, she thought she heard someone calling her name.

"Beth? What the hell are you doing here?"

It was Cal. She would know that soft southern voice

anywhere. He was here. But he was too far away to reach her in time. Because if she stayed in this terrible place a moment longer, she would be killed.

Moaning in terror, she struggled against the dream, and somehow she wrenched herself away. Literally wrenched her mind out of the nightmare, out of sleep.

She lay there on the bed, her breath coming in rapid gasps, her skin covered with perspiration. It had been a dream. Just a dream. But instinctively she knew that the danger was real, not only in her imagination.

The door opened, and her body jerked on the bed.

Then Hannah was crossing the room, coming toward her.

"Beth, are you all right? You were moaning. What happened?"

She pushed herself up, leaning forward and pulling up her knees. Wrapping her arms around them, she looked at the other woman. "I had a nightmare," she said in a small voice.

"It must have been bad. We could hear you thrashing around. Then you screamed."

"I...yes." She raised her face toward Hannah. "I'm sorry I woke you."

"No, I wasn't asleep. Do you want me to stay with you?"

"No. I'll be okay."

Beth felt a small surge of relief when Hannah turned and left the room. She wanted to be alone, to figure out what had happened to her. She had been pulled into a nightmare—a place where she knew it was impossible for her to stay and keep her sanity. Yet, at the end, she had heard a voice. Cal's voice. Although it had been far away, it had seemed very real, as if he actually were there.

She considered that idea for a moment. Then, with a shiver, dismissed it. She couldn't believe—didn't want to believe—that he had really been in that horrifying landscape. He was downstairs in the ICU, unconscious. Yet she couldn't entirely rid herself of the conviction that he had been in the dream with her, that he needed her.

If she dared go back to that place, could she find him?

She made a low noise that was almost an hysterical laugh. Make that—could she find him before the monsters tore her apart?

Clenching her jaw to keep her teeth from chattering, she huddled down under the covers, her thoughts chasing themselves around in circles. Sleep was impossible now, so that when Hannah knocked on her door at five in the morning, she'd simply been lying rigidly in bed, feeling torn first one way and then the other.

"None of us could sleep," Hannah said. "Do you want to go down to the cafeteria and get something to eat?"

Beth didn't think she could eat much. But being with people who cared about Cal was better than lying in bed, she decided.

She staggered to the bathroom, looked at her bleary-eyed face in the mirror and grimaced.

When she entered the lounge ten minutes later, she noted that Lucas, Sam and Hannah all looked almost as bad as she did.

"I have to call the man who works at my farm," she told them, "and get him to take care of my dog. Poor Granger's never been alone before. He's going to miss me."

"If I could slip him into the VIP suite, I'd do it," Lucas told her, and she gave him a little smile, knowing he was telling the truth.

They stopped by the ICU, where she was granted another ten minutes with Cal. Apparently there was no change in his condition. He was still unconscious, still unresponsive as she stroked her hand against the dark stubble on his cheek. And as she stood there looking down at him, she had the awful feeling that she'd failed him last night.

Breakfast was impossible. She was too miserable to eat, but she did manage to sip on a mug of coffee heavily laced with the half-and-half Sam poured into it. To fill the silence, Hannah told her about how she and Cal had worked together as uniformed officers and then as detectives in Baltimore City. Then Lucas related his adventures in Texas with Hannah. Beth went last, talking a little about the case she and Cal were working on. But she didn't have to tell them about the murder and assault at the reunion committee meeting because it had made the *Baltimore Sun.*

Some time during the morning when they'd gone back to the lounge, Sam Lassiter brought her a shopping bag with a clean T-shirt and underwear.

"Thank you," she said, grateful but a little embarrassed that he'd gone shopping for intimate apparel for her.

After she changed, she came back into the sitting area to find a man talking to Hannah, Sam and Lucas. He was short and compact in build, with close-cropped hair and hard features. He looked like a cop, she thought.

She could see his stance was belligerent. When he turned to her, his expression was angry.

"I already asked Lassiter. Now I'll ask you. What the hell was Cal doing going off in the middle of the night to some hare-brained meeting when he was supposed to be working undercover with you?"

She blanched, wondering if this man was always so graceless in his communications.

Lucas came up behind the man. "Beth, this is Lieutenant Ken Patterson of the Howard County Police. Cal's boss."

"Pleased to meet you," she said in a cold voice, her hand remaining firmly at her side. Raising her chin, she said, "Cal and I had a pretty traumatic couple of hours at the reunion committee meeting, as I'm sure you know. When we got out of there, I assumed we both had the rest of the evening off. Or do I have it wrong? Is he supposed to be on duty twenty-four hours a day?"

His eyes narrowed. "He's not supposed to get himself incapacitated on his own time."

Sam came up behind the man. "I told you, if you want to blame someone, blame me. Don't lay a guilt trip on Beth. She's got enough on her mind right now."

"Yeah, well, I don't much like this situation."

"Because you care about what happens to him? Or because you're annoyed that he ended up in the hospital unconscious and ruined your investigation?" Beth asked, making an enormous effort to keep her voice from trembling.

"Both. I need someone to work this case. And since he can't do it, I'll have to assign someone else."

After delivering that bombshell, Patterson turned on his heel and stalked out of the room.

"Nice guy," Beth murmured.

"He's got a lot of problems right now," Hannah said. "Like the fallout from the reunion committee meeting last night."

Lucas put a hand on her shoulder. "Sorry the guy had to be such a jerk. I don't envy Cal working for someone like that."

"Neither do I," Beth muttered

The lieutenant had set her nerves on edge. She was barely holding herself together as they took the elevator to the ICU. And she was even more dispirited to find there was still no improvement in Cal's condition. As the hours dragged by, she could feel one of her headaches descending.

Closing her eyes, she tried to will away the pain. But it remained, a dull throbbing in her temples and the back of her head that only got worse as the day wore into evening.

A triple dose of painkiller didn't help. Needing to feel as if she was doing something for Cal, she left her new friends and went down to the chapel off the lobby, sat in one of the pews near the back and clasped her hands. It had been a long time since she'd asked God for any favors. She asked now. "Please," she whispered, "please, let him get better. Please let him wake up."

She stayed in the chapel for a long time, her hands clenched as she repeated the words over and over. Then she took the elevator back to the ICU.

Cal wasn't there, and her heart leaped into her throat, blocking her windpipe. Running back to the nurses' station, she asked, "Where is Detective Rollins?"

"He's having more tests."

"What tests?"

"You'll have to speak to Dr. Koenig."

The doctor was with another patient. Unable to draw in a full breath, Beth waited for him, pacing back and forth across the tile floor.

When she saw the doctor's face, she knew immediately that any news she was going to get regarding Cal would be bad.

"What is it? What's wrong?" she demanded.

He shoved his hands into the pockets of his white coat. "I'm afraid Detective Rollins's brain activity is...deteriorating."

The words made her chest clench as though she'd been grabbed by an iron fist. "Why?" she managed to say. "What's happening to him?"

"We can't come up with any reason." He paused, sighed. "It's almost like he doesn't want to come back to consciousness."

"No!"

The doctor ignored her exclamation and continued, "The thing is, we just don't know enough about the brain. Sometimes with a patient in a coma, the problem is obvious. Sometimes not. There are times when I can't say why one victim of head trauma recovers and another doesn't."

The doctor had never talked about a coma before, and the word clawed at her throat. "You don't think Cal will recover," she said faintly.

"I wouldn't want to go that far," he allowed. But the tone of his voice was enough to plunge her into despair.

Chapter Ten

Unable to sit still, Beth paced along the length of the hall as she waited for an orderly to bring Cal back to his room. Once they'd transferred him to his bed, they gave her a few minutes with him again. The sight of him pale and still as death suffused her heart with a depth of pain she couldn't have imagined.

The only comfort was the warmth of his flesh, the rise and fall of his chest. But she sensed the same thing she had before—that his spirit was somewhere else.

"Cal," she whispered.

He didn't answer, of course. And this time she stopped denying what she had been afraid to face. Outrageous as it might seem, she knew where he was. In that dark, forbidding nightmare jungle that had scared her witless.

She shuddered. The man she loved was there. In that terrible place where the dream monsters were gnawing away at his mind, and he couldn't find his way back.

Which gave her no real choice. She had to go there again, even if the place terrified her to the depths of her soul.

"Cal, wait for me. I'm coming back," she whispered as she leaned down to press her lips against his cheek before walking out of the ICU.

Back in the private lounge area, she was unable to tell the others about her conversation with Dr. Koenig or about what she was planning to do, so she simply said that she had to get some rest. After shutting herself inside her room, she pulled the heavy blackout drapes, kicked off her shoes and stood with her fingers pressed to her aching temples.

Then, knowing she was stalling, she forced herself to cross the room and lie down on the bed.

The sensation of hitting the pillow felt strange, as though her aching head was sinking into the foam-rubber softness. As it had last night, the experience took her captive. Her eyes drifted closed, and once again she felt sleep pulling at her with a supernatural force. Once again, a jolt of fear shot through her, and she felt her heart begin to drum in her chest. But this time it was far worse than last night. This time she knew what was waiting for her.

There was almost no transition. One moment she was conscious of lying on the bed and the next, she was back in that dark, dank jungle where the thick canopy of foliage shut out the light and the underbrush was alive with creeping, slithering monsters.

Terror seized her by the throat, held her in its grip.

"Cal? Where are you, Cal?" she tried to shout, but her voice was only a croaking sound.

Cal didn't answer, and she was certain she had made a terrible mistake by coming here. The certainty increased as she zeroed in on the sound of something big moving through the leaves, padding toward her on what sounded like giant feet.

There was nothing she could do but turn and sprint away. As she ran, branches and thorns grabbed at her clothing like hands trying to hold her back.

Sobbing, she yanked her clothing from their grasp. Then above the roaring in her ears, she heard another sound. A voice.

"Beth. Where are you? Beth!"

It was Cal! Cal. And she felt hope explode inside her chest.

"Cal! I can't see you. Where are you?" she shouted.

"Keep talking to me. I'll find you."

If he could find her, so could the monster. Cal was just a man—and the monster was fast, strong, savage. "It's going to get me. It's right behind me," she screamed.

She heard Cal moving through the foliage, coming toward her, and she turned in that direction, quickening her pace.

But it was too late. Something tore at her back. Not thorns, animal claws. She cried out and threw herself forward. Then the sound of gunshots rang out in the darkness. Behind her, a massive body crashed to the ground.

Whirling, she saw the thing that had been stalking her with such single-minded purpose. Something with scales and massive teeth. Dark, beady eyes. Something that had never walked the earth.

Cal was beside her then, urging her away.

"Come on. We have to get out of here before something else tries to get us."

The rustling sounds in the underbrush confirmed that other creatures were moving toward them, following the sound of their voices and their scent.

"Where are we?" she asked, cringing against her protector.

"I wish to hell I knew." He guided her through the jungle, weaving his way around tree trunks, over fallen logs and around tangles of vegetation.

They ran toward a high brick wall. She could see a stout wooden door with a large, old-fashioned lock below the knob. Cal pulled a key from his pocket, fitted it quickly into the lock and shouldered the massive door open. Just as a dark, terrifying form emerged from a screen of leaves, Cal pulled her though the door and slammed it closed behind them.

Turning the lock, he sighed in relief as he leaned his shoulders against the barrier and reached for her. They were both breathing hard, and for long moments she could do little more than cling to him, her head resting against his shoulder.

"Cal, oh God, Cal," she managed to say, her arms tightening around him. He felt warm, solid, reassuring in a world of chaos.

"I figured out how to get away from the monsters by coming in here," he said.

"Good."

"But they're still outside, in the jungle. What were you doing out there? It's dangerous," he said.

She raised her head, blinked at him. The answer was so obvious, but he didn't seem to know it. "I came to find you. And suddenly I was just…there."

"You could have gotten hurt! I came here to hide out. You're not supposed to follow me." He stopped, looked confused.

"Cal?" She wanted to ask him what he meant. But his grip on her shoulders had changed, and the sudden smoldering look in his eyes made her go very still.

"Beth," he breathed. Quickly, decisively, he lowered his lips to hers. The kiss was hungry, passionate, and she knew by the way his mouth devoured hers now that in the past he had always been holding something of himself back.

No longer. Now his kiss seared her from the roots of her hair to the soles of her feet.

Always before, she had feared the power building between them. But in this place of unreality, the barriers were suddenly down, and it was impossible not to give him everything she could offer and ask for everything he could give.

Dizzy with need, and with relief too, she lifted her arms, anchoring one hand to his shoulder while the other curled around his neck.

He was like a drug flowing through her veins, pooling in sensitive parts of her body.

She made a small sound of pleasure when he deepened

the kiss, at the same time splaying his legs and pulling her aching body more tightly against his. When he took her bottom lip between his and gently sucked, she pressed herself shamelessly into the heat and hardness of him.

She felt him go still. Heard him draw in a sharp, disjointed breath.

Then his head lifted, and his hands were on her shoulders, setting her body away from his. Only a few inches away, yet the sudden absence of his warmth made her feel as if she'd stepped outside the house on a cold winter day.

Her eyes blinked open. "Cal?"

He looked as dazed as she felt. "What's happening to me? I shouldn't be kissing you like that. It's wrong."

"Why?"

"You're innocent. I came to the farm to do a job, not start anything with you. You shouldn't be getting involved with a guy like me."

"Because I'm innocent, or because you can't deal with it?"

He gave her a dark look. "Because I'm not going to make any kind of commitment to you. Not to you or any woman. That's who I am!"

"Suppose I don't need a commitment? Suppose I just want whatever you're willing to give."

"It's not enough. Not for you."

"Let me be the judge of that."

"No." Cutting off the conversation, he took her hand and led her away from the wall and toward another stand of trees. She saw that inside the wall, everything was different from the jungle outside. The grass was mowed short. The trees were planted on a neatly mulched plot, bordered by flower beds.

They emerged from under branches waving gently in the wind to face a curved swimming pool flanked at one end by a little waterfall. To the right was a small house with a veranda opening onto the pool deck. In the distance she could see a mansion with lights blazing through the windows the way her own windows blazed in the darkness.

Their radiance spilled out, illuminating the night. But that wasn't the only light brightening the scene. On this side of the wall, a full moon shone down, bathing everything in a silvery radiance.

In the swimming pool, a fish jumped from the water, leaving a trail of phosphorescence in the air before plunging below the surface again.

The fish was beautiful. The place was beautiful. The colors were bright and vivid, even at night. The wind carried the sound of low music and a rich woodsy scent that sank into her lungs and filled her brain with subtle pleasure.

"Where are we?" she asked.

"It's the estate of Cam Randolph and Jo O'Malley. They have a couple of parties here every year. I always thought it would be fun to stay longer. So here I am."

The casual way he said it sent a little dart of alarm through her.

"What do you mean, 'here I am'?" she asked in a voice that trembled slightly.

He looked momentarily uncertain, then gave an elaborate shrug. "I don't know. I guess I mean that I wanted to be here, so I am."

But she caught the doubt behind the surface of his dark eyes, as though there was no sorting through the logic of his own statements.

She stared around her, then back at him, feeling almost as unsure as he sounded, yet determined to figure out what was fantasy and what was all too real. This conversation—it was real. But the scene around them was the product of her imagination—or his—although she understood that what happened in this place carried power far beyond what was rational or logical in the normal world.

This might be a dream. Yet she sensed that staying here

was dangerous, even if the monsters were shut away on the other side of a wall.

She took a couple of deep steadying breaths. "You asked what's happening to you. Do you remember that Sam Lassiter asked you to cover him at a meeting with an informant?"

"Yeah."

"And what happened at the meeting?"

"He told me the guy who's after Lucas—Dallas Sedgwick—is in Baltimore. He's got some kind of scheme. Big plans, Deep Throat said." His expression turned urgent. "And he's using the name Sierra. I've got to tell that to Lucas right away."

"Did you find out anything else?" she asked.

His gaze turned inward, then a look of dismay crossed his features. "No. Someone started shooting. Deep Throat went down. I went for the gun in my boot."

"And?" she pressed.

"And nothing!"

"What do you mean nothing?"

"I don't remember anything else."

"You were hit in the head. A flesh wound."

She watched his face, watched the information sink in. "You're in the hospital," she added. "In a coma."

"No! I'm here. I'm here, with you." To prove his point, he grabbed her by the shoulders, his fingers digging into her flesh as he pulled the length of her body against his. "This is what's real," he said in a thick voice. "You and me."

She wanted to protest, wanted to tell him that he was fooling himself. Yet she clung to him with the same strength that fueled his passion.

Once more, his mouth came down on hers with a desperation she could taste, a desperation she could feel in every cell of her body.

He needed her. But no less than she needed him. Because what they could give each other had become as necessary as breathing.

She had come here with an urgent purpose—to connect with him—and she was doing that in a way that she hadn't dreamed was possible. As he kissed her, she forgot where they were, forgot the hospital and the urgency of her mission. The only reality was her and Cal, their mouths fused, their bodies locked.

The kiss broke, and he lifted his head, but only a fraction as his lips played with hers. "I want you," he said, his voice low and urgent. "I've wanted you since that first night at your house. I fought it because I knew it wasn't right. But now you're here, and I don't have to fight what I'm feeling."

She nodded, because it was true for her as well. In this place where the colors were more vivid and the feelings more intense, risks faded into the background.

If she wanted to make love with him here, she could do it, because all things were possible.

"Come inside," he murmured, leading her around the pool to the cabana. It was furnished not with lounges and chairs but with a four-poster king-size bed, the posts elaborately carved with motifs from her own weavings.

Had she put them there? Or had he? she wondered vaguely.

"Those flowing shirts of yours," he said thickly. "When you turn, the fabric clings to your breasts. Do you wear them to tease me?"

"I'd never tease you," she whispered, then dipped her head. "Well, maybe a little."

He threw back his head and laughed, an uninhibited laugh, because this was a place where the two of them could shed all inhibitions.

The laugh prickled along her nerve endings, setting off a wave of sensation that shimmered across her skin and sank into the marrow of her bones.

"Oh!"

"You know, I lay in bed thinking about which I'd enjoy more—undressing you or watching you undress for me."

"What did you decide?" she asked in a breathy voice.

"I decided that if you stripped for me, it would be the sexiest show in the world."

She had never thought of herself as a sexy woman, never imagined herself capable of such abandon. But in this place it was all right to let herself go.

Taking a step back, she reached for the buttons of her shirt. A flush rose in her cheeks, but it didn't stop her from enjoying the smoldering expression on Cal's face as she slowly slipped the buttons open one by one. She was certain she had put on a bra this morning. Now it had turned up missing, so she left the blouse hanging loose, hiding and then revealing glimpses of her breasts as she worked the snap at her waist and skimmed off her jeans.

She was wearing only the shirt now, and her panties. Wondering where her courage came from, she slid the blouse off her shoulders, playing with it as she slowly peeled it down her arms, aware that her nipples were tight with arousal as she divested herself of the garment.

Beth had never teased a man in her life. Never deliberately set out to be provocative. But she knew she had succeeded when she heard Cal make a low, needy sound.

"That's beautiful, so beautiful," he breathed as he came toward her, then slowly reached to sweep her hair over her shoulders, covering the tops of her breasts, then rippling the golden curtain.

"I love your hair. Your breasts," he said, his voice rough as he took her fullness in his hands.

She gasped as his fingers touched her, caressed her, swept the strands of her hair against her own flesh. Then he slipped his fingers between the strands, taking her nipples between his thumbs and fingers, giving her back his own brand of teasing. She arched into the caress, helpless to do anything besides respond to him—physically, emotionally, on every level that a woman could respond to a man.

Lifting her gaze to his face, she saw he was as captivated as she. She had never seen him like this. He looked younger, freer and totally entranced by the passion flaring between them.

He stripped off her panties. Then, lifting her in his arms as if she had no more weight than rose petals, he laid her gently down on the soft, yielding mattress.

Standing beside the bed, he stared down at her, looking as if he couldn't believe the two of them were here together.

''I want you naked, too,'' she said, astonished by the boldness of the statement.

''Good.'' He pulled his shirt over his head and tossed it away, then reached for the snap at the top of his jeans, shucking off his remaining clothing in one smooth motion.

She feasted her gaze on his body—the flat planes, the hard muscles, the jutting erection, thinking she should be embarrassed to enjoy his nudity so thoroughly. But she couldn't summon embarrassment, only gratification.

When she held out her arms to him, he came down beside her on the bed, gathering her close.

The feel of his skin against hers was so glorious that she thought she might die from the pleasure. But she quickly discovered there was more as he drew back so that his hands could travel over her body, finding all the sensitive places that responded so willingly to his touch.

She had never done this before and she thought in some corner of her mind that she should be nervous as his fingers slid over her belly, tangled in the curly hair at the juncture of her legs, then slipped into the warm folds of her feminine flesh. But there was no need to be nervous, not in this place, with this man.

No need for anything but her deep response to him. He had fueled her passion and fueled her dreams. And now here she was, making love with him, and it was everything she had imagined and more.

"You're so responsive, so ready for me," he growled.

"Am I?" she asked in a breathy voice, thinking she had never expected to be praised for something like that.

"Oh, yes."

"Responsive to you," she answered. "Only you, Cal. This feels so right because it's you."

He raised up on one elbow, his hot gaze burning into hers, and she reached up to press her fingertips against his cheek.

"Please, don't make me wait."

But he did make her wait while he pushed her higher and higher to a place where the only reality in the universe was the rich pleasure he was giving her.

Then his body was over hers. She had expected that this first time might hurt, but there was no pain, only the sweet sensation of his body filling hers and touching her very heart.

She took him deeply into herself, glorying in the knowledge of their joining, not just the physical pleasure of it but more, so much more. Then he began to move, setting a pace that carried her higher than she'd imagined possible. She clung to him, feeling small tremors shake her. They built to earthquake proportions, exploding through her in a shower of pleasure that brought his name to her lips.

She knew he followed her into ecstasy when she heard his deep shout of gratification.

He rolled to his side, kissing her, keeping his arms around her, and she snuggled against him, marveling at how content, how complete she felt.

She wanted to stay there forever with him. For a long time, they seemed to simply drift together in a private world where no one else could reach them. Yet slowly, under the contentment, a nagging feeling began to creep up on her, like an animal with sharp teeth nipping at her heels.

She pressed her palm to Cal's chest, feeling the beating of his heart. It felt strong and regular. His naked body next to hers was fit and firm. Yet this wasn't reality, she remembered with a jolt. This was his dream, and she had come here to be with him.

"Cal?"

"Hmm?"

"I have to go back. You have to come back with me."

"Back where?"

"Back to the real world."

"This is..." He raised his head and looked around as if seeing the setting for the first time. "You're right," he said slowly. "This is..." He stopped, then started again. "I could make love to you here. Back there, everything's too complicated. Here it's simple." He brought his hand to her breast and stroked the nipple, bringing it easily to arousal.

"I want you. You want me. We can give each other pleasure again."

It was so tempting to give in to the seductive tone of his voice, the heat he generated with his touch. But she couldn't let herself be seduced again.

"No. Cal, stop."

"You want me," he said again, his voice thick with satisfaction as he watched her nipple tighten. "We just made love, and you want me again."

There was no point in denying the obvious. "Yes. But that doesn't change anything. We have to go back."

His face turned hard. "You go back if you want to. I'm staying here."

"No." She reached for his arm, but he was too fast for her. He was off the bed and striding naked out of the summerhouse before she could stop him.

"Cal!"

She was running toward him before she had time to be embarrassed by her state of undress. But she was too late. He had already dived in.

Perhaps it was an illusion of the moonlight. But the moment his body disappeared below the crystal water, he seemed to vanish.

She ran to the edge of the pool, terror rising within her as she peered into the turquoise depths.

"Cal," she called frantically, even when she realized the effort was useless. "Cal."

The pool seemed to have no bottom. The crystal water went down and down into darkness. But there was no thought in her mind except to follow him and bring him back to her.

Plunging in, she kicked wildly downward. Then she found she didn't have to kick. She was being sucked down, down into the darkness where she couldn't see, couldn't breathe.

Then his hand was on her again, pulling her up and out of the blackness so that they stood on a beach with waves thundering and crashing.

She dug her bare toes into the warm sand, then looked up at Cal as he stood strong and naked beside her.

"You know this isn't real. Cal, you have to come back."

"It's better here."

She wrapped her hands around his arms. "You'll die if you stay here."

He stared at her, then looked away.

"Come back. Come back with me now."

His eyes burned into hers. He didn't speak, but she knew he had made his decision. And she wasn't going to change his mind.

Chapter Eleven

Beth woke choking, gasping for air, struggling against some terrible force that held her in place.

She realized that someone was holding her, his hands on her shoulders. And for a moment she thought they were Cal's hands. But they weren't. It was Sam Lassiter who held her down on the bed. He was on one side of her, Hannah and Lucas were on the other.

"Beth, you're all right. Take it easy." Sam's voice filtered into her consciousness. "It was just a dream."

She blinked. Just a dream? Was that all?

One moment she had been standing with Cal on a beach. Now here she was in the bed where she'd gone to sleep. She remembered it all. The terrors of the jungle, Cal's finding her, taking her to the other side of the wall where everything was different, where they'd made love.

She ducked her head, unwilling to let the people around her see the expression that must be on her face. She imagined she looked astonished, vulnerable—and embarrassed.

Grabbing the edge of the sheet, she clenched and unclenched her fingers. Lord, had she dreamed all that out of her wild imagination, because it was what she wanted so much? Or in some crazy way, had something real happened between her and Cal?

She saw a flicker of movement and glanced up through

her lashes to see a look pass between Hannah and the two men.

Sam cleared his throat. "Uh, we came rushing in here to find out if you were okay," Sam said. "We'll clear out."

"Thank you," she whispered. "I mean, thank you for being concerned."

Hannah waited until the door closed behind the men, leaving them alone. "Are you all right?" she asked.

Beth pushed herself up. "I had a dream," she said cautiously.

"It sounded like you were in considerable distress," Hannah said, her voice filled with concern. "Do you want to tell me about it?"

Beth knit her fingers together in her lap. "Distress," she murmured. "I guess you could call it that. I was trying to get Cal to face reality and wake himself up, and he ran away from me. We were in a garden with a swimming pool. He dived into the pool and disappeared. I went in after him, but he was gone. Then we were standing on a beach, still arguing."

"That's pretty upsetting, all right."

Beth kept her head bent. What if she explained that she wasn't upset by a mere nightmare? What if she said that she was pretty sure what had happened between herself and Cal in the dream was just as real as the reality of his unconscious body lying down there in ICU.

Her automatic reaction was that Hannah would think she was delusional, at best. Then she reminded herself that Hannah and Sam and Lucas weren't like the people she had known all her life, the people who had thought she was cracked in the head because she had no control over the psychic experiences that ambushed her.

Still, it was difficult to force the words out of her mouth. Finally she said in a rush, "Cal's in a coma. When you look at him, it just seems like he's unconscious. But his mind has gone somewhere—to a dreamworld where he's living. Because of my...psychic abilities I was able to communicate with him. When I went to sleep I ended up in that world with him. He saved me from a dangerous animal in a jungle, then he took me into a walled estate with beautiful grounds, a summerhouse and the pool I told you about. We talked and...touched each other..." Beth stopped and swallowed. "Cal told me he doesn't want to come back here. I think it's partly because of me. He feels guilty about our relationship. I mean, he thinks we shouldn't have gotten involved. It was all right for us to make love there, but back here, he thinks that his being attracted to me is wrong. Because he can't make a commitment to me, he said. So that's why he won't wake up. His feelings are all tied up in knots so he bailed out."

Beth stopped abruptly, realizing that she'd given away far more than she'd intended and wishing she hadn't said quite so much. Tension crackled through her as she waited for Hannah to say something.

"You know, Cal's mom left him and his father in the lurch. Cal's dad did his best to raise him, and for the most part, he did a pretty good job. But Mr. Rollins's own bad experience with marriage was the foundation for some of the attitudes he passed on to Cal. So I guess if he started falling for someone like you—someone who's sweet and natural and honest without an ounce of guile—that would call into question all the rules he's always relied on in his dealings with women who attracted him. I guess that would be hard for him to handle, all right. And maybe the only way he could cope would be to run away. The part I don't like is that he's using his medical condition as an excuse for not dealing with your relationship."

The unconditional acceptance of her story made Beth feel light-headed. "Then you believe me?" she whispered.

Hannah gave her a frank look. "If somebody else told me that story, I'd have a lot of questions. From you, it makes sense."

"And you don't think the coma is my fault?" Beth whispered.

"Certainly not! You go down to ICU and tell that jerk that if he doesn't come back to the world right now, you're going to take a stick to his worthless hide."

"I can't tell him anything. I can't reach him—not from here." She stopped, remembering something. "He said he had an urgent message for Luke. That someone named Sedgwick is in Baltimore. That he's using the name Sierra. Does that mean anything to you?"

"It certainly does! If I needed proof that you'd talked to Cal, you've just given it to me. Nobody knows about Sedgwick but the people close to me and Luke."

While Beth was taking that in, Hannah continued, "And that's proof you can do something about Cal. You reached him when you went to sleep. You can do it again. And you'd better get on it, because I didn't like what I heard in the last report from the doctor."

"He's worse?" Beth breathed.

"He's the same. And the longer he stays that way, the more dangerous it is for him."

Beth pushed herself off the bed. There was no thought of protecting herself now, no thought of what anybody was going to say about her odd behavior. She didn't even bother to put on her shoes as she dashed out of the room and made for the elevator.

She arrived breathless at the door to the ICU, then stopped short, thinking that they'd throw her out if she came barreling in like a madwoman. After giving herself a minute to calm down, she pushed open the door and walked to Cal's room.

The nurse looked at her, and she knew by the woman's face that she wasn't expecting Cal to wake up any time soon—if at all.

Ducking her head away, Beth tiptoed toward Cal's bed. The sight of him lying there pale and still, surrounded by monitors and hospital equipment sent a jolt through her.

When she had come to him in his fantasy world, he had wrapped his strong arms around her, kissed her, swept her away with his lovemaking. But that was only in his dream. This room was cold, sharp reality.

She came to a stop beside the bed, looking down at him, struck by the sensation that she'd had the first time she'd seen him here: his body might be in this bed, but his mind was far away. And now she knew where he was. At least she had known, before he had plunged into the swimming pool and pulled her up onto the beach.

Now he might be in some other place, farther away, where it was impossible for her or anyone else to reach him.

Her heart squeezed painfully. Maybe he didn't want her to find him, but she was damn well going to try.

After pulling up a chair and sitting down, she reached out and laid her hands on his arm, the feel of his hair-roughened skin making her body throb as it brought back vivid memories of their lovemaking.

Once again, she closed her eyes. Only this time she wasn't lying in her bed alone. This time the connection between herself and Cal was physical.

Once again, she was seized by a jolt of fear—fear of the unknown, fear of failure. Until she'd met Cal, she'd never deliberately tried to use her special abilities. She'd considered them a curse, and every time she'd succeeded in locking them away in some hidden part of her mind, so much the better. Now she was fumbling with the lock on that door, when she wasn't even certain where she kept the key.

She did know one thing for sure, though. She wanted desperately to reach Cal. The problem was, she didn't know how she had done it before. Didn't know how to accomplish that goal again. And there was one more terror as well. The idea of going back to that dark, dangerous jungle sent a wave of cold through her body. Cal had found her and rescued her but what if he didn't come this time?

She felt the cold fear penetrate all the way to the marrow of her bones, but she didn't pull away—either physically or mentally.

Teeth clenched, eyes squeezed closed, she tried to send her mind toward Cal's.

Cal, she called. *Cal, where are you?*

He didn't answer, yet she felt something. Some kind of barrier, too far for her to reach. Going there was impossible. But she would dare the impossible.

She wasn't conscious of falling asleep, only of images coming to her. The night sky, stars. At first they were above her. Then she wasn't seeing them from the ground. She was up among them, flying through them, the wonder of it almost canceling out the cold and the terror.

The stars stopped abruptly ahead of her, and she could see a massive barrier, a great dark wall, blocking out the light.

"Go back!" Cal's voice rang in her head. "You'll be killed."

There was no way to stop. She was flying straight toward the wall, her speed and trajectory out of her control now. She braced for the impact, knowing that her body was going to smash against that solid barrier.

Then at the last moment, she saw a tiny chink, a crack in the massive surface. With a little sob, she angled toward it, slipped through and found herself floating in bright turquoise water. In the swimming pool where she had followed Cal last time. Only the pool was much larger than it ever could have been. As large as the ocean. Cal was miles away, but he couldn't hide from her.

She swam toward him, kicking her feet, stroking with her arms, under the water like a fish with no need for air, moving impossibly fast, so that she caught up with him and clamped her hand on his arm.

He turned, his face fierce. "Leave me alone."

"No."

They were both underwater and there should have been no way for either one of them to speak. But they did.

"If you don't come back, I'll stay here with you."

His face contorted. "You can't. You'll die here."

"So will you, you bullheaded idiot. Is that what you want? To die here?" she screamed. "Are you a coward? Is that it? Did I finally figure out the secret of Calvin Rollins?"

"I'm no coward. Don't you dare call me that."

"What would you call it? You're afraid to face me in the real world."

"Don't let your head swell too much. It's not just you. Do you think I want to come back and hear everybody talking about how I walked into an ambush like a rookie cop and got shot?"

She stared at him incredulously. "Your macho pride is wounded? That's why you can't wake up, because you're not living up to your male image?"

His eyes were angry, defiant—and uncertain.

She went with the uncertainty. "Prove you're not a coward. Prove you're not afraid to face your life," she shouted.

"I don't have to prove a damn thing to you!"

She reached out to give him a rough shake, the action muted by the water around them. But then, suddenly they were no longer in the water. She gasped and found herself back in the ICU, sitting beside Cal's bed.

She felt a jolt of sensation as she looked down into his face. His eyelids fluttered, opened. And he was staring at her, a stunned expression on his face. "Where am I? What happened?" he asked.

"You're in the hospital. You were shot."

"You and I—" He stopped, gave her a look that she felt over every inch of her body. And in that instant she knew he was remembering what had happened. Not just behind the wall in the sky but earlier, in the summerhouse on the wide bed.

The expression on his face stopped her heart and then started it throbbing like a jungle drum.

"You and I...we...made love." He waited a beat before destroying her world. "That should never have happened."

That was what he thought about the most joyful experience of her life? That making love with her, even in his dream, had been a mistake?

She felt an iron fist squeeze around her heart, cutting off her breath. Struggling to her feet, she barreled through the door of the ICU, and almost collided with Hannah and the two men standing there.

As Hannah caught the expression on Beth's face, her own skin went pale. "What happened?" she gasped. "Is Cal—"

"He's awake. I'm sure he'd like to see you," she managed to say, then fled because she couldn't face these three people who had been so kind to her over the past few days.

SERIAL KILLER ARRESTED.

Cal set down his spoon with a thunk on the kitchen table. As he stared at the stark black headline in the *Baltimore Sun,* he cursed. He had been on medical leave for a week, rattling around his house with nothing to do. So he'd slept in, fixed himself a bowl of cereal and gone outside to retrieve the morning paper around 11:00 a.m.

Now he was hopping mad.

Damn! Nobody had bothered to tell him they had the bad guy in custody. And it was his case, dammit. His case!

But he knew why he was out of the loop. Because Patterson was giving vent to his ire. He supposed that was better than getting suspended, which would have been within the lieutenant's rights.

His heart was pounding as he focused on the text. The suspect was a little jerk named Wayne Jenkins, a guy who'd been teased and ridiculed by class members and had set about getting even. After the letters inviting everyone to the reunion committee had gone out, he'd been caught vandalizing the car of ex–football player Billy Nichols. Apparently he'd been charged with other acts of vandalism, too. And the tie-in to the killings was that he'd been spotted lurking in the parking lot of the Fairways Restaurant when the reunion committee had been meeting.

Cal read more of the story. When he came to the part about Detective Calvin Rollins of the Howard County Police working undercover, posing as the husband of Beth Wagner, he blanched.

How the hell had that piece of information gotten into circulation? Had Patterson let it out now that Jenkins was in custody?

He picked up his cereal bowl, dumped the contents into the trash and reached for the phone.

Patterson was busy, but Alex Shane, a fellow detective, was willing to fill him on the details. So far Jenkins hadn't confessed. In fact, he was steadfastly maintaining his innocence regarding the murders, although he had refused to take a polygraph test.

Still, Patterson was sure they had the right guy.

Cal hung up the phone and sat staring into space, so many emotions coursing through him that he felt his head start to pound.

Like Beth, he thought as he pressed his fingers to his throbbing temple. She got those damn headaches when she was having one of her psychic experiences.

Ever since he'd awakened in the hospital with a jackhammer pounding away in his head, he had tried not to think about Beth. But she kept stealing back into his mind.

It was tempting to dismiss the dream experiences with her as just that—dreams. But he couldn't. They were too real, too vivid.

She'd saved his life. He had no doubt in his mind about that. She'd used the psychic powers she hated so much to pull him back to reality when he'd withdrawn into his little dreamworld where he could pretend any damn thing he wanted.

And he'd thanked her by shoving her away, because he couldn't deal with what had happened between them. Couldn't deal with what he was still feeling. A gut-deep longing that he'd never felt before—coupled with the need to escape.

He clenched his fists. He'd told her he was embarrassed about getting shot. That was the least of what had sent him running headlong from the real world. Mostly he'd tried not to think about the trick his unconscious mind had played on him. Now he was forced to confront his demons. He'd been worried about what he was doing to Beth, so he'd bailed out. And it hadn't done him any damn good. Not with this article in the paper. Now his name was publicly linked to hers, in the most humiliating way possible.

His fists clenched and unclenched. He couldn't just sit here. He had to do something.

Twenty minutes later, showered, shaved and wearing jeans, a dark T-shirt, and a light jacket to hide his shoulder holster, he was on his way to McKinley's where it had all started—where Hallie Bradshaw was supposed to meet her friends for drinks after work.

As he suspected, the lunchtime crowd was talking about the *Baltimore Sun* article. And as he waited for a table, he spotted Candy Marks and Donna Pasternack having lunch together. Donna had been the reunion committee organizer. Candy was the football player's wife.

She saw him and bent her head toward Donna. Moments later, they were both staring at him. Hands in his pockets, he sauntered over to their table.

Donna pointed to an empty seat at their table. "Why don't you join us. It's Cal Rollins—not Roberts, isn't it?"

"Right," he answered, accepting the invitation. Why not? He'd come here for information, and this was as good a way as any to get it.

They asked him about Wayne Jenkins. He told them he

was on medical leave and didn't know any more than he'd read in the papers.

"Medical leave? Were you injured by Jenkins at the reunion meeting?"

"No. I got hurt on another case," he answered, thinking that it was true. Just not another official case.

"Well, it was very naughty of you not to tell us you were working undercover on a police investigation," Donna said.

"That's the nature of undercover work," he pointed out.

"Um, yes. And now it makes better sense. We were all trying to figure out how Beth Wagner...uh, snagged a hunk like you for a husband."

He felt his stomach muscles clench. "Well, it's true Beth and I weren't married," he heard himself saying. "She's an old-fashioned girl, so I knew she wouldn't be comfortable telling people she was living with me without benefit of marriage."

He saw Candy's mouth drop open. "You mean the two of you really were living together?"

He'd made it sound that way. Again, it wasn't strictly the truth. He'd lived with her, but not in the sense that he'd implied. He gave a tight nod. Then suddenly aware that conversation at nearby tables had stopped, he looked up and saw that the people around him were tuned in to his exchange with the two women.

"You'll have to excuse me. I guess I wasn't feeling as well as I thought," he said, scraping back his chair and heading for the door.

SERIAL KILLER ARRESTED.

The newspaper sat in the middle of Damien's desk like a newly acquired hunting trophy. He'd read the top story fifty times, savoring all the little details, all the information and misinformation.

"So the police think that Wayne Jenkins did all those nasty things?" Damien laughed. "Well, he might have done some of them. The small stuff. But he wasn't the one who was clever enough to kill eight people and get away scot free.''

And he wasn't the one who was even now plotting his next caper. This time the victim was going to be Beth Wagner, that little bitch.

A jolt of anger shot through him. Unable to sit still, he leaped up and paced to the end of the room, then came back to the article.

He'd thought she was so sweet and nice all those years ago. An outsider like he was. Then he'd seen her at that reunion meeting, seen her on TV with the cop Rollins.

''So, Miss Cop's Helper,'' he said aloud, ''I'm going to teach you a lesson you'll never forget. See, I've got a window of opportunity here because the stupid police are focused on the wrong guy. Trying to wring a confession out of him.''

He laughed. ''Maybe they will! Jenkins is such a wimp maybe he'd own up to crimes he didn't commit and give me even more breathing space. So I've got to plan this real good. Plan it carefully. I don't want to blow it. Not now.''

He'd already started keeping tabs on Beth. She'd been alone on her farm for the week—except for that big ugly dog of hers or when that guy who worked for her was out in the fields. He hadn't taken care of the dog yet because he didn't want to alert her to any danger. But he'd deal with the damn animal. After that, scooping her up wasn't going to be any problem now that her buddy the cop had moved out.

Chapter Twelve

Beth hcard Granger bark sharply. Reaching down, she patted the dog's back.

''What is it, boy?'' she asked.

She had been sitting at her loom, staring into space instead of at the tapestry that she was supposed to be weaving. She'd called the bank this morning and told them the wall hanging was going to be late.

Mr. Harrison had assured her that was all right. He understood that she'd been busy with that undercover assignment.

The words and the tone of his voice had made her cringe. She'd read the article in the paper and tried to tell herself it didn't matter that everybody knew she and Cal had just been playing house. Now she was pretty sure that the whole of Howard County was talking about it.

She shouldn't care what they thought. But Harrison's voice had brought back all the old pain she'd struggled with over the years. Now she couldn't even take refuge in her weaving the way she'd done so often, because since Cal Rollins had come into her life, she'd been too emotionally fragile to do more than two licks of work.

The dog growled again, then stood and walked toward the darkened window. He'd been skittish ever since she'd come home from the hospital. But she sensed it wasn't just her absence that had unsettled him. Her dog missed having Cal around, just the way she missed him.

Damn Cal. Damn him.

He'd made her care about him, then he'd as good as ripped her heart from her chest.

She stood up abruptly and followed the dog to the window. Since fleeing the ICU, she hadn't felt one psychic twinge. It was as if she were a radio with burned-out circuit boards and nothing was capable of coming through.

Only it wasn't radio waves that had been cut off. It was her psychic sense. It had been with her since that night of Dad's accident. She'd hated it, tried to deny it, fought against it. She hadn't realized that it was an essential part of her, even when it seemed to be quiet inside her. Now that it had vanished, she felt totally vulnerable and alone.

Granger barked and trotted down the hall. She followed him, then stopped to get a gun from her father's locked cabinet.

Twilight hadn't quite faded into darkness, but she turned on the outside lights anyway. Then, feeling clammy and uncertain, she stepped onto the porch.

Should she call the cops? And tell them what? That she and her dog were nervous? She remembered Officer Brodie, who had come here the first night and tramped around the farm. Remembered the pained expression on his face.

Then there had been Cal, coming out to check up on Brodie's story. She squeezed her eyes closed, trying to shut out all the vivid memories of Cal from that first encounter to the last.

When she opened her eyes again, she caught a flicker of movement down by the barn. Movement where there should be none.

She whirled, raised the gun, her finger squeezing on the trigger. But her dog was in the way, racing toward the open doorway and barking loudly.

"Granger, no. Come back!"

Then the man in the shadows stepped into the light, and she gasped.

She could barely utter his name as she stood there and stared at him in dumb-eyed shock. "Cal."

The last time she'd seen him had been almost a week ago when he'd been lying in a hospital bed, his skin pale as chalk, his body weak and his eyes fierce as he told her that he didn't want her.

Now…now he seemed to be recovered physically. Yet he was still staring at her as if she were the last person on earth he wanted to encounter.

"What are you trying to do?" he growled. "Kill me? Put that gun down."

She'd been so astonished that she'd simply frozen in place. "Lord, where's my brain?" she muttered as she stiffly moved her arm, then set the weapon down with a thunk on the table beside the porch chair. Turning back to him, she caught her breath, still hardly able to believe he was here at the farm. Not after what he'd said when his eyes had opened.

Well, maybe he was here on official business, or to pick up the clothing that was still in the room he'd occupied upstairs. She hadn't touched his stuff, and she hadn't been inside the room where he'd slept. She'd simply closed the door, thinking that she'd pack up his things sometime and drop them off at the police department.

"Cal, how are you?" she asked. "Are you back on duty?"

He made a harsh sound. "I'm still on sick leave. I'm here on my own time."

"Are you all right?"

"I'm fine, but they won't certify me to go back to work."

She was still trying to take him in as she stood there, struggling to speak around the lump in her throat. "If you were planning to come here, why didn't you call me and let me know? Or knock on the door? What are you doing in my barn?''

''Checking things out. I've been out in the fields, too'' he said, striding toward her, ignoring her other questions. ''There are tire tracks out in a couple of your pastures.''

''From Tim. He brings vehicles here sometimes.''

''A compact car?''

''No. Trucks.''

''So there's been a strange vehicle here. And someone who drinks designer water has been in the barn. I know you don't drink the stuff. Does Tim?''

''No,'' she breathed, struggling to take in the implications.

''If you come down here, I'll show you where the straw's been trampled. Right by a place where there's a spy hole in the wall. Don't tell me you haven't heard your dog barking any time lately.''

She watched him reading the guilty expression on her face. She'd been so out of it that she'd only shushed her dog. ''Granger did hear something.'' She took several slow steps forward. ''I thought...I thought he was reacting to a rabbit or a fox or something like that.''

''If you can't take care of yourself, somebody's got to.''

Had she heard him right? ''What did you say?''

Again he ignored the question. Turning, he swept his arm toward the barn. On unwilling feet, she came forward, let him usher her inside, let him show her the place where someone had been standing and spying on the house.

Beside her, Granger yapped, as if to reprove her for not listening to his warning.

She felt numb as she followed Cal back across the yard. She'd felt cut off from her ingrained psychic sense since coming home. Apparently her brain hadn't been working any too well, either. Apparently it still wasn't. She'd forgotten about the gun on the table, but Cal stopped to pick it up before walking into the house.

He was the one who put the weapon away and locked

the cabinet door, then turned to pace from one end of the room to the other.

When he stopped and ran his hand through his hair, she felt tension gathering in her chest as she waited to hear what he had to say.

"Somebody's been watching you. You're not safe here alone."

"I can't leave."

"I think you can."

"The sheep...my work."

"Your guy Tim will take care of the sheep the way he did when you spent the night in the hospital. And we'll move your loom someplace else."

She was still trying to take it in. "Where?"

"Someplace safe."

"I can't leave."

Ignoring her, he plowed ahead. "I won't allow you to be in danger because you helped me out with a case. So this time we're going to do things differently."

"Like how?"

"You read in the papers that Patterson thinks the case is solved. Well, I think he's wrong. But I can't prove it. And I can't prove that the killer has been out here watching you, although I *can* send that water bottle in for analysis."

"Why would someone be stupid enough to leave it?" she broke in.

"I don't know. To make you nervous?"

"If I were nervous, wouldn't I call the police?"

"Would you? Even after your recent experiences with Howard County's finest?"

She swallowed and ducked her head. "Maybe not."

"You're proving my point. I'm not going to take a chance on anything happening to you now. You're going to marry me so I can protect you—without setting tongues wagging any more than they already are. If you want to divorce me after this is all over, you can do it."

She felt her mouth drop open. "I'm going to what?" she managed to say.

"You're going to marry me."

The announcement sent a shock wave through her. When she could make her eyes focus again, she stared at the tense lines of his face, trying to take in what he had said, trying to think about what might be motivating him. He had just told her he was going to marry her because she was in danger. Given her a direct order, actually. He had also said he was worried about her, and worried about her reputation. But was that the sum total of his feelings?

Apparently the Cal Rollins standing in front of her couldn't admit to anything beyond those facts. But the Cal Rollins she'd met in a dreamworld had been quite different.

In the dream he'd let down his guard with her. Made love to her as if he cared. And that man who'd made love to her so passionately was buried in the subconscious of the Cal Rollins confronting her with his wild proposition.

So did that mean that deep down he did want her for his wife, for real and true? But he was incapable of admitting it to either one of them, especially to himself.

He was pacing again as he spoke. "See, I never thought I was going to need a marriage license, so I didn't have a clue where to get one. It took four calls to find the office where you apply for the damn thing. I tried Howard County information, and nobody answered the phone. I tried licenses, but that's not right either. They referred me to clerk of the court, who referred me to land records. Would you believe marriage licenses are handled by the same office that does land records?"

She listened to what he was saying and to the tone of his voice. He had never thought he was going to apply for a marriage license but he wanted to do it with her. And he had gone to a considerable amount of trouble to find out how.

Somehow that tipped the balance in his favor. Instead

of giving him a sane and sensible answer, she went with her heart. To her astonishment she heard herself saying, "All right."

His face momentarily registered astonishment, as though he'd expected a knock-down-drag-out fight, or at least some logical resistance. But as soon as she agreed, he swung into action mode. "All right. We're leaving tonight. You pack some clothing and I'll get the stuff I left upstairs."

"Dog food. I need dog food."

"Fine. Whatever."

OUT IN THE DARKNESS, the man standing beyond the range of the lights balled his hands into fists and cursed. The interfering, busybody cop was back. Just like that, he'd come poking around the farm. Tramping over the fields. Going into the barn.

He'd found that water bottle, probably. The bottle that Beth was supposed to stumble over and wonder who'd dropped it.

Lucky it didn't have any fingerprints or any telltale bodily fluids.

His attention switched back to the man. The cop. He'd gone inside with Beth, then lights had come on upstairs. In one room, then two. Were they up there making love or something? If not, what the hell were they doing?

The cop came down a few minutes later with a suitcase, and the watcher breathed out a little sigh of relief as the bastard walked to the car he'd parked several hundred feet down the access road. Not his unmarked cop car. His own car. He was leaving. And Beth would be alone again.

Even when Rollins drove toward the farmyard, the watcher figured he was just going to turn around. Then he pulled up in front of the door, cut the engine and climbed out. Moments later he was back in the house.

A string of curses issued from the watcher's mouth as he saw the guy come out again. He had another suitcase, a big old-fashioned leather one. It must be Beth's. She came after him, hugging an enormous bag of dog food. And the dog came next.

He felt his heart sink.

Then he reminded himself he had been patient before, always patient. Watching and waiting and doing little things that she would notice.

But maybe he should be more aggressive this time. Maybe he should make his own opportunity, like follow them and find out where the bastard was taking her.

"OKAY. YOU'VE GOT TO wait forty-eight hours to get married in Maryland. That's state law. So we'll get the license first thing in the morning. Meanwhile, you're going to stay with a P.I. friend of mine, Jo O'Malley, Sam Lassiter's partner."

Beth had heard that name before. She looked at Cal. "Jo O'Malley," she said slowly. "Isn't she…isn't that…" She stopped. "Isn't that the estate where—"

"Yeah." He cut her off before she could finish the question. The estate where he'd holed up in his coma dream. The estate where they'd made love. And he was taking her *there.*

The knowledge made her feel light-headed as the car looped around the beltway.

She saw Cal's hands tighten on the wheel, saw him staring intently in the rearview mirror and realized he'd been doing it off and on for the past several miles.

"What's wrong? Is somebody following us?" she asked.

"Maybe. But not for long." He speeded up, wove in and out of traffic, then took an off-ramp, careening around the curve, then on to the beltway again, heading in the opposite direction. He took the next exit again, this time heading back the way they'd been going in the first place.

When she saw him relax she knew he was satisfied that they weren't being shadowed.

They drove for several more exits, then got off at Owings Mills. When they turned off the main road, she tensed. Even though her reaction was totally illogical, she was half expecting to encounter the jungle where she'd run from the monsters stalking her. There was nothing, however, but ordinary Maryland woods.

The first thing she recognized was the brick wall. It was the same. But the gate was different. In the dream it had been like a solid door to keep the monsters out. This one was a more conventional metal fence.

Cal leaned out of the car and pressed the intercom button.

"Jo? We're here."

The barrier swung open, and he drove up a winding driveway to the house she'd only seen in the distance. It was the same house that she remembered, only bigger than it had looked in the dream. As they pulled to a stop in the circular driveway, the front door opened and a slim red-haired woman came rushing out.

Slowly Beth got out of the car, nervously smoothing her hand down the sides of her jeans.

"Hello, I'm Jo O'Malley," the woman said. "My husband Cam's away on a business trip, so it will just be us. And the kids. I hope you don't mind kids."

"Of course I don't mind. I like them," she said, glancing at Cal, who was busy getting her bag from the trunk. She had longed to have children of her own. But she hadn't been around many youngsters since her own early years. "I hope you don't mind dogs," she added as Granger lifted his leg against a boxwood bush.

Jo smiled. "The kids have been begging for a dog. This will give us a trial run."

Cal turned to Jo. "I appreciate your letting Beth stay with you."

"I'm glad to have some company. Come in and make yourselves comfortable."

Beth followed her hostess, still feeling disoriented as she glanced around the palatial residence, then at Cal.

He carried her bag to a spacious second-floor room, then, while she was settling Granger down, spoke to Jo in the hall. She could hear them discussing security at the estate. Quickly she walked into the hall, but before she could join the conversation, Cal said, "I've got to go."

She blinked. "You're leaving me here? Just like that?" *With some woman I don't even know. Here, of all places.*

"Yeah. I've got work to do." He shifted his weight from one foot to the other, then whirled away from them and trotted down the stairs, leaving her and Jo O'Malley staring after him.

Jo cleared her throat. "Is there anything you need? Anything I can get for you?"

Feeling like an intruder, she managed to say, "No. I'm bushed." Then, turning quickly, she escaped to the privacy of the bedroom.

BETH WOKE to the sound of high-pitched voices. Children. Crossing to the window, she pulled the heavy drapes aside and saw a boy and a girl playing on playground equipment that looked as if it belonged in a public park. The little girl, who appeared to be about three, was sitting on a small merry-go-round, squealing in delight as Jo O'Malley pushed her. The boy, who might have been five, was enthusiastically pumping a swing.

The girl said something and Jo stopped the merry-go-round, took the child's hand and led her to a seesaw. Granger was watching the action from the sidelines. If he was upset by their sudden move last night, he wasn't showing it.

The scene made Beth smile, until she remembered why Cal had left her here the night before. He thought she was in danger. Maybe he was right, but she still felt like an intruder in this grand household.

Still, she wasn't going to hide in her room. So she

crossed the thick carpet to the bathroom and took a quick shower before changing into a skirt, blouse and sandals she'd packed the night before.

Downstairs, she found a door at the back of the house and came outside. Granger bounded over, greeting her enthusiastically.

"Good boy," she murmured. "Good boy."

Jo O'Malley came toward her. "I fed him when I gave the kids breakfast. I hope that's all right."

"Thank you. I appreciate that."

The little girl had followed her mother over. "Finally, you're awake," she said. "I'm Anna. And this is my brother Leo. I like your dog."

Beth came down to their level. "I'm glad you like Granger. And I'm pleased to meet you," she said.

"Mommy says you're staying here before you get married. That means you're going on a honeymoon. And you're going to sleep in the same bed with Cal—like Mommy and Daddy sleep in the same bed. And you can make babies, too."

Beth flushed. Before she could think of what to say, the boy stepped forward. "Anna talks too much," he said, his voice scornful. "Because she's little."

"I don't mind," Beth said.

Jo made a quick change of subject. "What do you want for breakfast?" she asked Beth, ushering the children inside. "I've already eaten, but I can have a cup of coffee with you."

"I don't want you to go to any trouble."

"I'm not. Mrs. Marsdon made blueberry muffins this morning. And a ham and broccoli quiche. They're all ready."

"The muffins would be fine," Beth said.

After a maid came in and took the children away, Beth gave her hostess a little smile. "They're charming."

Jo laughed. "They were warned to be on their best behavior. But you see where that got me with Anna. She's really interested in mommies and daddies at the moment. Sorry about the personal comments.''

''That's okay. Um, can I help you do anything?''

''The coffee cups are in the last cabinet on the right.'' Jo pointed.

A few minutes later, they were sitting in the sunny breakfast nook.

''I should have thanked you last night for taking me and Granger in,'' Beth said as she broke off a piece of muffin.

''You looked shell-shocked last night.''

For more than one reason, Beth thought. Instead of focusing on the awkwardness of being dumped here like a displaced person, she said, ''I guess I was. I guess Cal talked to you about the reunion murders?''

Jo nodded. ''He thinks the killer has turned his focus on you.''

Beth's fingers clutched on the handle of her spoon. She hadn't expected Jo to be quite so direct. But then, she reminded herself, Jo was a private detective when she wasn't being a mommy.

''I don't know,'' she murmured.

''Then trust his judgment. He's a good cop.''

She set down her spoon and began crumbling her muffin into smaller pieces.

''I didn't mean to upset you,'' Jo murmured. ''Mentioning the murders.''

Beth sucked in a breath and let it out. ''Actually, I was thinking about me and Cal. The question is, did he bring me here because he feels guilty about dragging me into his case or because he really cares about me?''

''I think his asking you to marry him answers that question,'' Jo pointed out. ''He told me his plans when he asked if you could stay here.''

''I guess he was pretty confident that I'd give him the answer he wanted.''

''No. He wasn't. But he sounded determined.''

The news was a revelation to Beth. But she still felt

compelled to point out, "It wasn't a very romantic proposal. It was more like a bodyguard situation."

"Yes, well...some men are afraid to show what they're really feeling. You know, there was a study not so long ago about how divorce affects children. Long into adulthood, they still have commitment issues. And if just having your parents get divorced is traumatic, imagine growing up with a mother who'd abandoned you and a father who was bitter about his wife running out on him."

Beth stared at the woman across the table. "You must have been talking to Hannah."

"Actually, I have, since she works with me at the Light Street Detective Agency. But I'm a pretty good observer of people, too. Cal and I worked together on a couple of cases in the city, so I've had a chance to get to know him."

They were interrupted by a noise in the hall. Then Cal strode into the room.

His gaze shot to Beth, and she immediately felt guilty about discussing him. "Did you sleep okay?" he asked.

She nodded.

He seemed to relax several notches. "Then let's go get the license thing over with."

"The license thing," she repeated, unable to stop herself from sliding Jo a look as she pushed back her chair, leaving her muffin and coffee on the table.

As they drove back to Howard County, Cal seemed to withdraw behind a wall—like the wall in his sky. Only this time she couldn't find a way through.

His silence continued as they pulled into the parking lot up the hill from the county courthouse. Beth remembered it from trips to Ellicott City with her parents as a dignified stone building, but somewhere along the line it had been remodeled and expanded with white marble that left it looking like a puffed-up wedding cake.

The image was appropriate, she thought as they found the room where marriage licenses were issued. There was nothing romantic about the office, though, or about Cal's behavior. He was all business as he requested the proper form.

She'd memorized his early history for her role as his pretend wife. She knew his birthday and where he'd gone to school. Now she learned his address for the first time, learned that his middle name was William.

When she looked at the form and gave a startled laugh, he glanced up at her sharply. "What?"

She pointed to one of the questions. "They're asking if we're related."

"So?"

"Don't you think that's an odd question?"

He shrugged.

Shaking her head, she went back to the application.

He paid the fee, pocketed the receipt, then ushered her out of the building fifteen minutes after they'd climbed the marble steps.

As they walked back up the hill to the parking lot, she studied him covertly, wondering what thoughts were flickering behind his grim profile. Was he regretting his impulsive announcement of yesterday and now he didn't know how to back out? She was working up her nerve to ask him, when his phone buzzed.

Whipping it out of his pocket, he punched the button and spoke. "Rollins."

She couldn't hear the conversation on the other end of the line, but from Cal's face, she gathered it wasn't good news.

"What's happened?" she asked as he ended the conversation.

He looked around the parking lot. "Wait till we get in the car." Once the doors were closed, he turned to her. "That was a buddy of mine in the department giving me a heads up.

"There's no easy way to tell you this. There's a man out at the farm—dead."

Chapter Thirteen

Beth felt the breath solidify in her lungs. When she could speak again, she managed to say, "How?"

"It looks like he's been murdered. We're going out there to get the scoop," he said, backing out of the parking space and heading toward Route 40. He swung his head toward her briefly. "You didn't have any...vibrations."

"I haven't had any vibrations since that night in the hospital when you woke up! Maybe I—I used up all the power I had."

"You think so?"

"Do I detect a note of relief in your voice?"

"No!" he snapped. "I'm just trying to get at the facts."

He cut her another quick glance, then flicked his eyes back to the road, but his tense features spoke volumes.

"What aren't you telling me?" she asked.

"He was found in your bedroom."

"My bedroom?" she gasped. "What was he doing there?"

"I'd like the answer to that question myself."

"There's nobody I've entertained in my bedroom."

"Uh-huh."

She didn't like the neutral sound of his voice. Then another question struck her. "Who found him? I mean, how did anyone know he was there?"

"An anonymous tip—from a phone booth on Route 144."

She squeezed her eyes shut, pressed her fingers to her temple.

"Your head hurt?"

"Yes. But it's not because I'm getting any calls from the psychic hot line. A man is dead in my bedroom. I guess I'm not going to be sleeping there any time soon."

He gave a tight nod.

A police car was blocking the entrance to her lane, but when the officer inside saw Cal, he waved him through.

They pulled into the yard behind another cruiser, several unmarked cars and an ambulance.

Before getting out of the car, Cal took his gun from his holster and laid it on the floor.

"Why are you doing that?"

"I'm not here on official business."

As they walked toward the front porch, the burly man who'd confronted her in the hospital came down the steps.

Lieutenant Patterson.

His gaze shot to Cal. "What are *you* doing here?" he demanded.

"This was my case."

"You're on sick leave."

"And the department can't dictate how I spend my time. Beth is a friend of mine. I'm out here to be with her."

Patterson's gaze shot from Cal to her, then back again.

"And how exactly did you know to show up at a murder scene?"

"I could have been listening to my police scanner," Cal said blandly.

FROM HIS HIDING PLACE in the woods a half mile away, Damien watched the action through high-powered binoculars.

"Too bad I can't get any closer," he muttered. "But this is almost as good."

The binoculars had cost him a mint, but it was worth it to see the expressions on everyone's face.

"It's hard to know which is better," he murmured. "This stuff or what I got from that guy Harold Mason."

He hadn't planned on doing the poor jerk when he'd come out to the farm. But he'd known it was necessary as soon as the guy had spotted him poking around the house and demanded to know what he was doing there. Damien had pulled out a gun and explained that he was the one asking the questions.

Once he'd gotten what he could out of Beth's unwanted visitor, he'd killed him—to send her and her detective friend a message.

From the looks on their faces, the guy's murder had had the desired effect.

"Now all I have to do is find out where Rollins has taken her into protective custody, and I can snatch her up, because even if the guy's put himself on guard duty, he can't stick with her twenty-four-seven," Damien murmured as he watched them through the glasses.

AS BETH WATCHED Patterson and Cal eyeing each other like dangerous animals deciding where to strike to inflict the most damage, she had a better understanding of why he'd taken off his gun. If he wasn't here on official business, the weapon might have looked like a challenge to his lieutenant.

"I told you the guy you had in custody wasn't the reunion killer," Cal said in a flat voice.

"Oh yeah? What does this murder have to do with the reunion?"

"You're trying to tell me it's just a coincidence that Beth's face is flashed across the evening news after the meeting, she makes the morning paper, then a guy turns up dead at her farm?"

"Dead in her bedroom."

She cringed. There it was again. The innuendo.

Only this time Cal's attitude was a little different. "What's that supposed to signify?" he asked, his voice low and even.

"You tell me." Patterson switched his gaze from Cal to her. "Detective Shane has been trying to get in touch with you. Where were you last night?"

"At the home of Cameron Randolph and Jo O'Malley," Cal answered for her.

"Let the lady speak for herself," Patterson said.

Cal pressed his lips together.

Beth fought the queasy feeling in her stomach and, clearing her throat, said, "Cal was worried about me. He came out last night and asked if I'd mind staying with Jo O'Malley. I agreed."

"And you came back here when someone told him about the murder?"

"Yes."

"And you didn't leave the estate last night?"

"I think Beth told you where she was," Cal snapped. "She's through answering questions, so stop trying to get to me through her. Or are you planning to bring her down to the station and read her her rights?"

"What are you, her lawyer now?" Patterson asked. "Is there some reason she shouldn't want to answer questions about a murder in her house?"

"No. I'm just looking out for her interests."

The lieutenant turned back to Beth. "I'm not taking you anywhere, but I want to know where I can reach you."

"At the Randolph estate, like I told you," Cal said, reeling off the phone number. Then he asked, "You got an ID on the dead man?"

"Harold Mason."

"I...don't know him," Beth murmured. "Who is he?"

"You tell me," Patterson demanded.

"I can't."

"He's a land developer working in the county," Cal said.

Beth's head whipped toward him. "What? How do you know?"

"His car was parked at the end of your driveway a few days ago. I ran his license plate."

"You got any more information on him?" Patterson demanded.

"No. I wish to hell I had."

Patterson stared at him for a long moment. Then, turning on his heel, he walked back into the house.

Stunned, Beth stared after him. "Read me my rights?" she managed to say. "Are you saying I'm a suspect? In the murder of a man I don't even know."

"You sure as hell better not be," Cal answered. Firmly taking her arm, he escorted her back to the car.

"What was he doing here?" she whispered.

"Alex Shane will find out."

Beth was too numb to say much on the ride back to Jo's. This time, when they arrived at the gate, Cal had the number code, so he was able to buzz them right through.

There must have been an alarm in the house alerting Jo to their arrival, because she was standing under the portico when they drove up. From the look on her face, Beth was certain that she'd already heard about the murder.

In fact, as soon as he climbed out of the car she and Cal started talking about how to apprehend the killer—leaving her feeling like a third wheel on a bike as she stood beside them.

"I'm going back to that high-school database," Cal said. "I'm going to eliminate every name I can from the list. If I can narrow it down, then we've got a shot at finding the guy quickly."

"What do you want me to do?" Jo asked.

"Keep Beth safe." He stopped, ran a hand over his face. "I'll arrange for a wedding ceremony with one of the judges down at the courthouse on Thursday morning. Can you drive her there?"

"Of course. And I was thinking that Beth and I would

go looking for a wedding dress at Owings Mills Mall,'' Jo answered. ''But maybe we'd better stay on the estate until the ceremony.''

''I'll pay for extra security,'' Cal said.

''You don't have to pay. My husband owns Randolph Security, remember?''

''Yeah, right.''

At that point, Beth couldn't stop herself from breaking into the conversation. ''You're going to treat me like a prisoner? Don't I get any say in any of this?''

They both turned to her. ''I'm sorry if it sounded like we were ignoring you,'' Jo said quietly. ''If you have any suggestions, we'll be glad to hear them.''

Unable to think of any, she shook her head.

''Then it's settled.'' Cal started back to his car.

''Wait!'' Beth called.

He stopped and turned toward her with a preoccupied expression on his face.

''Then I won't see you again until the wedding?'' she asked in a low voice.

''Yeah. It's better that way.''

She wanted to ask him why. After the scene at the farm, she wanted him to at least hug her goodbye. She only gave him a tight nod, then watched him drive away.

When the car was out of sight, Jo scuffed her foot against a paving brick. ''Sorry.''

''About what?''

''About me and Cal taking over like that.''

Beth shrugged.

''I wasn't thinking,'' Jo said. ''I should have disappeared inside and given you guys some time alone.''

''It doesn't look like he wants any time alone.''

''Beth, he's worried. And nervous and scared.''

''Scared about what—my safety?''

''Your safety, of course.'' Jo paused. ''And scared that he's dared to take the step of asking you to marry him.

From his point of view, given his background, he's probably worried that you'll back out."

"I should."

"Don't!"

"I'll take that under advisement." Because she didn't want Jo to see the tears in her eyes, Beth turned and walked down one of the garden paths—and ended up at the swimming pool.

She stopped short as she saw the blue water surrounded by a curving band of concrete. It was much like the pool from Cal's dream, only now it sat placidly in the warm sunshine.

Mutely, Beth stared at it, then walked toward the cabana. There was no bed inside, only a rattan sofa, and table and chairs with bright cushions.

She let her eyes drift out of focus, conjuring up the bed, remembering how it had been with him that night and wondering if anything in life could match the magic of their dream lovemaking. Had it all been an illusion? Or was it real on some basic level that they just couldn't reach at the moment because they didn't know how to communicate with each other?

She longed to know the truth. Longed to know if she was making the worst mistake of her life. But there was no way to answer the question—not without Cal. And he had shut himself away from her.

She closed her eyes, trying to put the worry out of her mind, because she had something important to do. An experiment.

Since the hospital, her psychic powers had simply been gone. Could she call them back and make them work again? Did she want them back?

She'd thought that the biggest relief of her life would be if she could make them go away. Now everything was different. Now she needed those powers and they had deserted her.

Relaxing against the chair cushions, she tried to breathe deeply and evenly, tried to let her mind drift. Not so long ago, she'd felt the killer's touch, felt his hands on her body.

The memory brought a deep shudder, but she forced herself not to run away now. She'd been in contact with him once so she ought to be able to do it again, she told herself as she struggled to reach out to him with her mind and come up with some clue that would help Cal figure out who he was.

Maybe she could even find out his name.

Sweat beaded on her forehead and her head began to pound. But that was all. There were no flashes of intuition, no link, no sudden feeling of connection.

Nothing. Just an awful and final blankness.

Her psychic ability had vanished. And there was nothing she could do about it—just as there'd been nothing she could do about it when the power had taken over her mind bringing her pain and heartache.

CAL SAT before the computer screen, scrolling through the names of Beth's former classmates. He wanted to go ahead and eliminate the females, but that could be a mistake. Although it was unlikely that the killer was a woman, it was possible.

It was also possible that one of his earlier theories was true—that it wasn't actually somebody in the class.

That widened the search a hell of a lot. It could be somebody from a rival school, for all he knew. But in the next two days, he wasn't going to get very far with that line of thinking. And he wasn't going to be reassigned to the case by Patterson, so the best he could do was work with the list he had.

Five hours later, he rubbed his bleary eyes, stood up and stumbled into the kitchen. Opening the refrigerator, he grabbed a beer, popped the cap and gulped down half the bottle.

Then, realizing he was hungry, he got out the half pizza he'd bought two days ago and warmed it up in the microwave.

He thought about going back to the computer. That way he didn't have to think about the look on Beth's face when he'd left her at Jo's.

She'd wanted him to hold her, comfort her. He knew that with gut-wrenching certainty. And he'd wanted to put his arms around her so badly that his insides had been raw. But he'd been afraid that if he embraced her, he'd start to shake. So his only alternative had been turning and leaving.

Now he wrapped his fingers around the cold beer bottle, squeezing until he could steady himself. He didn't like being so scared for Beth that he could hardly think. And he didn't like being so scared she'd change her mind about marrying him that he could barely breathe.

With a grimace, he picked up the pizza and walked back to the computer, because the only way he could deal with both of his problems was to work until his brain was too numb to function.

OUT IN THE DARKNESS, Damien watched the lights go out in the room that police detective Cal Rollins used as an office. He'd called information and requested the cop's number, then he'd gotten the operator to read him the address by pretending he wasn't sure if he had the right party.

Now it was three in the morning. And the bastard had been in there at his computer screen for eleven hours.

Probably he was too tired to see straight.

"I hope you've worked yourself blind," Damien muttered. "Why the hell don't you go back to Beth and lead me to her? You've stashed her somewhere, damn you. Just give me a hint, and I'll take her off your hands."

CAL HAD SET the alarm for eight. Five hours' sleep was enough to recharge his batteries, he thought as he stood under the shower's needle spray.

Cold needle spray. Because in the unguarded moment of transition from sleep to waking, he'd known how much he wanted Beth. Wanted her with a primitive desire that made it difficult for him to drag air into his lungs.

Did you marry a woman because you lusted after her? Not just lust, he corrected himself. Need. Need that he didn't dare articulate. All he knew was that since the dream when she'd come to him, when they'd made love, he'd craved that again. Craved it with his heart, with his soul. Every moment of that dream was burned into his brain, into every cell of his being.

And that vulnerability to her was the most frightening thing that had ever happened in his life.

No, scratch that.

The most frightening thing was the fear that he would lose her to that bastard out there stalking her.

That was enough to dampen his ardor.

He was back at the computer with a mug of coffee in his hand by eight forty-five.

Last night, he'd come up with fifteen guys he wanted to take a closer look at. Guys who weren't married, hadn't done much with their lives after high school, were in financial trouble or who'd gotten into scrapes with the law. He'd even investigated Wayne Jenkins and he could see why Patterson had liked him for the murders.

But he'd been in jail at the time Harold Mason was killed. So that left him out.

Cal's prime candidate was a little dweeb named Dave Garwill. He couldn't say why he liked the guy so much. Gut instinct, he supposed. The problem was, two years ago Dave Garwill had dropped off the face of the earth. There were no phone records for him, no credit card records. Even his driver's license had expired.

So where was he? Was he one of the victims? Or had

he changed his name and gone underground so he could knock off his classmates?

Picking up the phone, Cal called Alex Shane, the detective working the Mason murder. Alex wasn't in, so he left a message, wondering if the guy would call him back or if he'd been put on notice by Ken Patterson that he was in big trouble if he dared to get in contact with Cal Rollins.

Cal grimaced. It would be counterproductive for Patterson to turn away help from someone willing to work the case on his own time. But somewhere along the line, this thing with Patterson had gotten personal, and he had the feeling that the lieutenant would go against the good of the case just to make a point.

AFTER TWO DAYS in the company of her down-to-earth hostess, Beth felt a lot more comfortable with Jo O'Malley. They'd talked to each other into the small hours of the morning for two nights now, trading confidences. She knew Jo had grown up poor in western Maryland. She hadn't been born to wealth, and she was well able to understand Beth's own background as the daughter of a Howard County farmer.

Beth had even been able to talk about the paranormal stuff—the past pain, the present frustration.

The late-night talks forged a bond between them. So it was a comfort that Jo was the one who drove her to the courthouse for the wedding ceremony.

She was even more buoyed up when she saw Hannah, Lucas and Sam all waiting with Cal on the steps of the massive marble building. Then she saw a contingent of the men she'd met from the Randolph Security detail: Jed Prentiss, Jason Zacharias, Hunter Kelley.

As soon as she spotted the security men, she realized that Cal hadn't simply invited his friends to the wedding.

They were here as protection.

IN THE PARKING LOT up the hill, Damien let loose with a string of curses.

"The place is crawling with security types," he muttered. "Private cops. So they're not wearing uniforms. So what? Anybody with a grain of sense can see who they are."

He'd been pretty excited for a couple of minutes. Finally, his surveillance had paid off. Cal had left the house this morning looking all spiffy in a blue blazer, rep tie and gray slacks. Then he'd headed for the courthouse.

Two minutes after he'd met two men and a woman on the steps, Beth had shown up.

And so had the security guys. Well, some of them had already been here, Damien realized.

"Do you want to take a chance on staying?" he asked himself. "Or is it time to beat a strategic retreat? Too bad you can't just drive by and shoot Rollins," he muttered. "But that wouldn't be too smart with all these bodyguards."

With an angry snarl, he drove out of the parking lot.

Chapter Fourteen

If the whole scene hadn't been laced with overtones of a stalker movie, Beth might have found it amusing. She and Cal were the classic nervous bride and groom. Only they had more reason to be nervous than most: there was a killer closing in on her.

At least Cal was convinced there was. So was Jo. She would be a fool not to accept their professional judgment. But did he really believe that she didn't know the mysterious Harold Mason from the man in the moon? She couldn't be sure he did, since he hadn't said a thing to her about it since their drive from the farm to Jo's.

Putting those thoughts firmly out of her mind, she studied the groom. He was so handsome that she felt a rush of warmth and secret pride. Then she took a closer look at his face, noting the way his features were set in rigid lines.

Looking away from him, she smoothed her hand down the skirt of the gauzy white dress she wore. She'd picked it from a selection Jo had had sent out from Nordstrom's. It wasn't the wedding dress she had dared to imagine in her girlish fantasies, but it was pretty. It looked good on her and she wished Cal had complimented her on it.

But he said nothing.

Sam broke the silence with a throat-clearing noise. "It's time for the ceremony. We'd better go in."

She could still bail out, she told herself. Instead, she followed Cal into the room where civil ceremonies were held. It was decked out like an indoor garden with plastic grass on the floor and a white arched trellis.

The judge got right to the service. Beth heard Cal say "I do" in all the right places. Then she did the same.

Cal had bought her a gold ring, but she hadn't gotten one for him because they hadn't talked about rings. Or anything else, for that matter.

Don't think about that, she warned herself. *Don't think about what's missing. Think about the good part. You're marrying the man you love. And you're going to show him how much a man and woman can give each other—if he'll let you.*

The judge pronounced them man and wife.

Cal leaned down and gave her a quick kiss on the lips before straightening. It was over almost before it started, and she wanted to grab his shoulders and hang on to him. But she allowed him to pull away.

Because another ceremony was scheduled right after theirs, the group moved into the hall and stood around a little awkwardly, until Cal said that he and Beth needed to leave.

The women kissed her cheek. So did the men, who also shook hands with Cal.

Beth was reminded once again of the reason why they'd all come when they fanned out in the parking lot, some following her and Cal to the car so that there was no chance to say anything private to him.

HE HAD DONE IT. Married Beth Wagner, Cal thought, feeling as if he'd just stepped off an amusement park thrill ride. His head was still spinning. Lucky the guys from Randolph Security were trailing him, because he wasn't capable of protecting his bride at the moment.

His bride.

He flattened his sweaty palms against his sides. He still

couldn't believe he was hitched, not after all the lectures he'd gotten from Dad over the years about letting a woman hog-tie him.

He couldn't wrap his head around the reality. He could only respond to physical feelings. The feeling of wanting her, like an ache that gnawed at his vitals, and the tight, wary feeling in his chest that made it hard to draw a full breath.

"Where are we going?" she asked. "Are you planning to drop me back at Jo's house?"

His head whipped toward her. "I'm not planning to drop you anywhere."

Unlocking the car, he undid the tie constricting his windpipe and tossed it in the back seat. He wanted to take off his damn blazer too, but that would leave him with a shoulder holster showing.

"What about Granger?" Beth asked.

"We'll pick him up later."

"You're sure Jo doesn't mind taking care of him?"

"No. I cleared it with her."

She didn't say she wished he'd let her in on his plans, even though she had a right to complain about that. Instead, she silently got into his car. But he could see her fighting to relax as they headed down I70.

He checked the rearview mirror. "This place where we're going is safe. I wouldn't take you there unless it was. I mean, it's safe because nobody besides Randolph Security knows I booked us a room there. And nobody's following us."

"I trust you," she murmured.

Trusted her safety to him? Or did she mean more than that? He wasn't capable of asking. And there was no question of idle conversation. His mouth was too dry. So he drove at a steady pace into the mountains, checking to make sure they weren't being followed by anyone but Randolph Security. After the Boonsboro exit, he slowed for a sign that said Wisteria Inn.

He'd checked some guidebooks for out-of-the-way inns and gone to the Web sites of ones that sounded promising. After talking to the owner and renting a couple of cottages, he'd sent two of the Randolph men on ahead, just in case.

The place lived up to the photographs he'd seen. He liked the beautifully restored Victorian house set on spacious grounds. After a quick stop at the office to get the key, he drove around to the cottage that he'd rented for them, which was surrounded by its own private garden. Did Beth think it was pretty? he wondered. Did she approve of his choice?

His hands weren't quite steady as he inserted the key in the lock, then stood aside as she walked into the small sitting room.

Hell, was he supposed to carry her over the threshold? No. That was too much for a guy like him.

"I've got some operatives from Randolph Security staying in another cottage. But they won't bother us," he said, hearing the stiffness in his voice.

"Okay." She was looking down at the tips of his dark shoes. Wedding shoes. Slowly she raised her face to his. "So now that we've established that we're safe, is that the only reason you brought me here?"

"No." His Adam's apple bobbed. "I wanted to be alone with you. Well, as alone as we could be."

"Then why did you leave me at Jo's when I wanted you to be with me?" she whispered.

"Because my computer's at home. I was researching the members of your class. I've eliminated ninety-five percent of them."

"Couldn't you have brought the computer to Jo's?"

"No. I didn't want any distractions."

He heard her voice hitch. "And you didn't think I might worry that you were staying away because you'd decided to back out of the wedding?"

All he could manage was a low sound in his throat as he reached for her and pulled her into his arms. As he held her, some of the terrible tension that had been building inside him seeped away.

"If I'd been at Jo's I wouldn't have been working," he whispered. "I would have been making love with you. And I told myself when I first met you that you weren't the type of woman a man could make love with unless he..." His voice trailed off. Then he started again. "I didn't exactly ask you to marry me," he whispered. "It was more like an order, and I didn't know if you'd start thinking it was a bad idea."

With a tiny sigh, she tipped her head up and looked at him. "I think a good rule of being married is that you talk to each other, so neither one of you is acting on assumptions that could be wrong."

"I don't know much about wedded bliss. My mom didn't stay around long enough for me to remember her face."

She moved her lips against the front of his shirt, and he could feel her trembling in his arms. "Cal, I know the idea of marriage scares you because of what happened with your father and mother."

He didn't bother to deny it.

"I know you're thinking I agreed because I was looking for a bodyguard. But when I said I'd be your wife, I wasn't thinking about your hanging around to protect me. I wasn't thinking about something temporary. I don't make life-changing decisions lightly. I said I'd marry you because I've fallen in love with you. Because I want to be with you—for keeps. If you think about how it was in the dream, you know that already."

The words stunned him. He longed to believe her, longed to believe she really knew what she wanted. "Yeah, the dream," he managed to say, wondering if either one of them would be here if they hadn't both dropped their guard in that world of unreality. Remembering it scared him because of the way he'd ached to feel that closeness with her again. But at the same time, he'd been secretly clinging to the memory. He realized now that it had given him the guts to make it this far.

She had tipped her head up again and was looking at him with such open longing that he felt his heart turn over in his chest. No one had ever looked at him like that. Probably because he'd made it clear he didn't want any kind of deep and meaningful relationship.

He still couldn't admit to either one of them what he wanted. Not in the long run. All he could do was dip his head and take her mouth in the kind of searing kiss he'd been craving for days, craving when the marriage ceremony had ended.

He'd been too self-conscious to do it then. But now that they were alone, he was helpless to keep from taking what he desired, needed. It was a kiss of hunger and passion, a very thorough kiss that left them both shaking when he finally lifted his head.

"Beth," he breathed. He would accept anything she was willing to give him. Now. In the present. Because he still couldn't contemplate the future.

His trembling hands skimmed her back, her gorgeous golden hair, then slid over the curve of her bottom just for a moment before pulling back to her waist. "I asked Mrs. Hawkins, the woman who owns this place, to fix us lunch and leave it here. We can eat if you want."

"Is that what you want?" she whispered against his lips.

"I think it's pretty obvious what I want."

"Then let's wait on lunch and get right to dessert."

He nibbled his lips over hers, little tasting kisses that moved to her cheeks and her jaw then back to her mouth, before he asked the question he was pretty sure he knew the answer to. "Have you done this before? Been with a man?"

"Only once. Only with you."

"That's what I thought."

Her breath caught. "Was my inexperience so obvious?"

"No. I was just thinking how much I want to do this right."

"You will." She giggled. "You already have, actually. That thought is very…bracing. It's working for me. Let it work for you, too."

He hadn't expected humor from her. "Okay," he answered with a grin. Reaching for her hand, he led her into the bedroom, then took a step back, gazing his fill. "You look so beautiful in that dress."

"You could have told me earlier."

"I could barely speak earlier. I'm lucky I could answer the judge."

Shrugging out of his jacket, he draped it over the back of a rocking chair. His gun and holster went on the dresser.

He knew she was watching him, knew she was nervous despite what she'd said earlier.

Clearing his throat, he said, "In the dream, you did a striptease for me."

Her cheeks flamed. A very stirring sight.

"You want me to do that again?" she asked.

When he heard the nerves in her voice, he silently cursed himself for not making his meaning clear. "No. This time, I'd like the pleasure of undressing you."

The look of relief she gave him made his throat ache. Wordlessly, he gathered her to him, his hands going around her to the zipper at the back of her dress. He tugged it down, then lifted the dress over her head and set it carefully on the chair, leaving her in the lacy slip he'd caught hints of through the sheer material of the dress.

When his fingers traced the lace of the bodice, her breath quickened. The slip went the way of the dress.

"You're not wearing panties," he breathed as he stared at her through the almost-transparent fabric of her panty hose.

"Jo said they spoiled the line of the dress."

"Remember to thank Jo for me," he murmured as he knelt to slide the hose down. He pressed his cheek against her middle, wanting to do more, but he had warned himself not to go too fast. So he only gave her tummy a nibbling kiss, then stood to unhook her bra.

He had seen her before. She had been naked for him, he reminded himself as she stood before him in nothing but her bare skin. But this was different. This was the real world.

"I kept wondering if you could possibly be as beautiful as you were in that dream. But you're more beautiful," he whispered as his gaze took her in.

Before she had time to blush again, he gathered her to him, kissed her, stroked his fingers over her silky skin, then turned to pull down the covers and lift her onto the bed.

His own clothing disappeared in record time. Then he came down beside her, cradling her naked body against his, his head spinning with the reality of feeling her soft feminine flesh pressed against him.

He felt her move her hips instinctively against his, but he eased away, his vision focused on nothing but her as he began to touch and caress her. First with his hands, then with his mouth, arousing her, bringing currents of heat to his own body, currents that sank from each point of contact to the depths of his soul.

Somewhere in his mind, he had been afraid that the dream was the ultimate pleasure. He had been wrong. This was more, so much more.

As he had done in the cabana by the pool, he ran his hand down her body, caressed the curve of her belly, then lower, before sliding into her hidden feminine place. She moaned her approval, arched into his caress, telling him she wanted more, wanted everything.

"Everything," she breathed, reaching for him, urging him to cover her body with his.

But he held back, just as he had in the dream, caressing her intimately until she was molten for him.

He moved over her then, pressed into her, feeling the resistance of the barrier.

"Beth, I—"

"Don't stop. Please don't stop."

Her hands locked around his waist and urged him forward. Taking her at her word, he plunged deeper, then stilled above her as he heard her gasp.

His gaze was urgent as he stared down into her eyes. "Beth?"

She sucked in a breath, and he heard her struggling to make her voice steady. "I'm fine."

"I hurt you."

She turned her face upward, meeting his eyes. "I think you can take the hurt away," she murmured, thrusting her hips upward, taking him deeper inside her.

He breathed her name, then began to move, slowly at first, watching her face.

"Everything," she whispered. "Give me everything. All of you."

He gave her what she wanted, setting a rhythm he remembered, except now he knew that the dream had only been a prelude to something deeper, more powerful. She gave him as much in return as they climbed upward together to dizzying heights.

He felt her hands on his shoulders, her fingers digging into his flesh even as she cried out his name, her body contracting around him.

Her pleasure cascaded through him, triggering his release, a burst of sensation so profound that there were no words to describe it.

Afterward he gathered her perspiration-slick body in his arms, feeling the pounding of her heart—and his. He bent to brush his lips against hers, then lifted his head so that he could look down at her.

"I thought nothing could be better than the way it was in my fantasy. But I was wrong."

"Oh, yes." She reached to touch his cheek. "Because this is real. You and me."

He nodded, still unable to entirely believe it, unwilling to let the happiness he felt sweep him away. It was still too new, too fragile. Too threatening.

But he was content for the moment, content to let her doze in his arms. A while later, when he eased away, she opened her eyes and smiled up at him.

"I don't know about you, but I'm starving," he said.

"Well, I was too nervous to eat this morning. I guess you had better feed me."

"Then we'll have a picnic in bed."

He gave her a few minutes alone and heard her disappear into the bathroom. When he came back from the living room, pushing a tea cart, she had straightened the bed and fluffed up the pillows.

She was sitting up, the sheet pulled over her breasts.

"We've got potato salad, sliced turkey, marinated artichokes with olives, curried chicken with pineapple and key lime pie."

"A feast."

"What do you want?"

"What you're having," she said.

He filled a plate for her, then for himself and climbed back in beside her, his shoulder pressed to hers.

They had been eating for several minutes when he cleared his throat, wondering how he was going to say what was on his mind.

When she tipped her head toward him inquiringly, he decided the best way was to just spit it out. "I never did thank you for saving my life. All I did was growl at you for daring to barge into my happy little dreamworld. But if you hadn't come there, I wouldn't have left. And I'd be a vegetable by now."

"I—" She stopped, found his hand and pressed it. "I'm glad you came back. To me."

"Yeah." He pushed a piece of potato around on his plate. "Talking about stuff isn't the easiest thing for me."

"I know. That's true for me, too. I was alone for a long time. I guess I was used to telling my secrets to my dog."

"Our dog now. We can both talk to him when we know the other one will be listening."

She laughed. "I'm hoping we can be more direct."

"More direct. Yeah." He reached to run his finger along the sheet where it covered the tops of her breasts. The touch sent an electric current arching between them.

"Here's a direct question. Do you want to finish eating later?" he asked in a thick voice.

"Yes," she answered, her tone matching his.

Cal moved the plates to the cart, took her in his arms and pressed her back against the mattress.

They spent the day glorying in the novelty of doing whatever they wanted. And when they woke the next morning it was to the same joyful celebration.

Cal didn't want to break the mood, to spoil their delight. But by afternoon, he figured they had to talk about some serious stuff.

"I was remembering what you said about not wanting to sleep in your bedroom," he began. "After the murder."

She shuddered. "I've worried about that."

"But you do want to stay on the farm?"

She gave him a conflicted look. "Before the murder, I couldn't imagine living anywhere else, but now..."

"We can move into one of the other bedrooms when we go back."

She nodded, then asked, "Does that work for you? Living out there?"

"Yeah, when it's safe. I grew up in the country. I like your farm."

"If we can't go home when we leave here, where are we going?"

"Jo has invited us to stay with her. That's about the safest place I can think of."

"We won't be alone."

"Actually, she's got a guest cottage where we can be as alone as we want."

She raised her face to his. "For how long?"

"I wish I knew." He reached with his bare foot to play with her toes, searching for the right way to bring up another topic.

"What do you want to ask me?" she said.

He looked up at her. "How do you know I want to ask you something?"

She shrugged. "I don't know. I guess I'm getting closer to you. I can tell you want to get further into this business discussion, but you don't want to upset me any more than you have to."

"Yeah. That's a pretty good description of what's going through my head." Not so long ago he might have been annoyed by her perception. Now it wasn't threatening. He cleared his throat. "Do you remember a guy named Dave Garwill?"

She thought for a moment. "A little runty guy? The other kids used to make fun of him. I felt sorry for him, so we'd talk sometimes."

"I can find records of him up to two years ago. Then he disappears from the radar scope."

"What does that mean?"

"He could be dead—although there's no record of that. He could have moved away from the area, but there are no records of credit cards in his name, or any other indication that he's moved. So my best assumption is that he's created a new identity for himself."

"Why would he do that?"

"So nobody can find him—or pin him to the reunion murders."

"You think he's the one who's doing it? The one who turned off the lights and...knifed people at that meeting. He wasn't like that. He was—" She stopped and thought. "He was a wimp."

''Yeah, well, from my research, I'd say he's the most likely candidate.''

''Then what are we going to do?''

''I'm going to get back on active duty and find him. Or if I can't get them to certify me as fit, I'll find him on my own.''

''How?''

''I'm going to get some help from Alex Shane, the detective assigned to the case. I want to give him as much information as I can. It would help if you could tell me everything you know about Garwill.''

She looked thoughtful. ''I haven't seen him since high school. I know he lived with his mother. That his father was dead. I know he liked electronic stuff—gadgets. I know—'' She stopped short.

''What?''

''I know he had a crush on Lisa Stapler, and she cut him dead. Laughed in his face, I heard.''

''Dead,'' he repeated, feeling the hairs on the back of his neck prickle as he thought about what had been done to her before she'd died. ''Yeah, Lisa Stapler is the one victim whose body we found. The body we were meant to find, because he left it right out in the open.''

''YOU'RE TOO RESTLESS to stay here, aren't you?'' Beth asked a little while later as she watched Cal shred a blade of grass with his thumb.

He tossed the mangled piece of greenery to the lawn. ''Sorry. I think I'm spoiling our honeymoon.''

She felt the corners of her mouth curve upward. ''Nothing could spoil the past couple of days. But I can tell you need to get back. Get to work.''

''I can't get the medical forms I need until Monday. I can't go back on the job yet.''

''But you want to be at your computer.''

''Yeah.'' He turned toward her. ''I rented this cottage for another day. I wanted time alone with you.''

"We'll have plenty of time alone once you catch Garwill."

"You think it's him?"

"You do!"

He nodded, coming toward her, reaching for her. She came into his arms and clung tightly to him.

"You sure you don't mind leaving?" he whispered.

"I think your mind isn't on making love right now."

"Yeah, it is. It is whenever I'm holding you or looking at you. But that bastard will still be in the back of my mind. I want you safe."

She nodded against his shoulder. When his hands slid down her back to pull her hips more tightly against his, she decided that maybe the honeymoon wasn't quite over yet.

An hour later he phoned the Randolph Security team down the road and told them they were going back to the city.

Then they carried their luggage to the car.

As they approached the beltway, Beth turned to him. "Can I go to your house with you?"

Cal thought about it for a moment. "No. I want you where you're safe. And the safest place I can think of is with Jo."

"Okay," she agreed, because that was something she could do for him, give him peace of mind.

He buzzed them through the gate, then pulled up in front of the house and set the luggage on the wide front porch.

She followed him, standing very close, reaching for him because she couldn't help herself. Now that the moment of separation had come, she realized she wasn't as prepared as she'd pretended to be. "Are you coming back tonight?"

"Yes," he said thickly. "No later than nine." And she sensed that if she didn't turn him loose, he might never leave.

She gave him what was meant to be a quick kiss, then

clung for extra moments, until she heard children giggling in the shrubbery. Looking up, she found Anna and Leo grinning at them.

She grinned back. But she couldn't shake a sense of foreboding as she watched Cal's car disappear down the long driveway.

Jo was waiting inside the front hall. "I take it the two of you worked things out," she said after she'd shooed the youngsters inside.

"Yes. I don't think he entirely trusts being happy, but I'm working on it." She found herself blushing as she thought about how good it had been. "Too bad his mind got stuck on business again," she added.

"Bad business," Jo murmured.

DAMIEN SLUMPED DOWN in the front seat of his Honda, moving to stretch cramped muscles. Hard muscles he'd developed through years of working out with weights.

He might have been a wimp in high school, but no more. Now he had a great body—to go with his excellent mind.

"I'm Damien Hardon," he muttered. "And that's a lot better than the wimpy name I was born with. Yeah."

Then he pressed his lips together. He was doing it again, talking to himself. Which was okay. There was nothing wrong with that. But not when he was on a stakeout.

He'd been watching the detective's house for the past two days, using a couple of different cars. So far the guy hadn't come home. He'd waited until the security guys were long gone before checking out the courthouse. There he'd discovered the names of Calvin Rollins and Beth Wagner on the list of marriage ceremonies that morning.

"Son of a bitch." He repeated the observation he'd been making since he'd discovered the marriage. "The cop's off on his honeymoon. But where? And for how long?"

Again he made an effort to keep his thoughts silent. If he knew Rollins, the cop couldn't stay away for long. Not a working stiff like him.

"Quiet little neighborhood," he muttered. "When it gets dark, I'll go up to the house and see if Rollins has an alarm system. Two to one he's too arrogant for that."

Damien stroked his chin, thinking. With his lock picks he could get inside most places. If he went inside, he'd probably get some prime information. On the other hand, maybe that wasn't such a good idea. The cop wasn't some naive civilian. He'd know somebody had broken in.

Damien was about to drive up to Route 40 and get himself some fast food when he spotted a car coming around the corner.

The cop. Rollins pulled into his driveway, got out of his car, then started for the back door.

Damien walked quickly toward him, the tranquilizer gun under his coat. "Officer Rollins. Thank goodness you're home. Can I talk to you for a minute?" he asked.

As the cop turned, Damien shot him in the shoulder with one of the powerful, fast-acting little darts. Rollins staggered as he reached for his gun.

Rushing forward, Damien wrested the weapon from fingers that were already limp. As he knocked the gun away, he sent the guy sprawling in the gravel driveway.

"Got ya," he said, excitement bubbling in his voice as he bent down and turned the bastard over, then looked up to make sure nobody had seen what was happening. "You thought you could get away from Damien Hardon. But you're wrong. You and I are going for a little ride together. And when you wake up, I'm gonna have you call your wife and get her to come rescue you. Only it's not going to work that way, because I'm going to kill you both."

Chapter Fifteen

Beth's body jerked.

Granger, who had been sitting at her feet, raised his head and whined, his brown eyes fixed on her face.

"What is it?" Jo asked. "Are you all right?"

"I don't know," she said slowly, pressing her hand to her shoulder. "Something...I felt this sharp pain..." She raised her eyes to the P.I. as if Jo could tell her what had just happened. "I have to talk to Cal," she said, feeling urgency tighten her chest.

"Did you remember something—some information he can use?"

Beth shook her head. "I...no. I'm worried about him. I have to..." She didn't know what she had to do. All she knew was that she had to hear his voice.

"He should be home by now. Why don't you call him?"

"Yes." She sprang up, then gave Jo a strained look. "I don't even know his phone number. He gave me his business card when I first agreed to work with him, but it's in my kitchen. I'm married to him, and I can't even call him on the phone." She could hear her voice rising, hear Jo trying to soothe her.

"Let's go inside. I've got his home number and his cell phone number."

They walked rapidly to a small office, the dog at their

heels. Standing by the desk, Jo picked up the phone, dialed a number, then held the receiver slightly away from her ear so they could both listen. Beth breathed a sigh of relief when she heard Cal's voice. She realized quickly that it was only an answering machine.

"Beth wants to talk to you," Jo said. "So please call us as soon as you get in. Unless we get you on your cell first."

He didn't answer on the cell either.

"I'm going to his house!" Beth said, starting toward the door.

Jo put a firm hand on her arm. "You can't do that. Cal wants you where he knows you're safe. But I can get one of the Randolph men to check out his house."

Beth closed her eyes for a moment. "I don't want to put anyone to a lot of trouble. But I'd feel better if somebody made sure he was okay."

"It's no trouble," Jo said, already making another call. "Hunter," she said into the phone, "this is Jo. Cal went home to do some research on his computer, and we can't get hold of him. Since you don't live too far away, I was wondering if you could stop by?"

After thanking him, she hung up.

"Let's go to the kitchen and have some tea," Jo suggested.

Beth nodded, not because she wanted tea but because it was something to do.

Both of them were tense as they waited, trying to make small talk.

When the phone rang, Beth jumped up and snatched it from the cradle.

"What about Cal?" she said as soon as the man on the other end of the line identified himself as Hunter Kelley.

"I don't like giving you bad news over the phone," he said. "But I thought I should get in touch with you as soon as possible. His car is in the driveway. But he's not there, and his gun is lying on the ground."

"Oh God," was all Beth could manage.

"Give me the phone," Jo demanded.

Obeying orders, Beth handed over the receiver, then she sank into one of the kitchen chairs because her legs would no longer hold her weight. She'd *known.* Not exactly the same way she'd known when she'd had her psychic experiences. There had been no premonition, no headache. Only a swift, sharp jab like a needle piercing her flesh.

Far away she could hear Jo's voice speaking to Hunter, giving more orders, it sounded like.

After hanging up, Jo knelt beside her. "It's all right. We'll find him."

Beth made a low sound and started to shake. "You know, I prayed to be normal. Prayed for my psychic ability to go away. Now I've got what I wanted! I should have known something was going to happen to Cal. But I didn't! I didn't!"

Jo rubbed her hands over Beth's back. "But you knew something was wrong. I saw you jerk, like you'd been hit."

Beth raised her eyes to the other woman. "Something. I felt something. But it was too late." Barely able to breathe, she continued, "Suppose one day you could see just fine, and the next day you were blind. Well, not quite blind. You could still see a little bit of light. Just a tiny bit. That's what it's like."

Jo nodded, although Beth wasn't sure if she really understood.

Forcing air into her lungs, she let it out again. Somehow she got a grip on her emotions. Because if she let herself fall apart, she wouldn't be doing Cal any good. If she couldn't help Cal through her former psychic powers, she had to use the same powers as everybody else. Raising her head, she looked at Jo. "Before you call anybody else at Randolph Security, call Alex Shane," she said.

"Who?"

"He's the Howard County police detective who came

to my house after that guy Harold Mason was killed. He'll want to be informed. He can work through the police department, and maybe he can get us a lead on Dave Garwill. Cal thinks he's the killer. But he's gone underground. Disappeared.'' She thought of something else, then rushed ahead. ''His picture's in my yearbook. Back at the house. If we get the picture, can't we get a computer to update it?''

CAL WOKE beside the pool, and a feeling of vast relief rolled over him. He was safe. Back at Jo's.

He sat up, looked around, rubbing his shoulder where it felt as if he'd been stung by a bee or something.

Looking up, he saw the sun shining in a perfect blue sky. The sight made him wrinkle his forehead in confusion.

Hadn't it been late in the afternoon when he'd headed for home? Almost dark, in fact. But now it was noon.

How long had he slept, anyway?

He stood, ambled toward the cabana, thinking he'd get a beer from the refrigerator. Then go find Beth and have a little fun.

Where was she? They were on their honeymoon, even if he was still working the reunion murder case.

He stopped when he saw the bed sitting in the middle of the cabana, feeling doubt crawl through his brain.

It was the bed where he and Beth had first made love. In the dream. But in the real world, there was no bed in the cabana.

Standing very still, he scrubbed his hand across his face, then noticed something else. He should have a five-o'clock shadow by now, but his face felt as though he'd just shaved.

Carefully, he looked around, thinking how quiet it was. Like he was all alone here. Like there wasn't another soul in the universe.

And at that moment he *knew*. There *wasn't* another soul

in the universe. Not this universe. He was back in the dream. Alone.

No! It couldn't be.

Why the hell was he back here? In the place where he had almost died.

Last time he'd gotten hit by a bullet.

This time...

His whole body went rigid as he strained to remember what had happened to him. This time...

And then in a terrible burst of memory it came to him, literally knocking him backward, almost off his feet, like a bullet to the chest. He'd been going back to his house to use the computer. Someone had called his name, and he'd turned. Then had come the pain in his shoulder, the woozy feeling in his head.

He'd been lying on the ground staring up at the bastard's smug, satisfied face, hearing him say, "You thought you could get away from Damien Hardon. But you're wrong. You and I are going for a little ride together. And when you wake up, I'm gonna have you call your wife and get her to come rescue you. Only it's not going to work that way, because I'm going to kill you both."

"No!" he screamed. "No! Leave Beth out of this. For God's sake, leave her alone."

The sound of his own voice roared in his ears. Then it was swallowed up by the terrible silence around him.

He staggered on his feet, sank into a fancy deck chair, cradling his head in his hands, trying to think this through.

The guy had shot him with some kind of tranquilizer dart. Lord, he had to warn Beth. Tell her to stay where she was safe.

He stopped short. Safe from whom?

The guy had said his name was Damien Hardon. But he'd looked like the picture of Dave Garwill he'd seen in the yearbook.

Cal thought about the man's face. And the name he'd given. Damien Hardon.

He gave a mirthless laugh. Could the guy really have picked something that stupid? Yeah. Probably he thought it was macho and full of hidden meaning.

But it didn't matter what the killer was calling himself. Cal had to warn Beth to stay away from him. No matter what the maniac told her.

Warn Beth. Again his brain lurched. There was no way to warn Beth. Or was there?

His head throbbed as if he were deep underwater trying to work his way to the surface before his brain exploded. The last time he'd been here, she'd joined him in the dream. She'd pulled him back to reality and saved his life. And that had used up all her psychic reserve of energy, or whatever you called it.

Since then she hadn't had a damn extrasensory twinge. He gave a bark of a laugh, caught in the irony of the situation. Just a few weeks ago he'd been convinced that all psychics were charlatans. Now he was absolutely convinced that Beth had been blessed with extraordinary powers—until she'd gotten mixed up with him.

He cursed, roaring the words at the top of his lungs because there was nobody here to cringe at the vile language.

Then he calmed himself, thinking that cursing wasn't very constructive.

Lord, was there any way to reach her? Any way to break through? Could he be the one to make the mind-to-mind connection?

He'd always had hunches, feelings about people that turned out to be right, insights that came to him like a gift from the ether.

Was that some kind of minimal psychic talent? Could he boost that little bit of talent and use it to communicate with Beth?

He didn't know. He didn't even know where to start.

FORTY-FIVE MINUTES after Beth had first spoken to Hunter, the house was full of people: Hunter Kelley and his wife,

Kathryn, Jed Prentiss, Jason Zacharias, Steve Claiborne and Thorne Devereaux from the Randolph Security team, and Alex Shane from the Howard County P.D.

Cam Randolph himself had come back from his conference in Oakland to find a command post had been set up in the living room, with banks of computers and phone lines.

Jed and Jason were scraping up every piece of information they could find on Dave Garwill. Alex was relaying everything the police had on the case. Sam Lassiter was evaluating other members of the class, on the chance that they were going after the wrong guy. Jo was asking Beth questions about Garwill, helping her dredge up every scrap of memory. And Kathryn Kelley was interviewing other members of the class, starting with Donna Pasternack, who had organized the reunion committee. Kathryn, of course, couldn't say they thought Garwill had abducted Cal. Instead, as a psychologist, she was pretending to be doing an article about the in-crowd and the out-crowd in high school and how they had changed or were the same.

Beth looked up to see that Lucas and Hannah had also come in.

Hannah came straight over to her, knelt down and hugged her. "I'm sorry," she said. "But we'll get him back."

Beth nodded, because she knew that if she tried to speak, she would start weeping.

HOURS DRAGGED BY like centuries. Finally, Hunter, who had been typing steadily at the computer terminal, looked up. "Garwill's parents are dead. But there's no record that their property has been sold. It's an old farm. You reach the house up a long driveway off Linkletter Road. I got the specs from the county planning commission computer because it's on the right-of-way for a highway across the upper end of the county."

"I can go in to reconnoiter," Sam said. "Then if he's there, we send in a team."

"I'm going along," Beth told him.

Hunter gave her a direct look. "I assume that when Cal left you here, he told you to stay where you are safe."

She glared at him. "It doesn't matter what he told me, I'm going."

In the end they compromised. Beth and Jo went along in the SUV with Hunter and Lassiter. They also had portable phone equipment with them that was connected to the line at the house, in case Garwill wanted to talk to Beth.

They parked down the road from the property. Beth sat in the back seat with her heart pounding, trying to pay attention as Jo gave her a quick course in what to say if the killer called while they were in the midst of this operation.

She suspected that only a quarter of what Jo was telling her was getting through, because so much of her attention was focused on the patch of underbrush where Sam had disappeared.

Eventually, Jo must have realized it was a lost cause because she stopped talking.

Finally, Beth spotted Sam trotting back to them and she was out of the SUV and running toward him before Jo could pull her back.

"Is he there?" she asked. "Did you find him?"

Sam shook his head, looking disturbed.

"What?"

"The house is abandoned, as far as I could tell. Nobody's inside. But there's a room where it looks like he took his victims."

Beth made a low sound of distress.

"Cal's not there. At least we know that. I'm sorry we didn't find him," he added.

"It's not your fault. I guess it couldn't be this easy."

"I do have a piece of information, though. There were

some pieces of junk mail dumped in a corner—addressed to Damien Hardon at an Ellicott City town house. I think that's the name he's been using.'' Reaching for the phone, he reported the information to Randolph Security.

THERE WAS a faint glow of light in the eastern sky as they rode in silence back to the Randolph estate. Finally Hunter, who was sitting in front of her, turned and leaned over the seat. ''I have been thinking about this problem, and I have come to several conclusions. I think that Damien captured Cal because he wants to get to you.''

Beth nodded miserably.

''He is making you wait. Making you worry. He is giving us the chance to trap him.''

Her heart leaped. ''How?''

''You must contact Cal.''

The slender thread of hope snapped. ''I can't communicate with him! I've lost the ability.''

Hunter gently laid his hand over hers. ''I was thinking about how you could do it.''

''How?''

''I want to talk to Kathryn first.''

Again conversation in the SUV came to a halt. When the phone rang, they all tensed. But it was only Cam calling to say that the name Damien Hardon had turned up in area credit records.

''Hannah and Jason are on their way to the Ellicott City town house,'' he added. ''But I don't think they'll find Cal there. It's too populated an area. But we're checking it out.''

They were back at the estate fifteen minutes later. Beth kept her eye on Hunter as he drew his wife aside for a quiet conversation. Watching them together made her heart tighten. They loved each other, and they seemed so in tune. That was what she wanted with Cal if they got him back. No, *when* they got him back, she corrected herself before her eyes could start to swim with tears.

To her relief, Kathryn approached her as soon as she and her husband were finished talking.

"Hunter's had the idea that I could hypnotize you. That way, I can accomplish two things—I can suggest that you've got your psychic powers back, and you'll be in a state close to sleep. Hopefully, that will allow you to reach Cal—if he's sleeping. If not, I don't know."

"All right," Beth agreed, not because she was confident that it was going to work. There were too many problems. But she was willing to try anything that had a chance of panning out. And willing to try anything that would put her in communication with her husband.

The others kept to their tasks in the command center. Kathryn took Beth down the hall to a television room, then gestured toward a recliner. "Why don't you kick off your shoes and make yourself comfortable."

Kathryn sat opposite her in a small armchair. "Let's talk for a few minutes," she said. "Can you tell me something about your previous psychic experiences?"

Beth sighed and fought to damp down her anxiety and her impatience. She didn't want to take up time explaining, but she knew that she had to give Kathryn some information if this plan had any chance of succeeding.

After a few moments of thinking about what to say, she began to tell the psychologist her painful history, starting with her father's auto accident. As she spoke, she watched Kathryn's face, looking for some sign that this woman saw her as a freak. But she only detected sympathy and understanding.

When she finished, Kathryn nodded. "You have rare talents that appear to have started developing at puberty. And even though you've fought against them, they've grown. Your getting into Cal's dream when he was in a coma and bringing him back was extraordinary. And it shows you can adapt to new circumstances. You'd never done anything like that before, but you reached a new level of proficiency."

Beth gave a mirthless laugh. ''Since then, I haven't been able to muster up more than a psychic twinge.''

''That twinge means the power is coming back,'' Kathryn said with assurance.

She nodded, unsure whether the psychologist was trying to bolster her confidence or whether she really believed it. Silently she prayed that it was the latter, and that she could really control a process that had controlled her for so long.

''The guys out there are desperate to know where Cal is being held. Do you mind if I have Hunter monitor what's going on in here from out in the other room? He'll use earphones, so it will be just him listening.''

She might have been uncomfortable about one of the other men observing the session. But she'd sensed that Hunter was more sensitive than most guys, so she gave her permission.

Kathryn flipped a switch on a box that sat on the desk and spoke rapidly into the receiver. ''All set,'' she said, turning back to Beth. ''Let's see if you can go where Cal is, see if he can tell you something.''

''I want to,'' Beth murmured.

''You can do anything you want if you just stop worrying about your abilities. You know, from what you've told me, it sounds like they're connected to people and animals you care about.''

Beth had never thought in those specific terms. ''Yes,'' she breathed.

''And you care deeply about Cal.''

''Yes.''

''So go out and find him. I'll be here, helping you achieve your goal. But first, let me explain the hypnotic-induction process.''

As Kathryn talked, Beth listened eagerly.

''Hypnosis is really self-hypnosis,'' the psychologist began. ''I'm only here to help you relax.''

''Now raise your eyes to the line where the ceiling meets the wall and relax. Relax...let yourself drift...''

Kathryn took her into a light trance, then into a deeper state of hypnosis as she mentally descended a flight of stairs, counting her way down from fifteen to one.

When she reached the bottom she felt deeply relaxed.

"Can you hear me?" Kathryn asked.

"Yes," she whispered.

"I want you to go find Cal. Send your mind away from here, the way he sent his mind away from his body when he was in a coma. Only this is a little different. You're the one in control. You're going where he is. You're going there because you want to find him."

"I can't," Beth whispered, feeling a surge of panic.

"Just relax. Let yourself float there. Don't resist. You want to be with him. You want to be with him very badly."

"Yes."

"Then use your power. Go to him."

For an eternity she felt nothing besides a deep, surging panic. *I can't! I can't do it.* Despair was like a monster crouching on her chest, making it impossible to breathe.

Just when she had given up all hope, she thought she heard Cal's voice. She felt a surge of joy.

"Cal?" she whispered.

"Stay away!"

"No. I've got to find you," she answered.

She felt the force of his will, trying to hold her away, hold her where she was. But at the same time there was a bond pulling her toward him.

She felt a swirl of motion around her and made a small sound as she felt herself leaving the room, leaving her body. Suddenly she was standing in the darkened stillness in a field beside a house. And she knew what that house was.

When she gasped, she heard Kathryn's reassuring voice. "Beth, are you all right?"

"Yes."

"Where are you?"

In amazement, she stammered, "I—I'm at the farm. My farm. But I'm not at my place. I'm at the little house Mom and Dad used to rent out until there were too many things wrong with it. I can see a light inside. It looks like it's from some kind of big flashlight."

"Is Cal there?"

"I don't know. I have to get close enough to find out." She started across the twenty yards separating her from the dilapidated dwelling, walking rapidly until she could see through the film of grime over the living-room window. Inside, a man was pacing back and forth. It wasn't Cal. Not at all.

Chapter Sixteen

Beth made a low sound of distress.

"Talk to me," Kathryn said softly. "What are you seeing?"

"Dave Garwill is there," she breathed, suddenly remembering what was happening. She wasn't at the farm—not really. She was at the Randolph estate, and she'd only sent her mind here. She had prayed that she would find Cal. Instead, she'd found the killer.

He was pacing back and forth across the room. Suddenly he stopped and strained his eyes toward the window as if he knew she was there.

But he couldn't see her, could he?

Hands clenched at her sides, she moved forward, one step at a time, slowly then more quickly.

"Is Garwill alone?" Kathryn asked.

"It sounds like he's talking to someone." She felt a shiver go through her as the utter strangeness of this whole situation overtook her. It was hard to shake the sense that Garwill could see her. But this wasn't real, she reminded herself as she walked up to the front porch and peered through the window into the small living room. It was empty of furniture except for a card table and a folding chair.

When she tried to open the door, there was no feeling

of connection with the handle. So she moved to the window and knelt to peer inside.

Garwill was alone. As she stared through the window, he spun around and for a terrible moment he seemed to be staring right at her through the grimy glass. She went stock-still, frozen in place. Then he shook his head.

"You're getting jumpy, Damien," he said, and she realized he was talking to himself, had been talking to himself all along. "It's that damn cop in the root cellar or whatever they call it. The bastard is still asleep. Screwing everything up."

It was obvious the man was angry. What had he done to Cal? What was he planning to do?

Beth made a small, whimpering sound.

"What is it? What's wrong?" a voice asked. Kathryn's voice. She had forgotten all about Kathryn.

"He says Cal won't wake up. He sounds angry. So angry."

Kathryn's voice turned urgent. "Beth, tell me exactly where you are. You're at a house that your parents used to rent out. But how do we get to it?"

Trying to stay calm, she said, "You go up Underwood Road about a quarter of a mile past Old Bridge. You turn in there and go up a separate driveway. You'll get to it. He says Cal's in the root cellar. He must mean the dirt cellar under the house."

Garwill was walking outside, crossing the porch. Beth followed him down the stairs and around the side of the house, her blood roaring in her ears so loudly that she felt like she was in the middle of a hurricane.

He stopped, looked down at a man lying unmoving on the ground near the back of the house, and Beth's heart stopped.

"Oh God," she moaned.

"What?"

"It's..." She bent so she could get a look at the man's

face. She had thought for a moment it was Cal. But it was someone else. Someone she didn't recognize.

"There's a man lying on the ground here," she whispered. "It's not Cal. I don't know who he is."

"Is he alive?"

"I don't know." She reached out her hand to feel his skin, but again there was no sense of touch. "His head is bleeding. Or it was bleeding. I don't know if he's still alive. But I do know Garwill isn't surprised to find him here. I guess he assaulted him. But I can't help him."

"Of course you can't. Only your mind is at the farm."

"I have to go to Cal."

Quickly she hurried to catch up with Garwill, who had stepped with casual unconcern around the body. Turning the corner, he stopped in front of a set of slanted, almost horizontal doors that led to the cellar. Tucking his gun into the waistband of his slacks, he inserted a key in a padlock, twisted the hasp, then lifted the doors. They flopped to the side, the boards shuddering. Garwill's gun was back in his hand as he clumped down the steps into the cellar. Like a shadow, Beth followed.

It was dark and damp in the cellar. In one corner, Cal was lying curled on his side on a blanket tossed on the dirt floor. He was breathing deeply, his arms pulled behind his back. As she hurried toward him, she could see that his hands were tied with thick rope.

Garwill went over and kicked his thigh. Cal made a sound, but he didn't wake up.

"Don't!" Beth screamed, rushing toward the killer and trying to seize him by the shoulder. But the effort was as futile as all her other attempts to manipulate the physical environment.

For a frozen moment he stopped and raised his head, and Beth stood there barely breathing. Shaking his head and making an angry sound, Garwill turned back to Cal and gave him another vicious kick. Still he didn't respond.

Her former classmate cursed loudly. "Wake up so you

can get your wife on the horn,'' he growled. ''I want the bitch here.''

There was no reply from Cal.

''I'll give you another half hour. Maybe that tranquilizer dart was too strong, but that's your problem, not mine. Asleep, you're no good to me. So I'm gonna put a bullet in your soggy brain. Then I'll tell Mrs. Rollins you're too groggy to talk, and she'll come running out here.''

Beth felt the words like a needle of ice piercing her heart.

Unable to move, she watched the killer spin around and march up the stairs, slam the doors back into place, and snap the lock closed.

HUNTER KELLEY SPOKE urgently to Alex Shane. ''You've got to send a Howard County SWAT team out to the former rental property on Beth's farm. Garwill is getting ready to kill Cal.''

The detective gave him a doubtful look. ''You're sure it's Garwill? How do you know? How do you know what he's doing?''

''My wife has hypnotized Beth Rollins. She's, uh, she's sent her mind to the site where Cal is being held. She knows what's happening.''

The detective stared at him. ''You expect me to get a warrant and send in a SWAT team on the basis of that kind of information?''

''Yes,'' Hunter answered simply.

The detective regarded him with narrowed eyes. ''If you're wrong, my job is on the line.''

''If *you're* wrong, Cal Rollins is a dead man.''

Alex ran a hand through his hair. ''You're sure of your information?''

''Yes. And the longer you wait, the more likely it is that Cal dies. What do you want? For us to send in an unofficial team to get him?''

''I wouldn't recommend it.''

"Then what do you suggest?"

Alex was silent for a moment, then he began to speak, picking his words carefully as if he was thinking through the technicalities. "Okay, I can get a warrant based on corroborated information from a known and trusted confidential informant. That's *you.* We'll worry about how you got the information later."

"I don't care what you call it," Hunter snapped. "Just do it."

IT WAS DARK in the cellar now, except for some shafts of light filtering in through cracks in the door frame and at the top of the wall. Quietly, Beth knelt beside the blanket. When her eyes had adjusted to the dark, she saw that Cal wasn't asleep at all. Now that Garwill was gone, he was lying with his teeth clenched, working the rope that secured his hands, sawing the fibers against a rusty knife that he'd wedged into the dirt floor. Angling her head, she could see what Garwill hadn't figured out: Cal had cut about halfway through the rope.

"Cal! You're awake," she breathed.

His head shot up, and his gaze frantically probed the dark corners of the cellar. "Beth. Oh God, Beth, did he get you to come here? I tried like hell in my mind to warn you away," he added, his voice filled with horror and defeat.

"I know. I know," she murmured. "I heard you. I think that's how I got here. I heard you."

"Where are you? I can't see you. What the hell has he done with you?"

"It's all right. I'm not here. Not really," she whispered. "It's like the dream. Sort of."

She watched his face as he tried to assimilate that. "More likely I'm hallucinating," he said with a raw laugh.

Dimly Beth thought she heard somebody calling her name. A woman. But the voice was too far away for her to pay any attention, and of no real importance now that she was with Cal. She longed to wrap her arms around him and hold him. But when she tried to touch him, the frustration of not being able to feel anything physical tore at her.

Perhaps he did feel the ghost of her arms around him, though. "Beth, are you really here? Oh, sweetheart."

She made a small, frustrated sound. "I'm here. But not here. This is like the dream, only it's different, because you're not sleeping." Then the implications sank in. "But you were pretending to be asleep. Oh, Cal, he's going to come back and shoot you."

"Not if I can help it." As he spoke he began sawing at the ropes again.

"Why did you want him to think you were asleep?" she asked.

"To keep you the hell away from him. If I'm out cold from his damn tranquilizer gun, I can't call you on the phone, can I? I can't lure you here."

She swallowed convulsively as she realized what he was saying. He was putting his life in danger to protect her.

"The Randolph people are guarding me pretty tightly," she whispered, afraid her voice would crack.

"Good." He laughed again. "I thought the dream was strange. This is...beyond weird. I can't see you. But I can hear you. And—" He stopped and swallowed hard. "Maybe I can feel you. Just a little."

"Lord, Cal, I wish I could help you with those ropes," she breathed, clenching her hands in frustration.

"Just your being here helps. Just my knowing you're okay," he added.

As he spoke, he kept working at his bonds, his movements steady, but she could see the strain on his face as he stopped and pulled at his hands, twisting the binding. His wrists were raw, and she clamped her teeth together to keep from screaming.

He sawed without pausing, then tested the ropes again.

This time, when he gave a tremendous pull, the fibers parted and his hands broke free.

"Thank God," she cried.

He lay there panting, his forehead beaded with perspiration. Then he pushed himself to a sitting position, his back against the wall. When he gingerly touched his wrists, he winced, and she felt her stomach knot.

"Cal," she whispered, aching to hold him.

As she watched helplessly, he climbed to his feet, swaying unsteadily until he pressed his shoulders against the wall.

"I feel like crap," he said. "Maybe there's something I can use as a weapon."

"Cal, you can't fight him. You have to get out. There's a coal chute in the wall in back of you. You can climb through there, if you stand on one of those boxes over by the furnace."

"Maybe." He staggered across the floor toward the boxes just as she heard the lock rattle on the cellar door.

"God, no!" she cried. "He's coming back."

Cal's head jerked up. Then like a movie when the film has snapped, the scene vanished from view, and she screamed in terror and frustration.

"BETH."

Her eyes blinked open and she stared into Kathryn Kelley's face, struggling to orient herself.

"Oh, God," she moaned. "Garwill's coming down there to shoot Cal."

"The SWAT team is on their way. They're following your directions."

"It'll be too late."

"No. They'll get to him in time."

"Please, you've got to take me there."

Kathryn nodded. "Come on."

They dashed through the house, the command post strangely empty now that the rescue team knew Cal's location. As they burst through the front door, into the driveway, Beth expected to find a car waiting to speed her to the farm. Instead, she heard the whoosh of helicopter blades. She stared in wonder at the machine.

Kathryn motioned, ducking her head low as she headed toward the open door.

Beth followed. Scrambling inside the chopper, she watched the other woman fasten her seat belt, then did the same. As soon as they were belted in, the helicopter lifted off the ground, swinging away in the direction of the farm.

AS HE HEARD the familiar rasp of the lock snapping open, Cal braced his shoulders against the wall near the stairway, a five-foot length of two-by-four clasped in his hands like a baseball bat.

The bastard was coming down again, and this time he was going to even the score. Cal heard the doors flop open, saw gray morning light seeping down the stairs. Then Garwill started down the stairs, his footsteps confident.

Cal waited, his breath shallow, his gaze focused on the man's legs. His heart was thumping inside his chest, but he held himself still, waiting, waiting until the right moment. As Garwill reached the fourth step from the bottom, Cal slammed the piece of wood into the killer's knees, his adrenaline surging as he felt the thwack of wood against flesh and bone.

Garwill screamed and tumbled down the rest of the stairs. Cal was on him, kicking the gun from his hand as he hit the floor near the blanket where Cal had been lying for hours in the dark.

He had raised his club to deliver another blow, but the killer grabbed the blanket, whipping it up and throwing Cal off balance as it hit him in the face.

Cal backed up. Blinded, he might have torn at the fabric. Instead, he swung the stick again, aiming at the shout issuing from Garwill's lips as the killer leaped toward him.

He felt the stick connect solidly with muscle and bone, changing the shout to a groan.

The killer fell back and slammed into the wall, giving Cal enough time to sling the blanket aside, then swing his weapon again.

Somehow, Garwill managed to bring his arm up and deflect the blow as he grabbed for the piece of wood.

Cal danced back, but he could feel his body slowing. Then, with strength that came from some hidden reserve, he swung the piece of wood again, brought it down in another savage blow. And then another, hitting the killer on the head and shoulders.

When Garwill went still, Cal turned and staggered toward the stairs, forcing one foot in front of the other as he climbed into the sunlight, leaning heavily on the two-by-four, using it as a cane instead of a club to keep himself from falling on his face.

After the darkness of the cellar, the light blinded him as he stood there, grasping the wood, swaying on his feet. Dimly, he could make out a ring of men wearing dark uniforms, body armor and helmets. They were armed with rifles—pointed at him.

Then he heard Beth scream, "No. It's Cal. Don't shoot. It's Cal."

In a blur he saw a running figure leap through the circle of men.

"Beth, no. Get back."

He braced for the impact of bullets. Bullets slamming into her flesh, not his.

But it didn't happen.

"Red light. Red light. Hold fire," a voice ordered.

He breathed out a sigh, seeing the rifles lower as Beth flung herself into his arms. She was real and solid, a burst of brightness after the dark nightmare of the past eighteen hours. The two of them swayed together, and he tried to absorb the enormity of what she'd just done.

"Thank God," she sobbed. "Thank God you're safe."

Beyond words, he gathered her to him, holding on for dear life, feeling her warm and pliant in his arms, knowing that she had risked her life for him again.

When he found his voice, he growled, "Don't you *ever, ever* put yourself in the line of fire again! Do you hear me? Don't ever do it!"

She nodded against her chest, and he was oblivious to the scene around him, lost to everything but the joy of holding her close when he had thought he would never see her again. She clung to him, her lips against his chest.

Then suddenly her body stiffened.

"Beth?"

"Down. Get down," she shouted. "He's coming. Get down."

He had heard nothing beyond her words. Seen nothing. But he had learned to trust his life to Beth's sixth sense. He didn't resist as she pulled him to the ground just as a bullet from behind him whizzed past the place where he'd been standing only seconds earlier.

As he pushed Beth to the ground below him, a volley of shots rang out over their heads, and he turned to see Garwill teetering at the edge of the stairway, a gun in his hand and a pattern of red spreading across the front of his shirt.

Then, in slow motion, the killer fell backward into the cellar, his body clattering down the steps and landing with a thud on the dirt floor.

It was over. Finally, it was over. And all he could do was hang on to Beth for dear life.

SOMEONE APPEARED at her side. It was Alex Shane.

"You all right, buddy?" he asked Cal.

"More or less."

"You can thank your wife for saving your ass."

"I intend to," Cal answered, pushing himself up, then pulling Beth to a sitting position.

"And you?" Shane asked Beth.

"I—I'm all right."

Lieutenant Patterson came trotting up and scowled at them.

"Are you here to make trouble?" Beth asked him.

"No." He cleared his throat. "I'm here to say I'm glad things turned out okay." He dipped his head, then met her gaze again. "I'm sorry I gave you a hard time before. Will you accept my apology?"

She swallowed. "Yes."

He turned toward Cal. "You were right. I was wrong," he said in a low voice.

Cal nodded tightly, and helped Beth to her feet.

She saw the red lights of an ambulance flashing. Then paramedics appeared at Cal's side.

He looked from them to Beth and back again. "I'm fine. I don't need anything from you guys."

"You need to have those wrists treated."

Cal looked down at his raw flesh as if he'd just realized he'd been injured.

"I'm going with him," Beth said, sticking by his side as they led him toward the ambulance.

They climbed inside, and she sat beside him on the stretcher, after he told the paramedic that he was damned if he was going to lie down. Before the doors closed, Alex Shane joined them.

"I thought I'd entertain you on the ride over," he said as he pulled down a seat along the wall.

"With what?" Cal asked as the vehicle started rolling slowly forward. A paramedic was leaning over him, taking his blood pressure.

"Some information about Harold Mason and Tim Fillmore."

Beth raised her head. "What does Tim have to do with Harold Mason?"

"With everything else going on, I haven't had a chance to tell you, but we interviewed Fillmore. He was upset by Mason's death—and scared. It looks like he and Mason had a scheme to get you to sell the farm. That's what Mason was doing out there. When you went to Jo's, Fillmore called him and said it was a good time to inspect the property.''

She stared at him in dumb-eyed shock. ''What?''

''I'm sorry to tell you this, but the two of them worked out a systematic policy of harassing you. Mason started a fire in one of your fields and poisoned your sheep. Fillmore did most of the inside work, though. He could get close to the house because your dog didn't bark when he came around. He took the cover off an old well. Left a water bottle in your barn so you'd wonder who'd been there.''

Beth heard the words, but they made no sense. ''Tim's my…my friend. Why would he do any of that?''

''Apparently, he wanted to be more than friends. He wanted you to turn to him for help. Marry him. He was attracted to you. But he also had an eye on making big bucks off your property.''

''No,'' she whispered.

''I'm afraid so. He was pretty upset when Cal walked into the picture, I can tell you that. Cal was in danger from him—a lot more danger than any of us knew.''

Before Beth had time to contemplate that, Alex introduced another topic. ''Did you know there was another man found outside the house a few minutes ago?''

Beth's gaze shot to him, saw him watching her and cringed. She had seen the man on the ground. Now she didn't know what to say in front of Alex.

''Beth,'' he said quietly, ''I authorized the SWAT team to come in based on the information you gave Kathryn. In the official report it will say that I used Hunter as a known and reliable source. But it was really you.''

''Me?''

''Yeah.''

She let out the breath she'd been holding. Here was yet another person who was willing to accept her psychic abilities. In fact, he had come to Cal's rescue based on her say-so. The knowledge sent a surge of emotion through her. For so long she'd felt like a freak. Now everything had suddenly changed.

The paramedic had stopped hovering over Cal, and she felt his hand press over hers as she said, "Yes, I saw him. Who was he? Is he dead?"

"No, I think the guy is going to pull through. He's Jamie Naylor, the brother of Sean Naylor, the kid who was shot down in the drug bust in Baltimore. The one involving Hannah Dawson. It's likely he's the man who killed one of the other officers involved in the incident, Ron Wexler. He's admitted to following Cal around, hoping he would lead him to Hannah. I guess that's what he was doing out there. Unfortunately, he got in Garwill's way."

"Was he the one who killed Deep Throat and shot at me?" Cal asked.

Alex shook his head. "It's more likely the shooter was protecting the interests of Dallas Sedgwick, the drug lord who's still after Lucas."

"Which means Lucas and Hannah are going to have to stay undercover," Cal muttered as the ambulance drew to a halt at the emergency room door.

Inside, Cal got priority treatment, and Beth was allowed to stay with him while his wrists were cleaned, slathered with antiseptic and bandaged.

Then, finally, the doctor stepped out of the room and they were alone.

Wordlessly, she turned to him where he sat on the edge of the exam table. Wrapping him in her arms, she held tight. For a moment he pulled her to him fiercely, then eased away.

"I guess you're sorry I ever came riding up your driveway that day," he muttered.

"We're finally alone and that's the first thing you want to say to me?" she asked in a voice barely above a whisper.

"You said we were supposed to be honest with each

other. You married me because you were in danger. Now what are your plans?''

Not so long ago the question and the tone of his voice might have put her off. Now she understood where he was coming from.

Taking a step back, she raised her head and looked him square in the eye. ''My plans are to love you, make you as good a wife as I can, have children with you and grow old with you. That is, if those plans don't interfere with yours.''

He looked stunned, as if he couldn't believe what he'd heard.

''I told you on our wedding day, I married you because I love you, not because I was looking for a bodyguard. What do I have to do to make you believe that? Did you think I was lying?''

''I thought—'' He stopped, unable to go on.

''What?'' she demanded. ''Say it.''

''I thought that once the danger was over, you'd change your mind.''

''No. Never.'' She would have launched herself back into his arms again, except that she was afraid she would hurt him. Instead, she inched slowly toward him, watching him, seeing that he was holding his breath as she moved into the vee of his legs, into his warmth. Slowly she angled her head so that her lips could press against his.

His hands simply dangled at his sides for several moments. Then they came up to clasp her, and she felt as if she'd moved from a storm-tossed sea into a safe harbor.

She felt his lips soften against hers, felt his mouth open as he took what she was offering. The first wave of urgency changed to a lazy exploration as they relaxed into the kiss.

''Oh Lord, Beth, how I love you,'' he sighed as he finally lifted his head.

She stared at him, her heart brimming over as she realized that she'd finally heard the words from him that she'd been longing for, praying for.

Still, she needed to be sure of one important thing. "You mean, you don't mind a wife who has psychic episodes at inconvenient times?" she murmured.

His expression turned serious. "You saved my life with a couple of those episodes. When I was in that coma. And that's how the SWAT team knew where to find me, how you knew Garwill was coming up the stairs, wasn't it?"

She nodded gravely.

"I wouldn't call that inconvenient. Or this morning when you were in that dirt cellar with me. You gave me hope—hope that I could cut through those damn ropes in time. How did you get there?"

"I don't know. Kathryn hypnotized me. I thought it wasn't going to do any good. Then I heard your voice warning me to stay away...and I came to you." She gave him a direct look. "So maybe I'm not the only one with psychic abilities. Maybe we never would have connected in your dream if you hadn't been able to call me there." She swallowed. "How do you feel about that?"

"Whatever works."

She let out the breath she'd been holding. "I guess you've traveled a long way from that first afternoon when you came up the driveway. I guess we both have."

"Yeah." His expression grew very serious. Clearing his throat, he said, "I told you, I'm not so great at saying stuff. But I want you to know...I think before I met you, before I fell in love with you, I had convinced myself that marriage was an institution with no meaning. That's what I kept telling myself, but I'm pretty sure I was really afraid that I'd be as big a failure as my parents. Then..." He dragged in a breath and let it out before continuing. "Then I met you, and I wanted you, but I knew I couldn't make love with you and walk away. I had to take the honorable route. I'm still nervous about it. But I can't give you up."

"Oh, Cal," she whispered, folding him close, overwhelmed by what he had told her. ''We'll make it work. Because we both want this so much.''

''Oh, yeah.''

''Do you think you could take me home now? I mean, to your house, where we can be alone.''

''As soon as I get a doc to discharge me,'' he answered, easing down off the table and slinging his arm around her shoulder. ''Then we'll get back to the honeymoon that was so rudely interrupted.''

''It's going to be a long honeymoon. I think a hundred years is a conservative estimate,'' she murmured as she followed him to the door.

He stopped, turned and looked at her with a gaze so fierce she felt her heart melt.

''After we get started on the honeymoon, do you think we could do the wedding again? I mean in a church, with music and flowers and all the trimmings? And a reception afterward for our friends.''

She felt her eyes brimming. She hadn't had many friends in recent years, but through Cal she'd met a whole group of people who accepted her in a way she never would have believed possible. ''I think that could be arranged.''

''Good. And oh yeah. You need to get me a wedding ring. A thick gold one. Because I want the world to know I belong to you as long as I live.''

* * * * *